Thank You

Reef Steve

TWO HEADS
ARE BETTER
THAN ONE

Reef Stone

ISBN: 9798377283942

Cover design: James Mossop

This book is available in print from KDP and
Amazon.

To my wife and family for your support,
understanding and the odd glass of wine.

ONE

'Hey, DS Blackmore, get your feet off the desk, your cute ass off your chair and go and see Chief Constable Mondell,' shouted Tuppence.

'What, now?'

'Yes, now.'

'What the hell does he want me for at this time of day?'

I was shattered and talking out loud, but within earshot of Tuppence.

'There is only one way you will find out,' she said, sarcastically.

It was six o'clock in the evening and I had just closed out the previous case with the investigation team. There had been a good team feeling with plenty of banter in the squad room and we were all on a high after a successful case conclusion. The vision of a nice cold pint was stirring my tired mind and wetting my very dry lips and it would be tantalisingly waiting for me sitting nicely on the end of the bar; I could virtually taste it. The team had already left for the pub. I would be with them soon, but I just wanted a little time to myself.

I sat wondering what Chief Constable Mondell wanted to talk to me about and slowly dragged my tired legs off the desk and walked slowly down the maze of corridors in this old, rattled police station.

The station, in my eyes, is ancient and built with brown depressing bricks. There is no character to the station and the bland architect must have imposed his own personality on it. I guess the station is a design with no style or thought to architecture, just functionality. The station has a fuzzy odour built up from many years and reflects the age of the building and some of the lags who have been here. It desperately needs a coat of paint and reorganisation, but alas this is out of my hands and there's no money in the station budget to do the work, or so I have been told.

If I become a Chief Constable one day, I will push for a tin of paint.

I was met by Tuppence, who was standing at the door to the corridor to the Chief Constable Mondell's office. I stopped. Tuppence slowly opened the door with a sarcastic smile, with her head leaning on the door. I said nothing. I made my way to the office of Chief Constable Mondell. I knew Tuppence would be waiting for me at the pub; she would be keen to know why Chief Constable Mondell wanted to see me at this time on a Friday night. So was I.

Chief Constable Mondell is a forty-five-year-old large man with an imposing stature. He is stern but fair and takes no shit from anyone; it has been said he can smell bullshit before a word is spoken. I guess he could be described as old school, as he embraces technology reluctantly. However, he has a team of people around him to deal with technical problems. I was raised on technology, but even I need technical support at times when problems occur.

I like and respect the Chief Constable Mondell. I know exactly where I stand with him when it comes to the job. He stands six feet four inches at full height and has broad shoulders, and hair that is showing signs of turning grey. He is an ex-rugby union player; he is very proud to wear his second-row battle scars from many a year on the rugby field.

His physical presence is awesome. One look has frozen many a member of the police force and public to the spot. They learn very quickly not to cross him. I think he misses his glorious rugby days, as the opportunity to take out his frustrations on his poor opponents would be very welcome to him.

He broke his leg during a fierce local derby a few years ago when a maul collapsed and he fell awkwardly. He recovered physically, but in my view the incident left mental scars. He was at a critical stage in his career as he was moving through the police ranks, so he felt it was time to retire from rugby and concentrate on his career. He has been quoted as saying, 'Rugby does not pay the mortgage.' He is still involved with the Mortley rugby club, but purely in an administrative capacity.

The Chief Constable's job is more political these days and he does it, in my opinion, very well. He is very tactful, but he works through gritted teeth at times and the urge to smash someone who bugs him if he could get away with it, is, I think, never far from his mind.

I have a vision of him on the rugby field, charging for the line, ball under his arm, an opponent under his other arm, a thunderous face as he charged for the line to score an imperial try. There was no way anyone was going to stop him from scoring, such was his prominence.

I knocked on the door and waited for what seemed like an eternity, then the booming voice called out, 'Come in, DS Blackmore, and take a seat.'

He said this in his usual deep voice and direct manner. I duly carried out the request. Although his stature was imposing, he had a way of making you feel at ease and I was not about to argue. I was too tired, anyway. I could sense from his body language something deep was on his mind and my senses kicked into full alert for the forthcoming conversation.

'Congratulations on the result of the case – and in such a short time; very impressive. You have been making a good impression in your time here.'

'Thank you, sir.'

'The team and the station in general have been making favourable comments about you and your exam grades are exceptionally good. I believe at this rate it will not be too long before another promotion comes your way.'

'It was a good all-round team effort, sir. It was unfortunate we sustained a hospitalised injury to Constable Davis. I intend to go and see him.'

'I went to see him this afternoon. He is doing well

and looking to get back on duty as soon as possible. He doesn't blame anyone, just those he calls those "bad-ass losers". There will of course be an investigation into the incident. Another department will carry this out in due course. I do not foresee any problems and the whole thing should be wrapped up to history,' he concluded. His expression changed.

'I will come to the point. There is a problem in your hometown of Cromley, more specifically at Cromley Hall. There is a bit of a panic at the hall, with two elderly members of the Holmes family murdered. Expensive family heirlooms, two antique George IV candlesticks, have also been stolen and they have no bloody idea how they got into the hall. Quite frankly, the whole thing is a bit of a mess.'

'I am aware of what is going on back in Cromley, sir, but not the details. My mother keeps me informed of everything that goes on back home.'

'For sure. Chief Constable Gregg, based at Cromley police station, and I met when we were at police college together and we have been friends and colleagues ever since. We spoke earlier this afternoon regarding a police college twenty-five-year reunion. Chief Constable Gregg raised the events at Cromley Hall and his concerns about the way the investigation is going. He is concerned with the slow progress and the media interest in the case. We feel a fresh pair of eyes would be the way forward. I agree with his reasoning based on everything he has told me.'

I went to say something, but he held up his hand to stop me.

'Chief Constable Gregg and I discussed the case in detail, and we agree a strategy that you, as a local lad, could focus fresh eyes on the case and pick up a trail they could be missing. I wanted to discuss it with you before I agree to his request. However, it has been a long day and now is not the right time to make a clear decision. Think it over overnight and come and see me at ten o'clock tomorrow morning. Yes, I know it's a Saturday, but you can see the urgency of the matter. In the meantime, go and enjoy your celebrations with the team; it is well deserved. So I bid you goodnight. This conversation will remain confidential,' he said in his direct and straight-in-the-eye manner.

There was no way I would ever consider it otherwise.

I got up and made my way from his office. I am sure he would have loved to have joined us at the pub, but he only does this on special occasions, such as retirements. I guess if he went to every occasion, he would be pissed every night of the week and that is not good for a Chief Constable. I think he might have enjoyed a few of them.

The conversation brought home to me the seriousness of the events in my hometown. I knew there and then I would be going back. I just needed to be clear in my mind how I wanted to do it. In the meantime, the pub beckoned. I made my way along the long, twisting corridor and then to check my car was OK in the car park. All right, I know it is a police station, but old habits die hard. I would collect it tomorrow.

The team were in good form when I walked in, and my pint was ready by the time I got to the bar. It tasted so good. I did not feel it hit the sides of my mouth as it went down, and a smile of satisfaction spread across my face.

'Where is Chief Constable Mondell?' yelled Sergeant Brown.

'Still at the station.'

'I thought he would buy us all a drink.'

'Are you going to ask him?'

'I think I will pass on that one.'

'Good decision.'

Everyone laughed and added to the mood of the squad.

'Chief Constable Mondell asked me to pass on his congratulations to you all for the positive outcome of the case and passes on his best wishes for the evening.'

With that, the serious celebrations began.

I spoke to individual members of the team over the course of the evening. I could see Tuppence out of the corner of my eye, and I knew she was anxious to know of my discussions with Chief Constable Mondell. I thought I would let her stew for a while such is the nature of my humour.

Later, when I was quite close to her, she leaned over and whispered in my ear.

'When are you going to tell me why Chief Constable Mondell wanted to see you, you shit bag?'

Typical of her to be so direct. I laughed and received a gentle punch in the side. Tuppence is a civilian employee working at Mortley police station for the last twenty years. I know there is talk in the squad room that we are having a relationship, but it is not the case. I like her a lot, though, and we have become exceptionally good friends. I have learned to trust her implicitly. She is the most tactful and discreet person, outside of my family, I have met. We hide nothing from each other.

Later we sat down, and I told her of my conversation with Chief Constable Mondell without going into detail: just some murders at Cromley Hall and that I would be going back to my hometown. She asked me how I would handle it, but I told her I was still formulating what I wanted to do. Although I have been in the pub laughing and joking, it has been on my mind since I left Chief Constable Mondell's office; I knew it would be a long night as I would work on my strategy for a while yet.

The next morning came soon enough.

I knocked on the door and waited for the call, which came straightaway. I entered Chief Constable Mondell's office and found him in a buoyant mood. He was looking directly at me. I guess he knew my answer.

'How were the celebrations last night?'

'They were good; the team were on a high and deservedly so.'

'Let's get down to it,' he said. 'You have given the matter some thought, and your answer is…'

'Yes, sir, I will do it, but I do have some concerns and a strategy on how I am going to go about it.'

'Good. Chief Constable Gregg and I feel it is too good an opportunity for you to turn down and you will have full support from him and, of course, from me.'

'Thank you, sir. That is good to know.'

'I have arranged a video link call with Chief Constable Gregg at ten thirty so we all can discuss the case together and your strategy.'

I made us some coffees and returned to his office. I knew the next few minutes would be tough, and I was determined to put a good case for my reasons.

The appointed time came and after the usual polite exchanges took place, I said, 'Chief Constable Gregg, I feel it would be to the benefit of everyone for me to work alone. As you know, Senior Investigating Officer Cornelius Grainger and I have a bit of history. There is no T in his team just an I. I want to go in with fresh eyes.'

I outlined my plans, as follows:

• I would prefer to work alone to start with and report directly to Chief Constable Gregg. I had previous issues with SIO DI Grainger and felt a conflict would not be helpful in the investigation; and it would give me the freedom to work.

• I wanted an incident room of my own at Cromley station.

- I wanted three phones for Chief Constable Gregg and myself for direct communication.

- I did not want anyone to know I would be working on the case; let them find out naturally. I feel it would be advantageous if fewer people knew who I was and why I was there.

- I would not be telling my family of my return. I would call and see them when I arrived in Cromley.

- I needed a place of my own to stay and work; I couldn't stay with my family.

Tough further discussions followed. They eventually agreed that my plan for an independent investigation to work alongside the main investigation would be beneficial. I was overjoyed when we reached an agreement and after a few minor details, it was agreed I would move to Cromley on Monday.

'One thing,' they both said at once. 'Who is having the third phone?'

'Tuppence; I want to take her with me.'

'I'm not sure that is wise,' said Chief Constable Mondell.

'I do not intend to take her out in the field except to take notes for me. I cannot interview, take notes and write them up at the same time; I need someone I can trust. Tuppence is very capable of looking after herself and I trust her implicitly,' I put to them.

'Have you discussed this with her?' asked Chief Constable Mondell.

'No, sir. I would not do so without discussing it

with you and Chief Constable Gregg.'

'What makes you think she would want to go?' asked Chief Constable Mondell.

'I know she will,' I replied.

'And where would she stay?' enquired Chief Constable Gregg.

'She will share the accommodation with me, sir. It will be safer for her, and the continuity of the case will be good.'

'It is a highly unusual request!' said Chief Constable Gregg.

'I can assure you that it will be strictly work related. I get on well with Tuppence and there is nothing going on between us, despite the rumours in the station. It is important we keep things very tight.'

After further discussions they agreed to my request and all I had to do now was to discuss it with Tuppence. I was quite sure she would jump at the chance.

I left the Chief Constable Mondell's office with him telling Chief Constable Gregg all about Tuppence.

I returned to the squad room to collect some things and sat for a few minutes to think about Cromley Hall and my hometown in general.

I felt bad not telling Tuppence of the whole conversation I had with Chief Constable Mondell, but I would reveal all later that night. I went to my car and after checking it I sent a text to Tuppence to come round to my place tonight for a pizza and a chat. I received the reply: OK?

I decided to leave my car at the station as the alcohol I had last night would put me over the legal alcohol limit for driving. I would get it tomorrow. The station was close to the town centre, so I decided to walk and clear my head a bit. I need to buy some things to take with me for the coming week.

The town centre is not very inviting. It has one main street with a variety of shops. According to Tuppence, the shops are extremely low key, and she prefers to go elsewhere for decent clothes, etc. I walked around for a while, thinking and focusing my mind on the coming weeks. There was a homeless guy sitting in an empty shop doorway, so I bought him some food from one of the many fast-food outlets that are popping up everywhere.

There were a lot of people walking about with no sense of purpose, so I guess they were just killing time. I purchased the things I wanted, as I might not have a lot of time when I got to Cromley. I dropped my purchases back at my apartment.

I decided to visit Constable Davis. He had been off for a couple of weeks with a broken leg and damaged ribs, but he was still healing slowly. He had been back in hospital to have more pins inserted in his leg and he told me that was the end of the surgery and it was now a process of healing. He said he missed the banter of the station and was keen to get back, but he would follow the hospital advice with his rehabilitation. He is a good police officer, and we could do with more like him. He is a team player, and I would not have a problem having him on my team. There are some I know who, with the slightest injury, have a lot of time off; not my type of police officer. The constable was injured when one of the thieves jumped off a forklift and left it moving. The forklift hit some racking, causing a pallet to fall. The pallet brushed down his left side, damaging his ribs and breaking his leg. He was incredibly lucky the outcome was not worse. I spent around an hour with Constable Davis, I then bade my farewells and returned to my apartment.

Tuppence arrived around seven o'clock with a quizzical and searching look on her face. She knew from my invitation to my place she would be involved somewhere. I have never seen her look so pensive, but then again, she is in a situation she has not faced before or what I am about to put to her. I smiled and she relaxed a little. We talked a bit about my hometown whilst we devoured the pizza, drank some wine and had a bit of craic.

Then I said, 'Let us talk. Back in my hometown of Cromley there has been a serious crime at Cromley Hall. Cromley Hall dates back hundreds of years and has been home to the Holmes family for a long period of that time.

'Two elderly members of the Holmes family, Jake and Arthur Holmes, have been murdered and some family heirlooms have been stolen. The case is making slow progress and I have been asked, as a local lad, to return and work on the case.'

'Are you going as part of the team?' she asked.

'No chance of that,' I laughed.

'Well, how are going to do it?'

'I will be working alone and reporting directly to Chief Constable Gregg.'

I told her of my plans with a separate office, phones and accommodation. I left the best to last.

'Tuppence, I want you to come with me to Cromley to work with me on the case.'

'What the hell!?' she said in astonishment.

'I know it's way out of your normal daily life.'

'How is it going to work?' she asked.

'You will be working with me to take notes as I interview persons of interest and all other work, writing the notes up every day. We will be based in the office in the station. You will be reporting to me and Chief Constable Gregg. You will have some interaction with the personnel at the station, especially SIO DI Cornelius Grainger. I need an ear close to the ground and in the corridors. No one from Mortley station will know where we are and no one in Cromley will know we are coming, especially my family. I will go and see them when I arrive. They will all find out as things develop.'

'Where will you stay if your family don't know you are coming to Cromley, and where will I stay?' she asked.

'Chief Constable Gregg is arranging, although reluctantly, accommodation for us and we will be sharing the same apartment. That way we can keep things tight and work closely together and keep you safe. So, what do you think?'

'Hell, yes, I'm in! I need something different to stir my senses and to share a place with you will be cool, and many a laugh can be had.'

'Yes, but we are there to do a job so that has to be our main focus.'

'What about my job?'

'Do not worry about that. Chief Constable Mondell has taken care of it.'

'You knew I would accept the proposition. I guess it's what every girl wants,' she laughed.

'Say nothing for now and I will call you when things are set in Cromley.'

We spent time talking about the case and other things. I have always been defensive when it comes to talking about my hometown and Tuppence has picked up on this. I guess she knows there is a girl somewhere in the story. I can expect a grilling on this when the time comes.

TWO

Over the weekend I sorted out my things and Tuppence dropped round a suitcase for me to take for her. She was really looking forward to going to Cromley. It looked odd with a girlie case in amongst my stuff, but what the hell. I cannot imagine what is in there and no guy I know would ever look inside a woman's bag!

Chief Constable Mondell rang and said if I needed anything then to call him. It's good to know I have his support; I may need it.

Chief Constable Gregg rang me to say he has sorted accommodation for Tuppence and my good self. He told me where I can collect the key to save me going to the police station. The apartment was in a decent area of the town, far enough away, but close enough at the same time. I was grateful for that, so I was now set.

My mind turned to my hometown, I have been away now for four years. The time has flown, but I don't miss it. I miss my buddies, Yak, Yamma and BJ, and I am sure we will meet up at some time. For now, they have no idea I will be back and for an unspecified period.

Leaving Cromley has been good for me. The independence has forced me to mature, I have become more self-confident and assured. The reaction when I get back will be interesting.

I will surely meet up with Amber, the girl who stole

my heart and ripped it apart, and it has taken a long time to heal. I was crazy about her for several years, but I was not strong enough to cope with her at the time, which was one of the reasons I took this promotion in Mortley. It was an opportunity to leave home and stand on my own two feet. Now I won't fear her when we bump into each other, which I know will happen. I do not know what has become of her as I avoid any mention of her and Yak, Yamma and BJ know this. For all I know, she is still in Cromley.

It will be good to see my parents and siblings, and my mother will go nuts because I did not tell her I was coming back and not staying at the family home. It would not be practical to stay there; my father will understand this.

The population of Cromley is approximately fifty thousand. It is a town with largely good working-class people. It has its crime like everywhere else and the dickheads at night who spill out of the pubs and clubs out of their heads on whatever concoction they take. What a waste of a life.

Cromley is an industrial town based a bit further north than Mortley in Northamptonshire. It is a town of various industries, but socially, like Mortley, it is changing. Pubs are closing due to a lack of customers. Fast-food outlets are springing up everywhere as people are too lazy to cook. Supermarkets are on a mission to close every pub by selling beer in cans at ridiculous prices. When the pubs close for good, they will jack the prices up and then they will be stuffed. People do not go out as much and home entertaining is more common, along with takeaway food. That is my rant over with.

Joining the police force was always my career choice from an early age and I set out my plan to get there to get the school results I would need. This was never a problem to me and I had more than I needed. I had the support of my parents for my career choice and that meant a lot to me.

My application was successful and on my eighteenth birthday I set out on a two-year probation programme with eighteen weeks' basic training as a police constable, and passed the physical and written tests with flying colours. There was never any doubt the police station would be where my future lay. Perceptiveness and attention to detail were always strong traits of mine.

Being a constable was the first step, but being a detective is where my main interest lay. I knew there would be long hours, hard work and a lot of self-discipline to get the first workbook done. I was fortunate promotion went my way to the rank of Detective Sergeant in Mortley. I had spent twenty-four months as a Trainee Detective Sergeant. I enjoyed being at the station with a great team, led by Chief Constable Mondell.

My family, except my mother, were delighted with my promotion. My mother was not happy I would be moving away from home, as I was the youngest of the family; in my mother's eyes, I was still her little boy. I needed to get away from that.

The events in Cromley I felt would have a seismic impact on my career. I was under no illusions about the difficult time ahead, but man, I was ready for it.

I slept well that night and woke refreshed and ready to go. I always sleep well. I never allow myself to get stressed over a case; to me, stress clouds the mind, judgement and ultimately decision-making.

I could not be bothered making breakfast, so I decided to get something on the way. I arranged for a friend to watch my apartment while I was away. I gathered all my things and Tuppence's suitcase.

Just then I received a text from Chief Constable Gregg to say a hire car would be available for me. The car hire company is based next to the railway station, so I was to collect it from there. I was happy with this arrangement, as I could leave my car in the garage. It did mean I would have to take Tuppence's case along with mine, but if that is all I had to be bothered with I could cope with that. I received a *Safe journey* text from Tuppence and returned her text with a smiley face. I called a taxi and it arrived very shortly.

I enjoy travelling on trains. The journey was uneventful and I soon arrived in Cromley. The station had had a major facelift and looked a lot more modern in line with the town and I liked it.

I picked up the keys to the apartment at the rail station master's office; the station master was a good friend of Chief Constable Gregg. I collected the hire car and set off to the apartment. The route took me past the town centre with the police station close by. The local sights had not changed, with the parks and woods. I have walked these roads many times in my time in Cromley.

The apartment was on the second floor of a small block, with one of the bedrooms overlooking Cromley Park. The park was the place where I played youth team football with Yak, Yamma and BJ. There was a clubhouse that doubled as a social club and many a good time we had there. We would do the things all young lads would do and eventually took an interest in girls.

When it came to girls, we were very green, especially me. I was very shy. We would play a game on a points system; if a girl looked at you, you got a point; if she held your gaze for a couple of seconds, you got another point; if she smiled at you, you got another point; if you talked to her, you got another point; and if she went out on a date with you, jackpot, a total of five points. This meant the next time we went out the winner from the previous night did not pay for any drinks that night. As we were underage, we of course did not drink alcohol, honest!

We did try beer, as lads do, but this was away from prying eyes. There was a tree in the woods we called the monkey tree. It had so many bendy branches we could climb all over it and swing across the branches. We spent many a year running around that tree.

It was our general meeting place and is where we would try various types of alcohol. I think my dad knew what we were up to. However, we never abused it and we all remained quite sober, so I guess he was ok with that. The clubhouse was the first time I set eyes on Amber, and she just blew me away and would bewitch me.

The apartment was comfortably furnished, and I put my bags down in the hall and looked around. The apartment had three bedrooms off a small passageway, two larger ones and one small one between them. I decided the small one could be an incident room we could have here, as well as the station. The bathroom was practical but small. There was a separate dining room and kitchen. It would do us nicely and Chief Constable Gregg had chosen well.

There was a knock on the door, which surprised me. I looked out of the window and saw a police motorbike parked outside. I opened the door to find a police courier standing there with a package in his hand. After I showed him my warrant card, he handed over the parcel after I signed for it. I left it on the coffee table for the time being. I put my bags in the bedroom I'd decided would be mine and left Tuppence's bag in the other bedroom room that overlooked the park. I think she would like that. I had a view of the rubbish bins and yard, which I found enlightening – not.

I made myself a coffee and sat down. I opened the package to look at what was inside. The parcel contained the case notes, a credit card and two mobile phones.

I checked the kitchen cupboards and all were empty, so some serious food shopping was required. I was used to shopping for myself, but I had no idea what to buy for female company. I could not ring my sister as she had no idea I was in town; I would just do my best.

I decided it would be best to shop in the next town for two reasons: it would give me the opportunity to drive past Cromley Hall, and also I would avoid, at this time, bumping into anyone I knew, so as not to be asked awkward questions. Just driving past the hall would jog some memories of many a time I spent there with the lads, I was looking forward to visiting again, but the circumstances this time would be different.

I remember the lads and I ran into a field to chase some sheep. We thought it was hilarious, running and hollering, but the tables were turned when some of them chased me. I was hit in the butt extremely hard by one, so hard I flew into some nettles. I was soon covered in red blotches that became itchy and sore.

When I got home my mother asked me, 'What happened to you?'

'I fell in some stinging nettles. Me and the lads were messing around on the way home.'

It was not totally untrue. Yes, I did fall in some nettles. I just left the sheep bit out, so technically I did not lie to her; and yes, we were messing about. That was my line and I was sticking to it.

She made up a mixture of baking soda and water and dabbed it on my skin. She told me not to scratch and keep cool, as heat would irritate my skin. She then gave me that quizzical look that mothers do when they doubt the story they are being told.

Back at the apartment, I sat and started reading the case notes Chief Constable Gregg had sent me. I was surprised and amazed at how narrow the investigation SIO DI Grainger was leading. I felt it all centred on SIO DI Grainger's plan that it was carried out by a member of the family, due to no signs of entry from doors, windows, etc.

I felt it was too big a case for him to handle on his own. This level of crime was way outside the general scope that was dealt with in an industrial town. He would not take too kindly to my involvement when he found out, but that would be his problem. I knew some of his team and they were good at their jobs, but little involvement would isolate them. This was the reason I had to work alone; I could not operate in a restricted atmosphere like that, and further I could not work with SIO DI Grainger. I believe both Chief Constables knew this as well and was why they agreed to my plan.

I thought it best to go to my parents' house and get it out of the way now, as sooner or later it would surface that I was in Cromley.

I drove around for a bit to get used to the car and enjoyed driving it. I arrived just as my mother was removing shopping bags from her car; I walked up and spoke.

'Would you like a hand with your bags, missus?' I asked, very politely.

She looked at me in disbelief, taking a couple of seconds to realise it was me. She put the bags down ran to me and gave me the biggest hug she could muster and spoke, 'Why didn't you tell me you were coming home?'

I grabbed the bags and told her we would talk in the house. My dad was in his workshop on his lathe and could be found in there on most days. The pieces he makes are good and a willing home was always ready for his creations.

We put the bags on the kitchen table and Mum called Dad through the intercom between the kitchen and workshop – yes, there really is one – to tell him I was home. He appeared in a couple of minutes with a smile and a strong handshake.

We sat at the big wooden table my dad made a few years ago. It was so big and solid you could stand a tank on it; my mother loves it and so do I. He made it in sections and bolted it together in the kitchen with the help of my brother and my good self. The table is a legend in the wider family and visitors have often remarked on it. The kitchen is large and is the hub of the house. It leads out to the back garden where my dad's workshop sits in the bottom corner. My mum would often go to the workshop with a bottle and two glasses, and we would hear them talking and laughing. A lot of laughter was heard in the kitchen over the years and, yes, sometimes tears, as well.

I explained, without detail, why I was in Cromley, and they accepted this. My mother stood up and said, 'I will get your room ready.'

I stopped her and told them both I would not be

staying at home, but had a police apartment on the other side of town. I told them about Tuppence and before my mother would put two and two together and make three, I said she was a colleague, and we would be working together on the case. It made sense. Also, I had to consider her safety. I also did not want to bring work home to my parents' house as I could be in and out at all hours. They understood the logic of it and agreed.

I decided it best to speak to my brother and sister to let them know I was back in Cromley. We had a face to face through the marvels of technology and I explained to them why I was here. They have all been to Mortley and we've had many a good night out. I told them both it might be a while before we could share a night out, as I had to focus fully on the case. They both understood and we said our goodbyes for now.

Both my brother and sister are married, and both live out of town. My brother is an old-school carpenter; his interest was inspired by many hours in my father's workshop where he was ever-present since he could walk. He makes a lot of speciality furniture for a niche market, plus general work, and he does very well. My father has been known to make bits for him. My sister is a senior nurse working in the general hospital in Cromley. Like me, she decided on her profession from an early age. She studied hard and went to university to get the qualifications she required. She flew through all her exams, and we all had a great night out at her graduation. She now does the job she has always wanted.

My father is an accountant and a successful one at that. He works for himself and is based in an office at the far end of the house. His workshop is his release from the daily grind.

My mother does not work and now that we have all left home, she gets involved in charity work. She has a great, warm heart and a smile that would melt the snow off the mountains. She now has a passion for making wine and many a night my parents would have wine-tasting sessions in his workshop, in the house and at friends' houses. They are extremely popular and dote on each other.

I soon returned to the apartment, checked the time and called Tuppence. I told her I would arrange a train ticket for Wednesday morning at ten o'clock from Mortley, one change and then arrive in Cromley at twelve thirty.

'To hell with that. I will be in Cromley at ten thirty tomorrow morning, so make sure you pick me up!'

I laughed and said, 'OK.'

I should have learned by now that Tuppence is never predictable.

I was up early on Tuesday morning to make sure the apartment was smart and tidy. I did not want her to think I was untidy. I think she knows I am a tidy guy, but I was not risking it; after all, I was used to living on my own. My mother ensured my brother, sister and I could look after ourselves when it comes to things domestic.

I arrived at the station in good time and I waited

patiently on the platform. Cromley rail station has had a major overhaul and is architecturally pleasing, and it looks a lot better for it. The train arrived on time and Tuppence got off the train with a big smile across her face.

'Hi, cute ass,' she yelled. 'It's great to escape Mortley. I feel I am on parole.'

'Listen, let us make that the last time you call me that. Leave Mortley behind and now focus on the forthcoming case.'

'Yes boss,' she laughed.

We put the bags in the boot of the car, and I took her for a long drive around Cromley, which included a drive past Cromley Hall. I pointed out all the interesting parts of the town; she looked at me with a bemused look on her face. I just looked at her and laughed, then headed for The Lodge for some lunch and a general chat.

The Lodge is a listed building and I like its ambience. I sincerely hoped it had not been screwed with by people who like to screw things for the sake of screwing and screw its character. It was a nice day, so we sat outside in the garden where we would have more privacy. As we were talking Chief Constable Gregg rang.

'DS Blackmore, I had a briefing with SIO DI Grainger, so I informed him of your involvement in the case. He was not happy; in fact, he was raging. He felt he was making good progress and he was being undermined. I put it to him a fresh pair of eyes, especially local eyes at that, would be a great benefit on the investigation. I also put it to him you would be working independently and reporting directly to me based in Cromley station.'

'Thank you, sir.'

I turned to Tuppence. 'Well, the cat's out of the bag. That was Chief Constable Gregg telling me he briefed SIO DI Grainger of my involvement in the case.'

'What will that mean?'

'It means the aggro stakes have risen, but, you know, let him bring it on. I am no shrinking violet anymore.'

Tuppence looked at me and smiled, but said nothing.

We arrived at the apartment. I made some coffee as she looked round and put her bags in her room and sorted her things in some sort of order for now.

'Nice view,' she said.

I nodded. She went to look at my view turned to me with a thank-you smile.

We sat and talked as we drank our coffee and then sorted our stuff in the apartment. There were no personal pictures, as I wanted the apartment to function as an office to concentrate fully on the case. Tuppence agreed to this.

'There are some shops just across the road. I will pop out and get the things you didn't get,' she laughed.

Women's shopping, I guess, is not something I am well versed in.

'As you are going shopping,' I said, 'I will pop into the police station to look at the room we will be using.'

I gave the spare key to Tuppence and the credit card.

The station was around three miles away, so I set off, taking in the old familiar sights. I saw BJ walking purposely, but now was not the time to stop and talk. It would have taken too long, with the inevitable invitation to have a pint. There would be time later for that. Anyway, he had no idea I was in Cromley, so what he didn't know at present would not hurt him.

I swiped my pass card at the barrier and parked at the first available spot. I entered the station. I was not nervous; I felt strong, good and strode with a purpose. I went to the reception desk and was met by Sergeant Phillips; he was very much in SIO DI Grainger's camp, we had crossed swords when I was stationed in Cromley a few years previous.

He looked at me with a raised eyebrow, as was his fashion, and said, 'DS Blackmore, Chief Constable Gregg informed me you would be arriving and would be here for a time. He left this key for you. You will be based on the first floor, room ten. You will find all you need in there.'

I thanked him, took the key and made my way to my designated room. It was far enough away from the main squad room; I liked that. Inside I found laptops for Tuppence and me. There were whiteboards with pens, etc. I decided I would take them to the apartment, as no doubt there would be snoopers when we were not there. Although the door would be locked and it was a police station, SIO DI Grainger could still get in if he wanted to. I went to the stationery office and picked up some pens, pads and two memory sticks, just for a bit of backup.

As I was setting things out, I heard the heavy footsteps of SIO DI Grainger pounding down the corridor. Sergeant Phillips did not waste any time, I thought. He barged into the room. I decided to ignore him, as I knew this would wind him up; SIO DI Grainger was used to people jumping to attention when he arrived.

He grabbed me by the shoulder and spun me round. His face was red and contorted and right into mine. I grabbed him by the throat and pinned him to the wall.

'If you put your fucking hands on me once more, I will tear you apart,' I said about an inch from his face.

He was shocked and stunned, so I let him go. I felt the anger increasing inside me, so I took a few slow, deep breaths. SIO DI Grainger was startled, his face fully red and convulsing with anger. He came over to me and spoke.

'I am the lead detective in this case. I expect you to report to me anything you find. Are we clear on that?'

I walked over to him and again about an inch from his face, I looked him square in the eye and told him, 'I have been assigned here at the request of Chief Constable Gregg; I will be reporting directly to him. I will have no part in your investigation, so if you have a problem with that, I suggest you go and see him. Now, if you do not mind, I have things to do.'

I turned my back to him and carried on sorting the

room. With that, he turned and left. I knew sorting the room would be something Tuppence would take care of, but I just needed something to do with my hands, as I was sure as hell I would end up putting my fist through his face. I found him to be the most obnoxious man I had ever come across. His very presence made my skin crawl.

He was a heavy smoker, so his body odour was akin to an ashtray. He always looked like he needed a shower, but I guess it was just his normal show to the world. He was scruffy, had unruly fair hair, a pock-marked face, and was arrogant and very self-centred. Crime investigation has advanced, and he has been left behind. In my opinion, he was way out of his depth with this case. There was just an I in his team of one and he never gave praise or credit to anyone. How he had managed to stay in his position for so long was beyond me, but it is sleepy Cromley.

I prefer to work with a good team with the following protocol: Task – the crime, Team – to solve the crime, Individuals – with experience to join the team to solve the crime. A simple ethic I feel, but it is a bit contradictory, as I would be working alone on this case as a detective. I would, however, have Tuppence working with me so I would not be completely alone.

There were further footsteps along the corridor and they were a lot lighter. It was Chief Constable Gregg. He entered the room with a concerned look on his face.

'I have been informed about a bit of commotion, so

I came along to see what it was,' he said.

'It was just SIO DI Grainger and me having a chat.'

'It was reported to be more like a fracas,' replied Chief Constable Gregg.

'No, we are fine, sir. We just laid some boundaries.'

'I wasn't expecting you until tomorrow morning, but now you are here, get yourself settled in.'

I knew SIO DI Grainger would not make a complaint or say anything to Chief Constable Gregg, or anyone else for that matter. It was not the thing he would do; it's not good for one's ego, due to too many questions asked. He would not want anyone to know I had my hand on his throat and pinned him to the wall. I also knew he would be out to disrupt my investigation. I think Chief Constable Gregg knew that, as well.

Chief Constable Gregg turned to leave, but stopped, gave me a knowing look and a nod of his head, and left. He knew why I'd come to the station and was ready for the task ahead.

I sat for a couple of minutes going over the last half hour and I felt good. I had made my mark. I left the room, walked through the reception, and smiled and winked at Sergeant Phillips, who looked somewhat awkward. I made my way to the car park, ready to return to the apartment. As I made my way to the barrier, I could see SIO DI Grainger standing at the squad room window watching me as I left the station. I made sure I was walking tall and assertive. I was feeling good. I phoned Tuppence to tell her I was returning to the apartment and would be fifteen minutes. I told her we would eat out tonight.

I arrived at the apartment and Tuppence had run a hot bath for me. Brilliant, I thought, as I was ready for it. I made us a coffee and took mine into the bathroom with me. I was lying there chilling when Tuppence called out.

'Do you mind me sharing the bathroom with you, as there is only one mirror and it happens to be in there?'

Before I could answer she pushed the door open with her foot and walked in with a makeup bag in one hand and coffee in the other, wearing just her bra, pants and a smile.

'Hi,' she said, as she put her stuff down.

I know there was no agenda, it is just the way she is; complete trust between friends. Tuppence is around five foot six inches in height; she has golden brown skin, with a fantastic figure that clothes just flow on. Her dark hair flows down around her shoulders; she has coloured streaks through it, which she says is her individuality. She has, like my mother, a smile that could melt the snow off the top of a mountain.

All right, I know you want to know more about Tuppence:

Tuppence is forty years old, born and raised in Mortley, and she is fourteen years older than me. She was wild as a child, she told me, but academically I find her to be very bright and intelligent. She is an only child from a mixed-race couple. Her mother was of West

Indies origin. Her father was British. She had a good upbringing, and her parents were good church-going people and fun loving.

She has a happy disposition, but her life changed when at the age of fifteen she fell pregnant. Her parents were horrified and after a lot of tears and recriminations, they stood by and supported her. She told me her carefree attitude changed after that, as she now had a child to consider. There was no way she would give up the child, as suggested by some of her friends. The child's father said he would stand by her, but Tuppence did not want a marriage because she was pregnant; she wanted more than that. For his part, the child's father supported his daughter and that has continued to this day.

'I was curious about sex and wanted to try it and didn't consider the consequences. I guess you learn the hard way,' she said.

She never had a serious relationship after the birth of her daughter, as she wanted to raise her daughter; and besides, she has never met anyone that she wants to share her life with. She is happy to be independent. Her parents were there for her and they have a good relationship.

When Tuppence started work at Mortley station, her mother would take her granddaughter to school and Tuppence would collect her from school. Tuppence said she would never shy away from her responsibilities, but she would never shut her parents out, either.

Her daughter is living in New York. She studied Journalism at university and gained a double first degree. She met up with an American female student who was also studying Journalism.

Through a connection the American girl's father had at a New York paper, a job was offered to Tuppence's daughter to work on an English section of the paper. After many discussions and tears and greatly encouraged by Tuppence, she took the job; she went straight from university to New York. Tuppence speaks with her daughter on a regular basis and plans to visit her later in the year. I have never met her, but the Mortley station lads say she is her mother's daughter. I guess she will be a stunner like her mother.

Tuppence has worked at Mortley station for twenty years and is extremely popular with everyone, although a few of the lads are intimidated by her. I guess her directness will cause guys to hold back. She will not suffer fools gladly and is not frightened to tell them, no matter who happens to be there. I, on the other hand, like that in a person. You know exactly where you are with them.

Tuppence is not her birth name; I found that out from Sergeant Brown at Mortley station. He said her real name is Gladys and she hates it. I was told her mother is a massive fan of Gladys Knight and the Pips. Her mother decided, after a Gladys Knight gig she attended with her husband when she was pregnant, if she had a daughter she would call her Gladys.

Sergeant Brown informed me in the early days at the station, Tuppence would put her pennyworth on any subject discussed, and sometimes more, so the name Tuppence was mentioned. When she found out they thought she would go ballistic, but she loved it and has been with her ever since. Although Tuppence, they say, is not so vocal these days, I find her comments to be generally correct and I would listen to her views.

Sergeant Brown also told me of a little song Tuppence sings quietly to herself, but loud enough for the irritant to hear when they are annoying her. When you hear *Bibbledee, babbled and bobbledee doo*, it is time to get out of there. I have never heard her sing it, so I guess I am one of the chosen few.

I kept the conversation away from the impending case; I would save that for the return to the apartment over a relaxing drink. Oh yes, I am driving. Tuppence wanted to know more about Cromley, and she was especially interested in Yak, Yamma and BJ. The names conjured up to her mythical characters. I laughed out loud and told her they were far from that. She was curious and wanted to meet them.

'Time enough, but not now.'

She understood and smiled.

We arrived back at the apartment around nine o'clock. I poured Tuppence a drink; I grabbed a can of beer out of the fridge, sat down, took a swig and spoke.

'I will outline the case to you and what I have managed to find out. I will tell you how I want to play it and your role in it.'

'OK, you have my undivided attention.'

'From reading the case notes, SIO DI Grainger has convinced himself a member of the Holmes family carried out the murders and robbery.'

'How did he come to that conclusion?' asked Tuppence.

'The fact that there was no visible forced entry to the building or exit the building. All have been checked thoroughly, so I believe the conclusion was based on that.'

'Somehow, from your body language and manner, I'm guessing you don't fully agree with that conclusion,' she stated.

'I can see why the conclusion has been drawn, but it just does not add up. Why would a member of the family murder two elderly relatives for some family heirlooms? Yes, they are of value, but to kill for them just does not sit with me. I also believe they will be hard to dispose of, due to the amount of publicity.'

'So, what is your plan?'

'I want to set up two incident rooms, one here and one at Cromley station. The main one will be here in the spare bedroom. I know there will be some of SIO DI Grainger's snoopers sniffing around the Cromley incident room when we are not there, that I can guarantee.'

'Why the secrecy?'

'Something just does not sit right, and I trust my gut

feeling, but I cannot put my finger on it yet. I do not want Grainger to find out anything regarding my investigation. You need to remember you are a civilian working *for* me and not *with* me; you can't get involved in anything or make any comments. If you have anything to say, then we will discuss it when the time is convenient. You have to be clear on that.'

'Yes boss. I was hoping I would carry a gun pushed down my trouser belt like they do in the movies.'
She then let out a roar of laughter and I laughed too.

'Tomorrow morning, we will go to Cromley station and set up the incident room, so for now it is time for some sleep.'

With that we called it a night. A new day beckoned.

***

'Hi, Tuppence here. Before I say goodnight, I had better describe DS Paul Blackmore to you. He is six foot two inches tall, with an athletic build and muscled toned body. He works out on a regular basis. His hair is short, dark in colour, and he also dresses very well. He wears sharp suits with a collar and tie when he is working, but jeans and T-shirts when off duty. He is super good-looking with a gorgeous smile. He has a calm way about him. He is extremely popular with the girls at Mortley station; the married ones, as well. Many a pass has been made to him, but he has a knack of fending them off without causing offence to them or embarrassing them, especially on a night out. He has been out on dates, but is not one for casual relationships. I have come to like him a lot and we get on very well and I would trust him with my life. We talk about everything knowing it stays between us. There have never been any sexual desires on either side, just a deep-rooted friendship, love and respect. I absolutely adore him.'

THREE

The morning came easily. I had slept well. The sun was shining into my room, deflected from the bins below. All was quiet, so I guessed Tuppence was still asleep. I quietly made my way to the bathroom, had a shower and a shave and got dressed. Tuppence appeared and spoke.

'Man, are you always so noisy in the mornings?' she hollered as she made her way to the bathroom.

I could hear her singing away in the shower, so I shouted that breakfast would be ready soon.

'My, you sure know how to impress a girl. It's a long time since someone, besides my daughter, made me breakfast like this,' she laughed.

I made an American-style breakfast with pancakes, syrup and a bit of bacon. I don't normally drink coffee this early in the morning, but I thought it would be fitting.

I outlined to Tuppence we would go to the station, and I would show her where everything was and set up the incident room. I told her when we were in the station she must react like a civilian and not a police officer. It would be easy to fall into this role as we discuss the case back at the apartment.

'Yes, boss.'

'Stop calling me that.'

She just gave me one of her big smiles, but I knew she got the message.

We arrived at the station and I showed her around; canteen, toilets, etc. I kept her away from SIO DI Grainger's incident room, but I pointed it out to her. I told her she would no doubt have visitors when I wasn't there, but I had no worries. She is more than capable of looking after herself. We met Chief Constable Gregg on the tour, and I introduced Tuppence to him. There was a lingering look between them, a look I have seen between my parents.

'Come and see me at ten o'clock,' he said.

I left Tuppence to it and headed for his office at the appointed time. It was just up the corridor, so I knew he would keep an eye on her.

I knocked on the door and was called in straight away.

'Have a seat,' he said. 'You have had time to think, so I am interested in your thoughts and plan.'

'Sir, SIO DI Grainger's thoughts are centred on the family. I believe he is convinced, purely by the lack of any forced entry, the crime was carried out by a member of the family, but it doesn't sit right with me. The heirlooms taken were valuable, but not, in my view, enough to kill Jake and Arthur Holmes the uncle's to the present owner John Holmes. The family have been in residence in Cromley Hall for an exceptionally long time and I see no sign of that ending any time now or in the near future. I will be going to Cromley Hall to see for myself and speak with the family.'

'Very well. I will let them know you are coming. John Holmes and I are members of Cromley Golf Club and we have shared many rounds of golf. Since this happened, I have not been near the golf course. I thought it best to keep my distance for now.'

'I understand, sir. I will take Tuppence with me, as she has amazingly fast shorthand skills. It would take me ages to write up notes and carry out the investigation at the same time.'

'Very well – and remember she is a civilian.'

'I understand that, sir.'

With that I left the office. I went to my incident room and heard voices: Tuppence and Detective Constable Harrow, one of SIO DI Grainger's team.

'Have you lost your squad room, DC Harrow?' I enquired.

'No.'

'Then I suggest you go and find it,' I replied, with a bit of aggression.

With that, he left the room. I turned to Tuppence and told her he was one of SIO DI Grainger's flunkies. He had been sent on a recce.

'You will have a visit from SIO DI Grainger,' I said. 'Mention a woman and he will be there.'

She laughed. She was more than a match for him.

I helped her organise our incident room. I wanted enough information to the visual eye to make sense, but for the more interesting information to be kept for the apartment.

I said to her we would go for lunch and then go to Cromley Hall to have look round and talk to the family.

'I need you to take notes for me, as I cannot write and interview at the same time. Be impassive and if you are asked any questions, defer them to me.'

'Yes…'

I knew what she was going to say, so I just laughed.

There was a quaint pub down the hill from the hall, so we went there. We walked in and my parents were sitting having lunch. We walked over and I did the introductions. We were invited to join them, and it would have been rude not to. The atmosphere was good and there was a relationship developing between my parents and Tuppence. My father looked at me with that knowing look in his eye. I just shook my head and mouthed, 'No.' He smiled.

Good as the lunch was, I told them we had to go as duty called. I paid the bill on the way out; we got in the car and Tuppence said, 'What a lovely couple. You have your mother's nature and your dad's steeliness.'

With that she smiled, and we went on our way.

We arrived at Cromley Hall security gate. I pressed the intercom and waited to see if the barrier would open. Cromley Hall is home to the Holmes family and is open to the public on certain days of the week. We waited for a voice from the grill of the intercom. Shortly, a soft Irish voice answered. 'Good afternoon. Can I help you?'

'Hello, I am Detective Sergeant Paul Blackmore of

Cromley Police; Mr John Holmes is expecting me.'

With that, the gate started to slowly open and the lovely Irish voice said, 'Please drive to the car park down to your right and then make your way to Blaggards' Door down to your left. Ring the bell and someone will come for you.'

I duly obliged and carried out the instructions to the letter. Whilst we were waiting, I said to Tuppence, 'What a name for a door. It conjures up all sorts of images over the years with robbers, rogues etc.'

The door opened and I was met by John Holmes, who I have to say looked dreadful. He was clearly stressed and looked as if he had not slept for days.

'Please come in.'

We made our way through some rooms and arrived at what appeared to be a library. He pointed to some seats and beckoned us to sit down.

'This is Tuppence,' I said. 'She is a civilian with security clearance attached to Cromley police station. She is here purely to take notes on my behalf. Is that acceptable to you?'

'Yes, that's fine. I am aware SIO DI Grainger is of the opinion one of the family, and that includes me, carried out this dreadful crime.'

'Yes, I am aware it is a line of enquiry that is being followed. I am working independently of the main investigation team. I want to look at other angles.'

He stopped pacing the floor and looked at me with what I saw as a sign of relief. I knew there and then the crime was not committed by him or indeed by a member of the family. I had no evidence at this point, but I did consider myself to be a good judge of character and body language. His demeanour seemed to lift when I said I was following different angles. I felt he saw me as someone who was on his side. He was right.

'Mr Holmes, are we free to walk round the Hall grounds? I used to come to Cromley Hall when I was younger and I would like to familiarise myself with everything again. I want to show Tuppence what a magnificent building and grounds you have here.'

'Yes, please do. I will inform the staff of your intentions.'

'I will need to speak with you again and the family members who were here. Can I have the names and addresses of all members of the staff from the last five years to present?'

'Yes, I will have Personnel arrange that for you.'

He led us out to the yard and made his farewell. I went to the north wall with Tuppence and showed her the fantastic views over the valleys, which are truly breathtaking.

Tuppence turned to me and said, 'He didn't do it, did he?'

'No, I do not think so, and now I am certain neither he nor any member of his family did carry out this crime. What I have to do now is prove it.'

I took her on a tour through the hall and its history, gardens and to the church. We spent time looking round the church. As we were about to leave, the verger, Mr Holloway, entered the church.

'Can I help you?' he enquired in his gruff manner, which seemed to suit Cromley Hall.

'No, thank you, we are just leaving.'

'If you don't mind me saying,' said Mr Holloway, 'I seem to know you.'

'Alas, I have one of those faces,' I replied, and at that we left the church.

We made our way to the Personnel office to collect the list I requested. It was ready for me and as the office manager handed it over to me, she spoke.

'Mr John Holmes or any member of the family didn't commit the crime. They aren't capable of it,' she said.

I was taken aback with the force of her words. I thought, this is the type of person you want in the trenches with you in times of adversary. I took the large envelope and thanked her for it.

We went back to the car and made our way back to Cromley station. When we got to our incident room, I asked Tuppence to type up this afternoon's proceedings while it was still all fresh in our minds.

'Leave out the lunch with my parents,' I laughed.

She just gave me one of her screwed-up faces as I left the room. I headed for Chief Constable Gregg's office. Chief Constable Gregg is made from the same granite as Chief Constable Mondell. He is forty-five years old, six feet tall and medium to large build. He has an authoritative manner and is very assured. It is easy to see why they get on so well. Sadly, Chief Constable Gregg's wife died some years earlier and a bit of spark has been missing from his life since then. He spends most weekends on the golf course, hence his association with John Holmes. I knocked on the door.

'Come in,' he requested. 'Sit down and tell me how the first day went.'

'I went to Cromley Hall to speak with John Holmes. I wanted to look him in the eye when he answered me; I needed to know from his body language if he was involved.' I put to him.

'And what is your opinion on this?'

'Without absolute concrete proof, I do not think he or any member of his family are involved. It does not make sense to me. Why kill two high-profile members of your own family for two pieces of heirlooms? The pieces would be hard to sell in the open market. A private collector would not really want them to be on display, as he could be implicated in a double murder.'

Chief Constable Gregg was thoughtful for a minute, then said, 'The conversations we have regarding this case are strictly confidential.' He was looking directly at me.

'Absolutely, sir.'

'I share your opinion; it has never sat right with me either. What is your next step?'

'I will interview each member of the family and staff at the hall. I have asked for a list of all employees past and present, starting five years ago.'

'You think it might be a disgruntled employee?'

'It had to be someone with knowledge of Cromley Hall, regarding all the doors, windows, etc,' I put forward. 'This is the line I will be following, sir.'

'Very well. The press have not cottoned on to you as yet, so be on your toes for when they do.'

'Sir, I am expecting it and I am ready. If I can make one other request, I will need background checks for all the employees past and present. Tuppence is not authorised to carry this out. I do think it is best if I could use Sergeant Brown of Mortley police station to carry out these checks.'

'I will speak with Chief Constable Mondell and let you know.'

His quick response caught me off guard. I left his office on a high and bounced down the corridor. I got to the incident room and Tuppence was typing furiously at today's events.

'Come on, save the work and we will go back to the apartment to discuss the day's events and what the next step is.'

We walked across the car park to the car.

'Can you feel them?' I said to her.

'Yes, I am aware SIO DI Grainger is at the window of his incident room, I can feel his eyes burning into the back of my neck.'

'Do not react or look. Keep walking. We need to be above this, and anyway, you have brightened up their miserable day.'

I could sense she wanted to laugh, but she stifled it. We got in the car and headed for the apartment. Tuppence wanted to finish her typing, so I left her to it.

'What was going on with Mr Holloway today? He seemed to know you?' she stated.

'You should have been a detective.' We both laughed. 'I was going to tell you later when we discuss the case. When I was around twelve years old, BJ and I were fascinated with Cromley Hall. We were convinced there was a tunnel from the church to the hall. We decided one day we would investigate the church. We set off early, planning to spend the whole day investigating. Naive, of course. We were banging away on the walls when Mr Holloway came in and grabbed us by the collar.

"And what are you two up to? Stealing I might say," he snarled.

"No sir, we are looking for a secret tunnel into the Hall," I pleaded.

"There is no such thing. I should call the police," replied Mr Holloway.

"What for?" I pleaded. "That is what we were doing, looking for a passageway. Honest, sir."

"Right, clear off," said Mr Holloway, "or I will call the police."

'With that he let us go and we ran out of there as fast as our little legs could take us. You know, I have never returned to the church until today.'

Tuppence was almost wetting herself laughing and I laughed as well.

'Do you think there is a passage between the church and the hall?' she enquired.

'I do not know, but I will find out.'

Just then my police phone rang; I said to Tuppence it was Chief Constable Gregg. She decided it would be a good time to go for a shower.

'Yes, sir.'

'I spoke with Chief Constable Mondell, and we both agreed to your request. Ring him in the morning to set things up.'

'Thank you, sir.'

Great – that meant I could crack on.

Tuppence emerged from the shower. I told her she would be working with Sergeant Brown at Mortley station, and she was pleased with that.

'He will carry out all background checks for you on the employees from the last five years,' I said. 'I will be speaking with Chief Constable Mondell first thing in the morning and when he gives the go-ahead, you can call Sergeant Brown.'

She went off to her room and I sat for a few minutes formalising things in my head. Tuppence emerged and sat with her laptop to do more typing.

Later, I outlined the next day's plan. Tuppence would be based at Cromley station in the morning liaising with Sergeant Brown. I would be going back to the church for a further look.

'What about Mr Holloway?' she enquired.

'I am ready for him. In the afternoon, we will go to

the hall to interview the family and staff, so it will be a long and tiring day with high levels of concentration needed.'

I headed to bed, thinking - as always with the cases I investigate – what the coming day would hold. The pace of the case, for me, was steady, but I was sure it would start to pick up as I got further into it. I would also be waiting for results from any analytical analysis, which I might need; patience is paramount.

FOUR

The new day brought new hope for me.

'Good morning,' said Tuppence. 'I thought I would make breakfast today and see if I can match your high standards,' she laughed.

I turned on the radio to the local station for the news bulletin. I stopped when I heard the news reporter say:

'There has been a development in the police case investigating the horrific murders of Jake and Arthur Holmes at Cromley Hall. It is understood a detective has been brought in from another force to assist the main investigating squad. We have also learned he is a former police officer at Cromley station. We will keep you updated once we find out more on this mysterious officer.'

'Well,' I said to Tuppence. 'The cat is out of the bag now and it will not take them too long to find out who it is. I guess SIO DI Grainger will see to that.'

I rang Chief Constable Mondell and briefed him on my investigation so far and he seemed happy with that. He also gave clearance to use Sergeant Brown to carry out background checks and he will contact Tuppence later this morning.

I told Tuppence she had clearance to speak with

Sergeant Brown and he would contact her later this morning. We set off for the station and when we arrived SIO DI Grainger was outside talking to some people I assumed were reporters. I guess the clue was all the mobile phones and mini-recorders stuck in his face.

'Who was that outside the station talking to those people?' enquired Tuppence.

'That, my dear Tuppence, was SIO DI Grainger.'

'Ouch,' she replied. 'He looks repulsive.'

'Wait until he speaks to you and is right in your face.'

'He won't get that close to me, I can assure you.'

'Of that I have no doubt,' I replied, laughing.

I parked up and we made our way to our incident room. I made sure Tuppence had all she needed at her desk to continue her notes before I set off for the church at Cromley Hall. I went to the car and drove to the end of the exit and paused for a minute. I chuckled as SIO DI Grainger looked flustered with what looked like a constant stream of questions. I put the car in gear and drove off, thinking that I must watch the local news to find out what he was grilled about.

When I arrived at the barrier at Cromley Hall I was again met with the lovely soft Irish voice that kindly let me in. I parked up and walked to the church and let myself in. My mind drifted back to the time BJ, and I searched thoroughly for a secret passage but never completed the search, due to Mr Holloway's intervention.

I was looking around the pulpit when I heard

footsteps behind me; I turned to look directly at Mr Holloway.

'You're here again?'

'Indeed I am.'

'Do you mind telling me who you are?'

'I am Detective Sergeant Blackmore assigned to Cromley police station as part of the team investigating the murders of Jake and Arthur Holmes and the theft of valuable heirlooms at Cromley Hall.'

I showed him my warrant card, and he seemed to relax.

'Your face is very familiar.'

I thought I had better put him out of his misery. 'I was in this church fourteen years ago with a friend of mine when you accused us of trying to steal objects from the church. You threatened to call the police, but we managed to convince you we were honestly looking for a secret passage into the hall.'

'Oh yes, I remember,' he said and then burst out laughing. 'Do forgive me. There has been so much tension in the hall lately, it is good to laugh.'

He sat down and looked very weary, and I realised he was not such a grumpy old fart, but someone who cared for the church, the hall and the family. I decided it would be a good time to interview him on the events of the night.

He told me it was a family occasion to celebrate the birthdays of Jake and Arthur Holmes; they have birthdays in the same week. Mr Holloway told me he locked the church after the evening service and returned to his quarters, where he remained until the following morning and heard the dreadful news.

I thanked him and said I would not detain him any longer.

'Tell me, do you really think there may be a tunnel from the church to the hall?' he asked earnestly.

'I do not know. There are no visible signs of forced entry to the building, so the suggestion is the crime was committed from within.'

'I somehow know you don't think that is the case,' said Mr Holloway.

'Quite frankly, I do not, so I am looking at other avenues.'

'I will continue to look for you. If it is here, I will find it.'

I thanked him and told him our conversation would have to be confidential and he agreed. Deep down he was a decent guy and I warmed to him. We parted with smiles and a handshake.

I walked around the churchyard looking for signs of fresh movement or anything else that might look out of place, such as footprints or disturbance around gravestones. I drew a blank. I decided to head back to the station to see how Tuppence was getting on with Sergeant Brown.

The excitement around the station from earlier was gone and things seemed to have returned to a level of normality. I made my way through the reception and

Sergeant Phillips was on duty.

'She's a bit of a stunner,' he ventured.

'Who might that be?' I asked.

'The woman you brought with you,' he said, with a level of frustration.

'Too stunning for you,' I replied.

I signed in and made my way out of reception without looking up. I think that put an end to any future conversation regarding Tuppence.

I could hear voices from the incident room as I neared; I recognised the voices of Chief Constable Gregg and Tuppence. I walked in and they were having a coffee and talking about the case. I sat down and joined the conversation. Background checks on the staff over the last five years showed nothing out of the ordinary. However, I was convinced there was a link somewhere and I would be pursuing that line a bit deeper.

Chief Constable Gregg stood up and said to me, 'Will you pop along to my office in ten minutes?'

'Yes, sir.'

I knocked on the door and was invited in, he indicated for me to sit down.

'I was in the corridor; I could hear Tuppence singing what sounded like a strange song I have never heard before,' he said.

'Was it *Bibbledee, babbled and bobbledee doo*?'

'Why yes, it sounded like that, although I didn't hear all of it.'

'Had SIO DI Grainger paid her a visit?'

'Yes, he had.'

'In Mortley, it is taken as a warning shot that you are annoying her. She sings it to herself to stop herself exploding at her annoyance. The person usually gets the message and leaves. I have never heard her sing it, so I guess I do not annoy her.'

We both smiled and then we discussed the case. I told him I would be going to the hall to interview the family and staff this afternoon. John Holmes has arranged for all the staff to be present on site.

Chief Constable Gregg also spoke of the press attention and the interview they'd had with SIO DI Grainger this morning. I said to him I'd noticed it as I was driving in this morning, I was quite happy to let him deal with the press. He said they would find out who I was sooner rather than later. I told him I was aware of this; I would deal with it when the time came.

I left his office and headed for the incident room, and said to Tuppence, 'I hear you had a visit from SIO DI Grainger this morning.'

'Yes. What an obnoxious dickhead he is,' she said, with a degree of venom. 'I kept my cool and told him I was on purely office and notetaking duties. He asked to see the notes, but I refused. I said he would have to ask you for permission. Just then Chief Constable Gregg entered the office and SIO DI Grainger left. Chief Constable Gregg asked what he wanted so I told him and that's when you entered the room.'

'Yes, we did discuss it when we had our meeting and I

assured Chief Constable Gregg you were more than capable of looking after yourself. He may return, and Chief Constable Gregg will not be far away.'

She smiled at my answer and seemed to relax back to her usual self.

'Come on, let us go to Cromley Hall.'

We arrived at the hall. I was looking forward to hearing that soothing beautiful Irish voice when I pressed the intercom at the gate.

'Can I help you?' asked an abrupt male voice.

'Detective Sergeant Paul Blackmore from Cromley Police,' I answered.

'Yes, we have been expecting you. Do you know where to go?'

'Indeed I do.'

With that he opened the gate and I made my way to the car park. We walked to the side door. I was met by Cynthia Holmes, wife of John Holmes.

'I'm sorry, but John is dealing with an urgent matter and will be with you shortly. We have prepared the library where you can carry out the interviews. I have prepared an interview order for you, starting with the family and then the staff.'

'Thank you, that will be fine. As you are here, can we start with you?'

She nodded her agreement and sat down.

'I believe it was your mother who found the bodies of Jake and Arthur Holmes?'

'Yes, she did, and she is experiencing terrible trauma

since. We all set out to search for them as they had been gone for a while. My mother went to the gallery and found them both lying on the floor.'

'I need to speak with your mother.'

'Of course, I will bring her to you.'

We sat in the library for a few minutes then Cynthia Holmes arrived with her mother. She was walking slowly, and she looked dreadful and clearly still distressed. She slowly sat down on the sofa with Cynthia Holmes sitting beside her.

'I have told my mother who you are and why you are here and why we have to go through this.'

'Thank you.'

'Thank you for seeing me, Mrs Drummond, and I know it will be difficult, but could you take me through the night of the party from your viewpoint?'

'The party had been going well with nothing unusual, we noticed Jake was gone for a while and Arthur went to look for him. When he failed to return, we all went to look for him and Jake. We discussed who would go where and I went to the gallery.'

'Why did you volunteer to go to the gallery?'

'There are no stairs to climb, and walking is easier for me.'

'What did you find when you arrived at the gallery?'

'When I entered the gallery, I saw Arthur lying on the floor and when I walked further in, I saw Jake lying on the floor. I let out a scream and Cynthia and John came running in followed by the family.'

'Did you notice anything else?'

'There was blood on the floor around their heads. I left the room as I was upset. Cynthia took me to the library and John rang the police.'

'Thank you, Mrs Drummond, that will be all.'

Cynthia Holmes took her mother back to her room and then returned to the library.

The interview with her went much as I expected and was consistent with her husband's comments when I first spoke with him. She told us she had arranged tea at three o'clock, as she felt we would need a break. I know Cromley Hall will be in good hands while she is around. I said to Tuppence she had work to do to meet that standard and I got a thump in the ribs.

The afternoon panned out, with all the interviews going as I expected. I spoke with John and Cynthia Holmes' children, cousins and other family members who were present at the party.

The only member of the family who was not with the family when the bodies were discovered was John Holmes nephew Roderick Holmes, Roderick told me he had gone to the kitchen to fetch some more beers from the fridge and when he returned, he heard the commotion and joined the search. The kitchen is at the opposite end of the building to the gallery.

I spoke with the hall staff, guides and ground staff and nothing stood out. I was now totally convinced there was no foul play with the family and staff. I thanked Cynthia Holmes for her hospitality and we made our departure.

We sat in the car for a few minutes, then Tuppence spoke. 'What is bothering you?'

'Did you notice the body language of everyone we spoke to? The heaviness in their hearts and the strain they are all under? It is too late to return to the station, and we need a drink.'

'Oh yes,' she replied with a smile.

'To The Lodge,' I said with purpose.

We dropped the car off at the apartment and walked to the pub and sat down. The pint of the lovely stuff went down a treat and, boy, did I need that. Then Tuppence said, 'What did you make of the interviews?'

'Let me turn the tables and ask you for your opinion.'

'I don't think any of them were involved. There was nothing outstanding from anyone. They are all good, decent, hardworking people.'

'Spot on and I agree totally. There was consistency across all of them, with nothing obvious standing out.'

'Are you going to tell them?'

'No, I want things to stay the way they are. It will help me and leave the focus on SIO DI Grainger.'

Just then, the local news came on the television in the lounge. I watched to see if the going's on outside the station this morning would air on the programme. I did not have to wait long. The television news presenter spoke of developments in the case and cut to the police station. SIO DI Grainger was standing there looking extremely uncomfortable; normally he loves this type of attention. Chief Constable Gregg has certainly hung him out to dry.

Tuppence and I watched very intently, with a sense of mischief.

'SIO DI Grainger, are you any closer to solving the case?' asked Sue Bentley of the Cromley Echo.

'The case is complicated, but the investigation is making progress.'

'I take that as a no. I have been reliably informed that another detective has been assigned to the case. I also believe he is a local man by the name of Detective Sergeant Paul Blackmore. Will you confirm this to be true?' Sue Bentley asked directly.

'As with all cases we investigate, we take every opportunity and resource to solve cases.'

'I take that as a yes,' Sue Bentley stated.

The camera cut away and back to the television studio.

'Bringing in a detective from another force, although he is a local man, raises profoundly serious questions on how this investigation is going or not going. As far as I have been able to find out, there has been truly little progress so far and a lot of serious questions have been asked regarding the investigation team. Sandra Roberts, Cromley News.'

'Wow!' I said to Tuppence. 'Sue Bentley is tough and direct.'

'She certainly is and doesn't mess about.'

'I could not put it any better myself.'

We both laughed.

'What does that mean for you, now your name's out there?' she asked.

'Well, my name is out there now, they will come looking for me, so I will just let them find me.'

We finished our drinks and slowly headed back to the apartment. I was enjoying the walk taking the air deep in my lungs. Tuppence was saying how sad she thought Cynthia Holmes looked and the strain she felt she was under. I guess the whole family and staff were feeling the same way. I thought that after dinner when we had our catchup, I would outline my thoughts and plan to Tuppence. It was time we moved on.

'Remember to keep an open mind and control emotions, as they can overtake and fog the mind. I believe no one from Cromley Hall is involved in this case, but we cannot fully rule it out at this stage.'

She nodded in agreement.

FIVE

The apartment was warm from the evening sun; Tuppence was standing by the window looking over the park. The sun created a silhouette of her body, she is a stunning woman.

Dinner, washing-up done and showers taken, she made a dig on how much room I take up in the bathroom. I had better do something about it or I might hear the dreaded song.

We went to our incident room to discuss the case. I went to the whiteboards and Tuppence sat down. I was about to start when my personal phone rang. It was Yak. I turned my phone off; I would ring him later.

'OK, let us see where we are. It is clear to me no members of the family or employees were involved in any way with the murders or theft of the heirlooms. However, I cannot rule it out, no matter how small the likelihood.'

'I agree. So, what's the next step?'

'I believe someone connected with the hall in some way is involved and I need to find the link. That person or persons must be intimate with the workings of the hall and especially entry and exit points. I also believe Jake and Arthur Holmes were killed because they were in the wrong place at the wrong time. They were murdered in the gallery and the party was in the main hall, which is situated on the other side of the building. There is no other logical reason to me to explain their deaths.'

'Wow, I can see your thought process.'

'We need to dig further to find the link. I will check with the forensic people tomorrow to see if they can reveal any clues.'

'I will see what I can find out from the main investigation team. I will take a wander down there to borrow some sugar and get to know them,' she said.

'Do not overstay your visit, as the tension in there will be very high. They will be suspicious of you.'

We called it a night at that point.

I checked my personal phone: four missed calls: My mother, Yak, Yamma and BJ. I laughed.

'Why are you laughing?' asked Tuppence.

'Missed calls from my mother and the lads, so I will ring them.'

I rang Yak.

'Hey, why didn't you tell us you were in town. Are you involved with the goings-on at the hall?' he asked.

'Hi mate. Sorry I could not tell you why I was in town, but yes, I am working on the case,' I answered.

'Hell, so much for sleepy Mortley. Who would have thought Cromley would be the hub of activity,' he stated.

'Listen, I cannot go into details on the case for obvious reasons.'

'That's fine. We can all have a catch-up soon.'

'I look forward to it.'

We spoke a bit more about general things and then hung up. I called BJ and Yamma and had similar conversations, and we agreed we would all meet up soon.

I stood for a couple of minutes, deep in thought. It occurred to me Amber would know I was in town. We had had no contact for some time and to be honest I was not in a hurry to see her. I slowly began to realise that Tuppence was standing watching me. I turned and looked at her.

'A girl on your mind?' she ventured.

I just stood and smiled, but said nothing.

'I will get us some drinks and then you can tell me about her and your friends.'

She poured the drinks, not my usual pint but a large Southern Comfort with ice and an Irn-Bru mixer.

'I felt you needed something stronger than a beer.'

She was indeed correct on that one; she has a great sense of occasion.

'Then you will begin.'

She was curled up at the end of the sofa with a large drink in hand and her face full of concentration. Wow, I felt intimidated.

'I will start with the lads. We met when we were all in the Infants and went all the way through the years and grades together. Wherever there was one, the others were never far away. We spent as much time in each other's houses. My parents had no problem with them crashing out at my house after a night out. The saying "All for one and one for all" applied to us. There was a tremendous level of trust between us.

'BJ, his real name is George Murphy. His parents moved to Cromley when his father accepted a new job in engineering. We started calling him BJ because he was always saying "Bejesus" and it has stuck with him ever since. He is a clever lad. He studied engineering at university and he is in engineering, and in fact he is working at the same company as his father. He is in a long-term relationship with his partner Evet. He has a young son.

'Yak, his real name is John Parker. His family settled in Cromley just before he was born. We started calling him Yak because he could never hold his drink and inevitably, he would throw up at the end of the night. He did not need a lot to drink; it just never agreed with him. He is now married to Shirley and has a young son and daughter, and rarely drinks alcohol. He went to university to study nursing, and he works at the Cromley hospital, the same hospital as my sister. BJ, Yamma and I were all his best men at his wedding. He refused to select one of us, so it was logical for the three of us to do it together.

'Yamma, his real name is Richard Moore. His family have had roots in Cromley over generations. We started calling him Yamma because he would always say, "I'm a" when he was going to do something, but it sounded like Yamma, so it stuck. He is also in a relationship with Lucy, and has no children. He went to university to study to be a teacher, got his degree and teaches at a school outside of Cromley. He has worked hard on his diction and has never said "I'm a" for a while now.'

'And what about you? What did the lads call you?' she asked, laughing.

'They called me Blamer,' I answered.

'What the hell! You had better explain that one,' she said, with a degree of laughter and sarcasm, and sat bolt upright.

'It was actually given to me by my father. When I was incredibly young, if something happened and I was involved, I would always blame someone else instead of myself. My father got fed up with it and decided to call me Blamer to teach me a lesson and the lads picked up on it.'

'Did it teach you a lesson?'

'It sure did, as I hated it.'

'And you have saved the best until last?'

'Amber. I first set eyes on her at the clubhouse after we changed after a football match. I thought she was the most beautiful girl I had ever seen, and she took my breath away. She was petite, shoulder-length blonde hair, she stood around five foot three, confident and very self-assured, with beautiful blue eyes and a great toned body. She was her own woman. To say I was intimidated by her is an understatement.

'She was extremely popular with all the guys; I was way down the pecking order. I tried to talk to her, but became tongue-tied and she would laugh. I shrank within my sensitive shell and just admired her from a distance.

'I did find the courage at one time to ask her out and to my astonishment she agreed, she had obviously seen something in me. We met at the club, but we were always interrupted, and she did not seem bothered. She relished the attention, and I became depressed and just let the night fizzle out and made my exit. I left her with her friends and admirers and made my way home. I made one further date and met her on a bench in the Queen's park next to the town, but again it never worked out. I saw her occasionally from a distance over the years, but there was an unfinished episode in my life and that has bugged me ever since.

'I decided I had to mature. I had to leave home and the promotion at Mortley station came at the right time. It gave me the chance to breathe and fend for myself, and to let the person within come out. So far, it seems to have worked.'

'Amen to that. I see the person I know before me now and I can't relate to the person you have described.'

'Yes, the Mortley therapy seems to have worked,' I laughed.

'What would you do if you saw her now?' she asked.

'I guess it was my insecurities rather than her, so I do not think I would react in any way. I really do not think a relationship with her would work. I look at my parents and how they are. They are still as much in love now as the day they met; they laugh every day.'

'I know you have been out on dates, but I have never known you to have a long-term relationship. The girls in the office love you,' she said, with mischief.

'I have never met anyone I want to spend my life with. I have no intention of being in a relationship just to be in a relationship. I look at my parents and see how much they love each other. They are very content with each other's company and often my mother would go to my father's workshop with a bottle of wine and two glasses. We would hear laughter coming from the workshop and it had a lasting effect just not on me, but also my brother and sister. I have not met that person yet.'

'You will. Time is with you,' she answered.

SIX

I woke fresh and ready for the day ahead. I like to feel fresh and business-like when dealing with people and situations, and then my phone rang.

'Good morning, DS Blackmore. Make sure you are at the station for eight thirty for a briefing, ready for a press conference at nine o'clock,' he ordered.

'Thank you, sir. I will be there.'

'What did Chief Constable Gregg want?' Tuppence asked.

'It is time to face the wolves.'

We arrived at the station in good time. I left Tuppence in the incident room and then made my way to Chief Constable Gregg's office.

'Where are you with your investigation?' he asked, directly.

He was agitated; he knew there was little progress with the case. I was also surprised SIO DI Grainger was not in attendance.

'I do not think the family or present employees are involved. I believe Jake and Arthur Holmes were murdered because they were in the wrong place at the wrong time. I believe the murderer or murderers know the layout of Cromley Hall and how to get in and out. Sergeant Brown and Tuppence are checking the employee records going back five years and I should have that information later today.'

'Very well,' said Chief Constable Gregg.

'Before we go, sir, I think there is a mole in the investigation team. Information is being deliberately leaked to Sue Bentley of the Cromley Echo. She knew of my arrival and knew I was working independently, I put to him.

'I will look into it, but for now let's get this press briefing over with,' he said, with a level of agitation.

We made our way to a room set aside for such occasions. I could hear voices coming from the room; at the appointed hour we made our entry. I could feel all eyes burning into me as we made our way to the head table. We sat down and Chief Constable Gregg made a start.

'Good morning,' he opened. 'I would like to introduce Detective Sergeant Blackmore. DS Blackmore has been brought in to assist with the investigation at Cromley Hall. It is my belief his local Cromley knowledge will be a great benefit to the investigation team. So now, if you are ready, we will take your questions.'

I noticed the female reporter from the other morning sitting intently. She was looking directly at me and ignored Chief Constable Gregg. I looked at her directly with a deadpan expression, I was hell bent on offering her no expression. She was on her feet in a flash.

'Sue Bentley, Cromley Echo. DS Blackmore, are you

taking over the case from SIO DI Grainger?'

'I am here as part of the team, to assist with the case.'

'It is my understanding SIO DI Grainger has made little or no progress on the murders of Jake and Arthur Holmes at Cromley Hall,' she said aggressively.

'We can't discuss specifics of the case,' Chief Constable Gregg answered quickly.

'It has been said the police are of the opinion the murders were carried out by a member or members of the Holmes family. What is your opinion on this, DS Blackmore?' Sue Bentley asked aggressively.

'As I answered earlier, we can't discuss specifics of the case,' Chief Constable Gregg got in quickly.

'It is my opinion, DS Blackmore, you do not share this view and you are carrying out your own separate investigation. Can you confirm this?' Sue Bentley again asked aggressively.

Chief Constable Gregg was again going to intervene, but I stopped him.

'This is a difficult and complicated case with no quick fixes. Progress is being made, but I cannot reveal any details as it may prejudice the investigation.'

'I will take that as a yes,' Sue Bentley again said with a hard tone to her voice.

'How were Jake and Arthur Holmes murdered?' asked the reporter from the television news programme.

'That question at this time cannot be answered,' I replied.

'Are there any questions you can answer? It seems to me the police do not have any evidence or suspects at this time,' Sue Bentley demanded angrily.

I felt she knew my train of thought and my comment about progress being made was progress I was making. She is no idiot.

There were other questions, but no more from Sue Bentley of the Cromley Echo. I felt this would not be the last time I would see or deal with her; I could feel her steely eyes boring into me. Chief Constable Gregg called a halt to the proceedings, and we made our way to his office.

'Well done,' he said. 'You handled it well.'

'She is one bright reporter.'

We discussed the case for a few more minutes and then I left and made my way to the incident room.

Sue Bentley was a tall, attractive woman with short, neat hair and elegant in her looks and manner, with a steely interior. She had long, perfectly shaped legs and dressed very well. She had a way about her that got her what she wanted, so I had better always be vigilant.

'How did it go?' Tuppence asked.

'Difficult. The media are restless for information. They sense we do not have anything at this time and they are not far wrong. No doubt it will feature on the local news tonight. Right, where are you with the checks on employees from the last five years?'

'Sergeant Brown has not turned up anything. No one has been sacked for stealing, etc.'

'There must be something somewhere. It is staring me in the face, but I cannot see it just yet. I am going out for a while.'

'Where are you going?' she asked.

'I am going to the park for some air, to walk around, and above all else I need to think.'

The park was quiet. The sun was out, but not too hot and that pleased me. I walked around as I used to not that many years ago. It had not changed at all. The football pitches were still set as they were with more or less the same teams playing on them. The clubhouse was much the same, except it desperately needed a coat of paint.

I walked through the woods and along the dirt track myself and the lads used to race on our bikes. We would race for hours and Yamma would win virtually every one of them. He was a natural racer; he eventually joined the local cycle racing team.

I need times like this to myself to think and get myself together. It is a trait I have always had and so far, it has served me well. Self-space and awareness are something I believe everyone should indulge in for inner peace, tranquillity and clarity of thought.

I made my way to the nearby burger stand to get a coffee, and a familiar voice from the burger van said.

'Hello, Paul. It's been a long time since I have seen you in these parts.'

It was the voice of my old football team manager, Graham Curtis.

'Hello, yes it has been a while,' I replied.

'No need to ask what you are doing back here; it's on the news and in the paper. Are you going to save Cromley Hall?'

'Do not believe everything you hear and read.'

'So, what's going on at Cromley Hall?'

'You know I cannot discuss it with you. I have local knowledge that may be helpful to the investigating team. What is it with the burger van? The last time I saw you, you were dressed in a sharp suit.'

'I got fed up with it, so I took early retirement and bought a burger van. I am never going to earn a fortune, but it keeps me out of mischief, and I answer only to myself – oh, and my wife,' he said, laughing.

'Are you still involved with football?' I asked.

'No. I come down when I can to watch the odd game, but no involvement.'

'Good to see you, Graham. Take care, and we will probably meet again.'

With that I made my way across the park and headed back to the station. I was almost at the exit when a female voice spoke, and I knew straightway who it was.

'Hello, DS Blackmore,' said Sue Bentley in a direct manner. 'What a coincidence we should meet,' she said with a level of sarcasm.

'I rather think not,' I replied. 'The station is just across the road from the Echo premises, so it would be easy to see me in the park,' I said sarcastically.

'Touchy. As if I would.'

I looked at her and raised my eyebrow.

'Any further developments?' she asked.

'You had your briefing this morning and I have nothing to add.'

'You don't get along with SIO DI Grainger.'

'What gives you that idea?'

'Why wasn't he at the briefing this morning?'

'Police work.'

'So, what is your line of investigation?' she asked forcefully.

'Have a good day.'

I turned and walked away and headed to the station, she called out to me: 'DS Blackmore, why don't we go out for dinner?'

I stopped, turned and looked at her.

'That will never happen.'

'We will talk again,' she answered.

Not if I can help it, I thought to myself.

I reached the incident room to find Tuppence was not there. I started to write my train of thought down on a pad. There was no way I was going to put them on the whiteboard for all to see. I would save that for later back at the apartment.

Just then, Tuppence arrived back in the room.

'Hi, did you enjoy your walk in the park?'

'Yes. I met up with my old football manager and we had a chat. I also met up with Sue Bentley of the Cromley Echo, or should I say, *she* met up with *me*.'

'Digging for more information?'

'Yes, and she invited me out for dinner.'

'Why is it every woman has the hots for you?' she said whilst laughing.

'No, she is desperate for information.'

I walked over to the door, checked the corridor and then closed the door.

'That reporter is getting information from someone inside the station. She knows about my temporary transfer to Cromley and my working separately on the case. What have you been up to?'

'I was invited for a coffee with SIO DI Grainger's team.'

'That means they are hunting for information.'

'Yes, I thought so, as well, so I was on my guard.'

'Well, we can use that to our advantage. They have opened the door and you have walked through it. They will try to sweeten you with smiles and compliments to draw you in. Be careful.'

I had only glanced over the lab report on the murders of Jake and Arthur Holmes, so I sat down and read it thoroughly. There was alcohol in their systems; it was their birthdays, so it was to be expected. The alcohol levels were extremely high; I would say they were fairly drunk.

No sign of recreational drugs and again I would be surprised if there were. They were both on medication expected of gentlemen in their late seventies and the levels matched up with their medical records.

The official cause of death was blunt trauma injury to

the head. Jake and Arthur Holmes were found later that evening when they were reported missing. I put the report down for now.

'Let us discuss the list of employees from the last five years.'

She duly put the file on the table and opened it. There were twenty-three names. Thankfully, it was as low as it was as it is a tedious, but necessary job to go through them. All of them left for various non-suspicious reasons, but I was convinced the answer lay in there somewhere.

I decided it was time for lunch, so we went to The Lodge; I was deliberately avoiding the police canteen. This was no reflection on the canteen food, which was generally good. I felt the less contact we had with the station personnel the better for them, as well as Tuppence and my good self. We arrived at The Lodge and sat looking at the menu.

'You were very quiet in the car,' Tuppence commented.

'Sorry, I am missing a link and cannot connect with it yet. I still believe the answer lies at Cromley Hall.'

'Put it to one side and enjoy your lunch. An hour away from it will perhaps do you good.'

She was right, as always, and we sat and had our lunch whilst talking about Cromley as a town and the comparisons to Mortley. We laughed at that, as they were remarkably similar in size, population, industry and the usual goings-on around the people on a daily basis.

Lunch finished, I drove Tuppence back to the station and walked with her to our room. I dropped her there and decided to go back to Cromley Hall; I wanted to look at the church again.

I was delighted the soft Irish voice had returned when I pressed the intercom button at the hall gates. She duly opened the gates to allow me to enter.

I slowly made my way to the church, looking intently at everything I could see, the front towers, corridors, etc. I could feel the answer, but was not able to touch it.

I walked into the church and found Mr Holloway inside preparing the church for a service that night dedicated to the Holmes family. I felt for the family, as they were all feeling the strain. I also felt for the staff. However, I must keep my feelings under wraps for now. Mr Holloway saw me and stopped what he was doing. He walked towards me; we shook hands.

'I have been over every part of this church; I can't find any sign of an entry to a secret passage,' he said, frustratingly.

'If you do not mind, I will have a look round to satisfy my own curiosity.'

'Of course.'

I started with the pulpit. I was looking for signs of stone slabs, steps being moved recently, but alas, everything was in place. I spent two hours in the church looking intently at everything I could put my hands on, but came up with a blank. I pushed and pulled the pulpit, pews, etc. I left defeated. I bade farewell to Mr Holloway and made my way back to the car and drove back to the station.

I walked down the corridor to the incident room and caught sight of Chief Constable Gregg going into his office.

'Had a visitor?' I asked her, with a raised eyebrow and half smile.

'Yes, Chief Constable Gregg popped in to see if I was OK.'

'Let us wrap up here and head back to the apartment.'

'Amen to that.'

We made our way to the car and drove to the barrier. I stopped for a few seconds and then swiped my pass to open the barrier and we drove off.

'Why the pause at the barrier? You appeared to be looking at something.'

'The offices of the Cromley Echo newspaper are across the road from the vehicle entrance to the station. I have noticed Sue Bentley at one of the office windows on a few occasions. I feel she is watching my movements more rather than SIO DI Grainger's. It is my belief Sue Bentley has an informant in SIO DI Grainger's team. To hell with it, let us go for a drink.'

'Amen to that.'

I parked the car at the apartment, and we walked to The Lodge. I got our drinks and we sat in the corner out of the way. I had just taken a mouthful when Yak walked in with his wife, Shirley.

'Hi, John,' I shouted over.

He was stunned for a moment and then realised I was sitting in the corner and then looked at Tuppence. I invited them to join us and after the introductions I got them some drinks and I told them Tuppence was working on the case with me. Yak threw me a raised eyebrow, but I shook my head as a no.

We sat going over our teenage years, much to the amusement of the girls. However, I had a case to investigate. We made our farewells and promised we would all meet up when the case was over and before my return to Mortley.

'What a lovely couple,' Tuppence said, as we walked back to the apartment.

'Yes, they sure are. It was good to see them; It was good to have a diversion from the case, to have a laugh and clear the head.'

'Yes, it was,' she replied, with a smile.

We arrived back at the apartment and headed to our incident room. I spoke openly to Tuppence; what I was really doing was emptying my mind of my thoughts.

'I am more and more convinced the murders are associated someway with someone who has a connection with Cromley Hall. There has to be a connection; we have to dig deeper. That person or persons knows of a way into the hall from an external source. I have to find it. That is why I am convinced of the link. I need to press on, as the answer will not come to me. I have to go and find it and find it soon. Chief Constable Gregg is not pressuring me, but his patience will run out at some stage.'

'I haven't picked up on any impatience from Chief Constable Gregg. My view is he believes in your line of enquiry, so carry on,' she said, with a smile.

I looked at her and stopped short of asking how she knew that, but let it go.

SEVEN

I woke from my night's slumber fresh and with a purpose in my stride. I made a coffee and headed for the bathroom, singing quietly to myself. I was feeling the power of the summer's morning and the birds were singing in tune with me. I must sort out my things in the bathroom; maybe I will do it this evening.

I could smell the aroma of breakfast, so Tuppence was obviously awake and in the kitchen. She enjoys cooking and prefers to do it; she assures me it is not my lack of cooking prowess – hmm, I am not so sure.

We listened to the local news and there was a brief mention of the murders of Jake and Arthur Holmes. The forthcoming local elections are now becoming centre stage. I know this will not be the case with Sue Bentley. She is no mug and I believe she does not go along with the view that the murders were carried out by a member of the family, hence her interest in me.

I called Tuppence and said it was time to leave. The drive to the station was uneventful. I parked up and we walked across the car park to the entrance to the station. I looked up and saw some of SIO DI Grainger's team standing at the windows, and they were sure as hell not looking at me. I stopped and looked towards the Echo newspaper building. I saw Sue Bentley standing at one of the third-floor windows. She waved at me when I looked at her; I looked away and headed inside. We signed in and made our way to the incident room. I caught sight of SIO DI Grainger leaving Chief Constable Gregg's office. He had a smug look on his face, and he waved to me. What is he up to? I thought. We had no sooner sat down when I got a call from Chief Constable Gregg to go and see him, so I guessed my thoughts would be answered very shortly.

I went to his office, knocked and duly waited. The call came:

'Sit down,' he ordered. He was looking very pensive. 'Update me with your investigation,' he said forcefully.

'I am still convinced the murders and thefts were carried out by someone associated within the staff, but not directly. The person or persons entered the hall by means of an entry point I have not, as yet, located,' I answered.

'Interesting! SIO DI Grainger has just informed me he has made a breakthrough.'

'That is interesting, sir. On what evidence?'

'He has found the murder weapon and it has been confirmed by the forensics laboratory; the murder weapon was a wooden sculpture that was on display. He also has fingerprints and DNA from the murder weapon that have also been verified by the forensic people. He is on his way to Cromley Hall now to make an arrest and bring him to the station.'

'Wow!' was all I could muster in answer. 'Who he is

bringing in?'

'Roderick Holmes, nephew of John Holmes.'

'That will never hold up, sir,' I said, frustrated. 'He lives at Cromley Hall, so his fingerprints and DNA will be everywhere in the hall.'

'His case is backed up by the forensics team,' said the Chief.

'All the forensics team have done is confirm the fingerprints and DNA. They could go over the whole of Cromley Hall and find the same results,' I said angrily.

'You had better get on with your investigation. Time now is not on your side.'

I left his office and felt the feel-good factor I had this morning slowly draining out of my body and being replaced with anger. I walked into the incident room seething. Tuppence turned to look at me and sat opened mouthed when she saw the expression on my face.

'What the hell has happened to you?'

'SIO DI Grainger has told Chief Constable Gregg he has made a breakthrough in the case.'

'What? What is it?'

'He has told Chief Constable Gregg he has found the murder weapon with fingerprints and backed up with DNA. He has said the suspect is Roderick Holmes, nephew of John Holmes. He is on his way to Cromley Hall to arrest him,' I said, angrily.

'That is dramatic. How do you feel about it?'

'It is bollocks. Roderick Holmes lives at Cromley Hall, so his fingerprints and DNA are going to be all over the building. It is a sign, to me, a mark of desperation. If the Crown Prosecution Service agrees he has a case, Roderick will be charged and will go to trial.'

'So how is that going to affect your investigation?' she asked in a concerned voice.

'Chief Constable Gregg has told me time is not on my side. I still believe one hundred percent that I am following the right path and I will continue to follow it,' I said determinedly. 'I am going out for a while; I need to clear my head.'

Tuppence nodded her head, and I left the incident room. The reality was I needed time to think and take in the events so far. I was going to walk to the park but remembered Sue Bentley of the Echo; she would be looking out for me.

I decided to head to another park on the other side of town. I would leave the car as I felt it would indicate I was still in the building. I walked down the corridor and made my way to the side door.

As I opened the door, I caught sight of SIO DI Grainger driving into the yard with the police car's blue lights flashing like it was Christmas, for all to see. As usual, he was making an entrance and statement, as was his style. It was obvious to me Sue Bentley would also have seen it and would be on to it in a flash.

I grabbed a cab and headed for West Cromley Park. The cab dropped me at the gates to the park. In all the years I have visited this park, I have never walked through the large iron gates. I walked down the long drive between the trees to the main visitor centre; the sun danced between the branches of the trees as I walked. The park is very scenic and has good, strategically sited benches to sit and think. I came here many times when I was studying; I would sit on the same bench, if it was available, to read and revise. The view over the valley is serene.

I walked to the café, which had had a major overhaul since I last was there. It was a lot more commercial and had less of the town's history and heritage. I guess income has a higher priority than looking at objects and what life was like during the war years in Cromley.

I bought a coffee and made my way to my favourite bench, then I sat for a few moments. I let my mind wander free just to disengage from everything. I was watching the world go by, people walking their dogs and dogs walking their people, I chuckled to myself.

I caught sight of Amber who was pushing a pushchair with a young child in it. There was another older woman with her with the same blonde hair, so I deduced she was her mother. Well, I am a detective!

She was a bit away from me, but I knew her features very well. She is petite, blonde hair bouncing on her shoulder, gorgeous body and a great sense of dress. As always, she looked stunning.

She did not see the bench I was sitting on. I had no idea if she knew how, at one time, I really loved and wanted her; did she even care? I guess I was too shy, awkward in nature with absolutely no chat-up lines. I looked at her now and those teenage feelings did not rise; I guess I had matured and moved on.

I finished my coffee and thought, I cannot, much as I want to, sit here all day; I needed someone to talk to away from Cromley. I decided to give Chief Constable Mondell a call.

'Mondell,' he said, in his normal direct manner.

'Good morning, sir. DS Blackmore.'

'It's early for an update, so how can I help you?' His tone was of concern, and it relaxed me.

'There has been a development in the case where a member of the Holmes family, Roderick Holmes, has been arrested and he is at Cromley station under interview. The murder weapon has been found with fingerprints and DNA all over it. If the Crown Prosecution Service agrees, Roderick Holmes will go to trial charged with the murder of his two great uncles,' I said, in a nutshell.

'I take it from the tone in your voice you are not in agreement with this, so why?' he asked, directly.

'The fingerprints and DNA evidence are weak; Roderick Holmes lives at Cromley Hall so they will be everywhere in the building; he has no history of violence, he has never broken the law, nothing. Why would he kill his great uncles for a couple of family heirlooms? I still believe the murders were carried out by someone outside the family and that is the line I am following,' I replied.

'There is still time for you to follow that line of

enquiry. The process of a charge to court to conviction will take a while; he will plead not guilty, and, in a way, it will be of help to you. You will be able to work behind the scenes, so stick with it. Speak with Chief Constable Gregg tomorrow morning. Let today settle, as there will be highly charged atmosphere in the station,' he said with finality.

I thanked him for his advice and decided it was time to go back to the station. I made my way along the drive to the park entrance and called a cab. I took in the scenery as I waited for it. I had never really noticed the church across the road on the opposite side of the park. In all the years visiting the park, I have always arrived by car and driven through the gates and parked under the trees. The cab duly arrived.

I opened the cab door and heard a car coming along the drive. I paused for a moment and looked towards the oncoming car. I noticed the car driver was Amber; she had to stop as the cab was blocking the exit. I saw her looking at me intently as I got in the cab. She would know I was in town as it was all over the local news and newspaper. I could feel her gaze as she followed the cab back to the town. That is the closest I have been to her for a few years.

I got the cab driver to drop me at the market square and I walked across to the station. I walked in the main entrance with my head up and a brisk step. There was no way they were going to see me totally pissed off. SIO DI Grainger was in the interview room with Roderick

Holmes. I arrived in my incident room to find Tuppence looking thoughtful.

'Have you cleared your head?'

'Yes, I have.'

'What have you decided?'

'We carry on.'

'Great!' she said happily.

'Why?'

'Sergeant Phillips was in here earlier; they are on a high in their incident room. As far as they are concerned, the case is over, and you will be scuttling back to Mortley very soon.'

'Come on, we have work to do. I am missing a link, but at this time I cannot see it. I have to find the key that will open the door.'

'The checks Sergeant Brown and I have made on the staff at Cromley Hall revealed nothing,' she reported.

'I believe that is where the answer lies. We have to delve deeper,' I put to her.

'You appear to be getting regular visitors whenever I leave the building.'

'Yes, I am, and they are slowly opening up to me. I put on an impassive face when they mention you. As far as they are concerned, I am just someone who takes notes and writes them up,' she said, laughing.

Just then the desk phone rang, and Tuppence took the call. 'Yes, sir, I will tell him straight away. Chief Constable Gregg wants to see you straight away,' she said directly.

I jumped up from my chair and headed to his office. I knocked on the door, waited and the call came. I entered the office and was ushered to sit down.

'DS Blackmore, Roderick Holmes has been charged with the murder of his two great uncles. As expected, he is denying all charges. He will make his first appearance at the magistrate's tomorrow morning.'

I looked at him in disbelief barely able to take in what he has just told me. My mind was racing at a rate of knots. Chief Constable Gregg looked at me with a concern on his face. I was doing all I could to control my emotions and stop myself from exploding. He brought me back down to earth.

'I know you do not follow SIO DI Grainger's line of enquiry and now everyone is expecting you to return to Mortley. I brought you here for a purpose and as far as I'm concerned that purpose has not been completed. I want you to carry on your line of enquiry. I have spoken with Chief Constable Mondell, he has agreed to you staying on for a bit longer.'

'Thank you, sir.'

I left his office and went back to the incident room.

'Come on Tuppence, I have had enough of this place for one day, Let us go back to the apartment and then The Lodge.'

'Amen to that.'

EIGHT

We made our way back to the apartment. It was quiet in the car as I was in a pensive mood and not very sociable at that point, I guess Tuppence was feeling the same way. We had some food and got ourselves ready to go out. We walked to The Lodge; I felt the evening air in our lungs would do us a power of good.

I got us some drinks and we sat in the corner for some peace to talk. I could see people talking and looking at me, so I guessed they now knew who I am.

I sat down and said to Tuppence, 'I have had my moment of sullenness and it is time to refocus. I feel everything at this time is going against me, I believe one hundred per cent Roderick Holmes did not commit the crime and the answer is somewhere connected to the hall.'

Tuppence did not say anything and sat there listening to me.

'The fact that Roderick Holmes is pleading his innocence has bought me more time and I need to use it wisely. I feel too angry, and that goes against my normal state of mind, to discuss the case anymore tonight, so let us enjoy having a drink and take our minds off the case.'

Tuppence just smiled, but in a relaxed way that also relaxed me.

We sat and watched the news on the TV and the lead story was the arrest of Roderick Holmes for the crimes at Cromley Hall. I could hear the murmurings in the pub and the looks across to me. I was not intimidated by the atmosphere in The Lodge, as I believed I was one hundred per cent right in my thought process of the events at Cromley Hall.

We finished our drinks and left the pub to walk back to the apartment. I was talking as we approached the main road we had to cross when I heard Tuppence scream, 'Look out!'

I could feel myself being pulled backwards and something hit me down the left side of my body. I could feel myself falling and I ended up sprawled across damp grass with the world spinning around me. I was stunned and I could hear Tuppence screaming for help and calling for someone to phone for an ambulance. I could hear a lot of voices and commotion and people running around. I was aware of Tuppence kneeling by my side talking to me, asking me if I was all right. As hard as I tried, I could not say a word. My mind was in a whirl, and Tuppence was holding me and telling me to stay still, and I guess my instinct was to get to my feet. I was moving my hands, legs, etc. Thankfully, I could feel them all, but, man, did I ache down the left side of my body. I lay still and I could feel Tuppence gently lift my head and put something soft under it. I could hear the distant sound of sirens gradually getting louder and eventually they stopped beside us. There were a lot of people crowded around and I could hear voices saying, 'That's the copper who is working on the murders at Cromley Hall.'

I was aware of someone asking me where I was experiencing pain. Through the darkness I could make out a paramedic and one was kneeling beside me. They were asking me again where I was experiencing pain, so I ran my left hand down the left side of my body. They took my vital signs and slowly got me on to a stretcher and with the help of the police got me in to the ambulance and shut the doors. The paramedics carried out an external examination of my body, but thankfully nothing seemed to be broken. They took me with all lights flashing to Cromley hospital. I was suddenly concerned for Tuppence and where she was. I called out her name; the paramedics assured me she was safe with the police officers.

In a short time, we arrived at the hospital. I was taken straight into the Accident and Emergency department to be met by a trauma team who set to work on me. They talked to me the whole time, asking where I was experiencing pain and taking lots of readings. The trauma doctor arranged for me to have a body scan to ensure they had not missed anything.

The technician asked me to remain still during the scan, but I was that sore I could not move anyway. After a while, the scan was complete, and I was taken back to the Accident and Emergency room. Chief Constable Gregg and Tuppence had been waiting for me and they came into the cubicle; I could see Tuppence had been crying. Chief Constable Gregg had a grave, concerned expression on his face. He came over and spoke to me, but I was still dazed and was later diagnosed with a bit of concussion. I was moved to a more secure room and Chief Constable Gregg posted a guard outside with no one to gain entry to my room except Tuppence and the medical team.

Chief Constable Gregg spoke, 'Tuppence has told me what happened, so I suggest you rest tonight. I will see you tomorrow.'

I did not sleep well that night despite painkillers. I spoke with the nursing night team about everything and nothing. They are truly professional in their level of care and dedication to duty. I thought it was just my sister who was wholly enthusiastic when it came to nursing.

The morning came slowly, and the trauma consultant came in with his team and told me I was lucky. There were no broken bones or damage to my body except bruising and that would heal with time. My head was still a bit fuzzy so they would keep me in for a little longer under observation. I was feeling hungry and thirsty, but they would not allow me to eat anything and to just sip water in case I had a relapse.

Tuppence arrived. She told me Chief Constable Gregg had driven her back to the apartment and arranged for some police officers to watch the apartment overnight.

'They drove me to the hospital and escorted me to your room. Chief Constable Gregg also placed a police officer outside your room and there is one there now.'

'What happened?' I asked her.

'I have been instructed by Chief Constable Gregg not to discuss the events of last night with you. He wants you to rest and will see you later today,' she said with a level of firmness I did not have the energy to argue with.

The consultant came to see me later in the afternoon and examined and chatted with me. He was happy with my progress and was happy for me to be discharged, and left to make the arrangements. Tuppence had brought me some clean clothes and it was difficult getting them on, but eventually I got there. Tuppence rang Chief Constable Gregg and informed him I was being discharged. He arranged for a squad car to take us back to the apartment.

I made my way to the sofa and sat down. I was sore but I was also determined not to show how I really felt. It was important to me to show I was fit to carry on. I did not know how Chief Constable Gregg would be with me, but I had to show a determined spirit and willingness to carry on.

It was four o'clock and as I had not eaten all day, Tuppence decided to make a light meal for us and duly carried on. I went for a shower and the hot water felt good on the bruising down my left side and just stood there until Tuppence gave me the ten-minute food warning. Tuppence informed me Chief Constable Gregg would pay a visit at six o'clock. I had been thinking about the events of the last twenty hours and said to Tuppence, 'What happened last night? I want to know before Chief Constable Gregg arrives.'

She looked at me, picked up her coffee and sat down.

'We left the pub, talking as we were walking. Suddenly, as we got to the road, a car appeared with no lights on and headed towards us at speed. As I was facing you as you were talking, I saw the car as it came out of the darkness. I managed to grab you by the collar and pulled you backwards. The side of the car hit you on your left side, pushing us both backwards, and I fell on you as we hit the ground.'

'So, it was not the car that caused the bruising down my left side?'

'Your other side will hurt in a minute,' she said menacingly.

'Did you see who was driving?'

'No, the car lights were off. The driver was wearing a hoodie with it up over his or her head. They were hunched over the steering wheel so I could not see a face,' she added.

'Did you see the make of car, colour and number plate?'

'No, it happened so fast I just grabbed you and pulled you back.'

'So, you were also responsible for the scratches on the back of my neck.'

'The urge to cause you further damage is getting stronger,' she again said menacingly.

Chief Constable Gregg duly arrived at six o'clock. He looked pensive and serious. There was no way I was going to show him any signs of pain, just positivity.

'How are you feeling?' he asked.

'I feel fine, sir, just a little stiff, but that will clear up soon. It was a glancing blow down my side.'

'I will make some coffee,' said Tuppence. 'I have told DS Blackmore what happened.'

'What do you think really happened?' he asked.

'Someone made a great attempt to take me out, sir,' I replied with conviction.

'You don't think it was just someone stealing a car or a joyrider?' he added.

'No,' I replied with assertiveness. 'For me to be at that place at that time was more than a coincidence. I feel he or she was waiting for me and timed their attempt almost to perfection. If it were not for Tuppence, I would not be sitting here talking to you. I believe through the Echo paper reporter Sue Bentley, the opinion that the events at Cromley Hall were being investigated on a different line of enquiry to SIO DI Grainger. I feel this has spooked the real killer, which resulted in this attack. This has more than reaffirmed my belief the crime was carried out by someone who knows the layout of Cromley Hall and somehow there is a link to someone who has had a connection with the hall. There is no way any member of the family, in my opinion, carried out this crime.'

'From now the stakes have risen to a higher level. We need to discuss the way forward,' he added.

Tuppence returned with the coffees and turned to leave the room.

'Please stay,' I requested.

She stopped and turned towards us. I looked at Chief Constable Gregg and he nodded in agreement. I motioned for her to sit and she duly obliged. I thought I would put my line of attack in first as I was leading one line of enquiry.

'I agree the stakes have risen and that has confirmed my belief my instincts are correct. I do not believe the murderer is a professional, just a plan that went horribly wrong. The attack last night I believe was carried out in a panic and will now be very unpredictable. I believe we should feed the press it was a car theft, and I was in the wrong place at the wrong time. This will take the pressure off the murderer; I do not want him or her to go underground. It is important he or she stays within reach.'

'Go on,' said Chief Gregg.

'It will be beneficial for my investigation to carry on as it is. I feel for Roderick Holmes, but I have no concrete proof that will have him released anytime soon. I do not want the murderer to do anything rash and remain with a level of calmness,' I concluded. 'I have interviewed every member of the family; all the answers, body language, levels of stress and anxiety are all the same. There was consistency across them all. I have interviewed all the members of staff and my conclusion is the same as the family.'

'If that's the case,' said Chief Constable Gregg, 'the murders were carried out, as you have said, by someone with a connection to the hall.'

'The murderer has intimate knowledge of the hall, so my next phase is to look at the partners and children of the staff. I want to check for criminal records and if they have worked at the hall. I will also continue to search for the point of entry to the hall. All the members of the family say it does not exist and if it does it must have been found at some point in time.'

'Very well, carry on, but work from the apartment tomorrow and you can liaise with Sergeant Brown when it is required. This will be a good time to conclude for the night.'

Chief Constable Gregg stood up to leave and commented, 'You need to rest.'

He looked at me and nodded his head. He knew I was in more pain than I let on. As I said earlier, he is no idiot.

'We have kept the incident from the press for now, but I will have to make a statement tomorrow morning. I will put out that it was likely to be a car theft and you were in the wrong place at the wrong time and an investigation is in place.'

'Thank you, sir.'

Somehow, I could not see Sue Bentley falling for

that line and I can expect a grilling from her when she has the chance. Tuppence showed him out whilst I went over the last hour. She returned and seemed relaxed.

'The meeting went better than I thought it would go,' I put to her.

'He was relaxed. I think he believes in you and is willing to give you time, I don't believe he thinks the murders were carried out by a member of the family. Perhaps I am being cynical, it crossed my mind that SIO DI Grainger was behind the attack and wanted you out of the way,' she said it in a way that alarmed me.

'I can see why you would think that but no, I believe he was not. SIO DI Grainger may be a complete dickhead, but he is no fool. He will probably get great pleasure that I have been injured, and he thinks I will be out of the way for a few days or even returned to Mortley; I do not believe he would want to see me killed.'

As there would be a press release tomorrow, I thought that I had better ring my parents, as my mother would freak out if she heard it from the news bulletin first rather than me. I leaned over to get the phone and experienced a sharp pain that made me breathless for a couple of seconds. I dialled the number to my parents' house.

My phone call completed, I put my phone down and sat looking at the floor.

'A penny for them?' Tuppence asked.

'Do you not mean tuppence for them?' I said

laughing.

'Funny!' she replied.

'I think tonight we will not discuss the events of the last twenty-four hours or the case in general. Let us have a night off.'

'You're the boss,' she replied with a smile.

Tuppence went to her room to have a video call with her daughter, and I sat watching the television. Watching TV is not something I would do a lot of, as there are more interesting things to do in life. Tuppence appeared shortly and spoke.

'I thought you were having a night off.'

'What do you mean?'

'You are watching *Midsomer Murders*,' she said, laughing her head off.

'I happen to like watching this programme. I like the characters,' I said, laughing.

NINE

I did not sleep too well as it was difficult to settle due to my injuries. I got out of bed a couple of times and sat in the sitting room and watched some television. I made myself some tea, turned the lights out, and sat in the armchair and watched the sun as it rose majestically in the sky and slowly lit up the park. It is such a beautiful time of the day; the birds were singing to each other, but otherwise the morning was still. There is something poetic about this time of day, with nature at its finest and most beautiful.

I must have fallen asleep, as I was woken up with the gorgeous aroma of breakfast cooking. I must have slept in the chair for a couple of hours. I could hear Tuppence humming away to the radio. The table was set, and I looked towards the kitchen door just as Tuppence walked into the dining area.

'Good morning, and how are you feeling? I thought I would leave you sleeping as I know you had a restless night. I heard you get up and walk about. I got up and stood by the bedroom door and saw you looking out the window with the lights out. You look settled so I thought I would just leave you and went back to bed,' she said with a warm smile.

'What time did you get up?'

'Around an hour ago. I had a shower and sorted out a few of my things, and then made breakfast.'

'It smells good. I am starving and I've hardly eaten anything in the last twenty-four hours.'

'I guessed you would be. I have, however, only made a small breakfast, as it is best not to overdo it and leave you feeling uncomfortable.'

Breakfast finished and domestics done, I turned to Tuppence and said, 'I suggest we go to our incident room to plan the next step.'

'Not yet. I need to pop over the road to get some supplies, so we can do it when I come back.'

'OK. I know the shops are not far, but be careful,' I said with concern.

'Of course.'

I promised Tuppence I would stay where I was until she came back, I kept my word. I sat watching the daily life of the park. People diligently walking their dogs, stopping to chat to each other with a poo bag in hand and not a care in the world. Yuk.

There were the usual serious runners checking their watches as they did a circuit of the park, and the joggers who were so unfit and overweight, they put on their kit and struggled red cheeked around the park, blowing hard and looking as if they could keel over at any time. Kids kicking a ball around in the goals on the football pitch, pretending they are their idols with their numbered and named shirts, reminded me of the time when the lads and I used to do the same thing.

Tuppence duly returned with shopping bags in hand and without incident. She was quite chatty as she put the shopping away, and I said to her,

'Sit down and I will put on the news to see if anything has been said regarding the case.'

I turned the TV on to the news channel and just caught the newsreader saying,

'There will be a news conference from the Cromley police force at one o'clock regarding the crime at Cromley Hall, so we'll come back to that…'

I sat going over the events in my head from my arrival in Cromley, to the incident with the car and, I have certainly spooked someone and that to me is a very good sign. The rest of the morning I spent reading the notes that Tuppence had written up.

I turned the television on just before one o'clock and Tuppence joined me. We watched with great interest.

The conference opened with Chief Constable Gregg. He was on his own outlining how the case was going, and everything seemed to be going in a civil matter until Sue Bentley stood up and directed a question at Chief Constable Gregg.

'Was the incident with DS Blackmore, where he was knocked down with a car the other night, a deliberate attempt to injure or kill him?' she asked directly.

There was a stunned silence in the room, but Chief Constable Gregg remained resolute.

'We believe the car may have been stolen and there is no evidence to suggest it was a deliberate act; DS

Blackmore was unfortunately in the wrong place at the wrong time,' he replied.

'I believe DS Blackmore is working independently, looking into the killing of Jake and Arthur Holmes at Cromley Hall. Will you confirm this is true?' She was looking Chief Constable Gregg directly in the eye.

'As I stated before, I cannot make any further comment on the investigation at this moment in time,' he said firmly.

'Why is SIO DI Grainger not here today?'

'He is not available.'

'He has not been at the last two conferences. Are you shielding him?' she said forcefully and with menace.

With this, Chief Constable Gregg called a halt to the proceedings. I looked at Tuppence and spoke. 'She is one tough cookie.'

'She sure is.'

'I think I will buy the Cromley Echo tomorrow; I believe her article will be interesting.'

My personal phone started pinging with messages from Yak, Yamma and BJ. I messaged back to say I was all right and would catch up with them soon. I also sent my brother and sister the same message.

'Let us work – to the incident room and beyond,' Tuppence laughed in her best Buzz Lightyear voice.

Despite my discomfort, I was in the mood to work and felt I had sat on my arse for far too long. I needed to keep pace with the case and events as they were unfolding.

I went to the planner boards where they were split into sections: Cromley Hall, the Holmes family, the hall staff, the grounds staff and SIO DI Grainger's investigation.

'OK, let us review. If you have any comments or views, then please feel free to throw them in the pot.'

Tuppence smiled and nodded. 'Cromley Hall. This I firmly believe is where I will find the answer, so I have to find the evidence. The search for a secret tunnel in the church has been unsuccessful by Mr Holloway and me. We have covered every bit of the church and the churchyard. I even checked the graveyard, but there were no signs of anything being disturbed. I still believe there is another access to the hall known to the murderer or murderers. I will have to widen the scope. Mr Holloway is like a kid with a new toy as he is doing something outside his daily activity and greatly wants to help the family, so I will ring him tomorrow morning to discuss other parts of the outer buildings and grounds.'

'I would like to have a look around the kitchen,' Tuppence stated. 'That would be safe to do.'

'Ok, this is how we will play it. We will go to the hall together and visit the kitchen. I will pop out to see a member of the family and you can just have a look. If you see anything that might need pushing or pulling, do not do it; let me know and I will arrange whatever we need to do. I do not want you to risk any kind of injury; Chief Constable Gregg would crucify me.'

'It's a deal,' she said with a smile.

'Holmes family. We have interviewed every member of the family including Roderick Holmes; he has no criminal record or any misdemeanours of any sort. Roderick is living at Cromley Hall with his uncle John Holmes as his parents are working on a five-year project in New Zealand. As his workplace is closer to Cromley Hall it is easier for him to be based there; this has allowed his parents to let their house out whilst they are away. Roderick works in banking in Leicester, he leads what can be described as a modest life. I believe his father is returning from New Zealand due to the nature of the case. I do not believe anyone from that family carried out this crime. The body language and level of stress are consistent with them all. Their answers to my questions were all consistent, with nothing sticking out to set off alarm bells in my head. I passionately believe murder or any acts of dishonour are not in their hundreds of years DNA. It makes no sense for any member of the family to gain from this crime. The heirlooms stolen could not be sold on the open market as they are unique to the family and no dealer would touch them. It looks more and more to me it was an amateurish attempt gone very terribly wrong.

'SIO Grainger. In a word, desperate. Yes, there is evidence that the crime could be pointing at Roderick Holmes, but then again it could point to a number of people. The pressure for now is off him due to the arrest and I am surprised the Crown Prosecution Service agreed with the charges laid down. Surely, they would know this is flawed? A good defence barrister will tear them apart, but that, for now, is not my problem.

'Cromley Hall Staff. I do not think any member of the staff is directly involved, so we will look at their families and past employees. I believe the answer will be there somewhere. He or she will be in a high state of anxiety and stress and that is a dangerous combination, as we have found out. I believe the statement from Chief Constable Gregg's at the press conference will have reduced that person's stress levels, but they will be watching closely.

'So, let me recap. We need to investigate all the staff families for the last five years. We need to check for any criminal records, drugs, and financial records, anything that is not legal or close to it. A direct line has been set up with you and Sergeant Brown, so call him, work with him and dig deep. I will ring Cynthia Holmes to supply us with the names of spouses, partners, siblings and children. That will do for now. I will also ring Mr Holloway to widen the scope to search for a secret way into the hall.'

'Do you think Cynthia Holmes will supply personal staff details?'

'Yes, she will have no choice in the matter. Although I have not directly said no member of the family carried out the crime, she believes I know they did not do it. She will be keen to clear the family name and will work with us. So, let us crack on; we have a lot of work to do. I will make us a drink.'

'No!' she yelled. 'I will make it.'

'I have had enough of sitting on my arse. Moving around will help me, as sitting about causes me more discomfort.'

She did not argue.

'There is one other thing I need to investigate; Sue Bentley is getting her information from somewhere and I need to find out where.'

'How do you know?'

'Did you not notice how stunned the other members of the media were when she asked Chief Constable Gregg about the incident with the car? She was the only one who knew. How did she find out?' I said to her directly.

Tuppence looked at me with a blank expression on her face.

'I will speak with Chief Constable Gregg later today.'

TEN

The phone call to Cynthia Holmes at first was pensive. I asked her how the family were coping with the situation. She said they all felt under immense pressure and knew Roderick did not kill his great uncles and steal the family heirlooms. I wanted to tell her I believed her, but I could not. I explained the line of enquiry I was looking at and she appeared to relax. I asked her to write all of the staff family connections on some plain paper and put the list in a sealed envelope. I asked her if she would be kind enough to be at the gatehouse, I did not want anyone else putting their hands on it. I told her Tuppence would pick it up later before the hall closed for the day. We agreed five o'clock would be a good time.

'Tuppence, I have a small job for you.'

'Really?'

'Yes, I want you to drive to Cromley Hall for five o'clock and meet with Cynthia Holmes at the gatehouse. I do not want to arrange for someone from the station to collect the envelope; there is no way I want Grainger to get wind of my investigation. She will give you a sealed envelope with the names of the staff families; then drive straight back.'

'Am I insured?'

'Yes. I had that arranged right back at the start, just

in case there was a need for you to drive, but no speeding,' I said, laughing. 'Of course, you can decline the request, bearing in mind what happened the other night.'

'No way will I refuse. I know you would not ask me lightly and I don't feel in any sense of danger.'

I called Chief Constable Gregg and I outlined my plans to him, and he agreed. I also said again there is an informant in the station, probably linked to SIO DI Grainger's team. There was a stunned silence at the news conference; Sue Bentley was the only one who knew of the car attack on me; how did she know?

He said to leave it with him.

I was feeling tired, so I decided to rest and presently Tuppence went to Cromley Hall to collect the envelope from Cynthia Holmes. I was not concerned with her driving, as I felt the attack on me was a one-off.

I did not sleep, but just dozed on and off for a while, and I heard Tuppence return to the apartment. She came into my room and handed me the envelope. She had spoken with Cynthia Holmes, who had said to Tuppence:

'I believe DS Blackmore doesn't think Roderick killed his great uncles. This has given us all hope and we will help him in any way we can.'

Tuppence said she could not comment, but felt like giving her a big hug; perhaps she can when this is all over.

I decided we would do no more work this evening. We will set up a new email address in the morning and send the list name by name to Sergeant Brown to start background checks.

I sat in my chair looking out over the park and watched the early evening runners and joggers in the park, as well as the usual dog walkers. I noticed a familiar face running down the park in the direction of the apartment. I clearly recognised the face and shape of Amber; she is a serious runner in terms of her pace and gear. She is a stunning woman. She looked at her watch as she turned the corner and she appeared to be comfortable with her time. I watched her for a couple of laps, then dozed off.

Tuppence went to speak with her daughter, and she reappeared looking relaxed and after checking I was OK, she disappeared into the bathroom.

I sat thinking about Cromley Hall. I was thinking about the layout of the hall grounds and how they have changed over the years. The church had been there I guessed more or less from the beginning. Maybe I had been infatuated by my childhood dream that there was a tunnel from the church to the hall and that had clouded my thinking down a narrow tunnel. I need to talk to John Holmes regarding the changes to the hall and grounds over the years. I want to talk to Mr Holloway, as well. A trip to Cromley Hall tomorrow is a must.

ELEVEN

I was up early around five o'clock and ready to do some work. Tuppence was still asleep, so I made myself some tea. I stood by the window overlooking the park. No, I was not looking for Amber; I was just greeting with the early morning smile that I enjoy at this time of day. I sat for a while and started making breakfast.

'What the hell are you doing?' she yelled.

'Look, I am not crippled and doing things helps me. I cannot sit around all day long. It frustrates the hell out of me.'

Her face softened and then she broke into a smile. She set the table and we had breakfast. We had a rule never to discuss work over meals. Well, in all fairness, it was my rule, but Tuppence readily agreed.

We had just finished when Chief Constable Gregg rang. I took the call and sat in my chair by the window. He was in good humour and had rung to see how my injuries were coming along. I told him I was good and ready for work. I told him I would be going to Cromley Hall later this morning and I would be there for a few hours. I spoke with him again regarding my opinion that someone within the station was leaking information to Sue Bentley from the Cromley Echo. Chief Constable Gregg stopped me and informed me he was dealing with that issue. He wanted me to focus fully on the case without distractions. I had no option but to agree, but I was also incredibly grateful he had taken it on board.

The call ended and I went into the kitchen to see Tuppence and told her happily:

'Chief Constable Gregg is going to take care of the leak from the station to Sue Bentley of the Echo.'

She looked at me and before she could say anything, I said, 'He wants me to focus on the case without distractions and you know he is right.'

We made our way to our incident room to go over the day's work and I put in to place the following:

• Tuppence would ring Sergeant Brown and put into place background checks on the Cromley Hall staff.

• I would ring John Holmes to arrange to meet and discuss any changes to the Cromley Hall buildings over the years.

• I would ring Mr Holloway, the next phase of finding a secret entrance to the hall.

I have decided to remove the secret tunnel from my investigation; it was just a childish fantasy. Tuppence laughed when I said this, but could see where I was coming from.

I left Tuppence in the incident room to ring Sergeant Brown and I went to my chair by the window. I sat for a few minutes to take in the world going by and then rang John Holmes.

'Good morning, Mr Holmes,' I said formally. I did not ask how he or his family were as I already knew the answer to that question.

'Good morning, DS Blackmore,' he replied.

'I would like to come to the hall this morning to talk to you about the hall and grounds, in particular to changes over the years and any drawings you may have.'

'Of course,' he said.

'I would like to have our meeting at eleven o'clock, if that is agreeable to you.'

'Yes, that will be fine with me; I will inform the security gate of your visit.'

'Could I also ask you to keep the reason for my visit strictly confidential?'

'Of course.'

I ended the phone call and sat thinking for a few minutes and then I thought of Mr Holloway. I rang and he answered in a jovial mood.

'Good morning, DS Blackmore,' he said with positivity. His positivity made me think he may have found something.

'Good morning. I will be at the hall later this morning, so I would like to meet with you early this afternoon to have a chat, if that is acceptable to you.'

'Yes, that will be fine. Where do you want to meet?'

'I will meet you in the church.'

He agreed and I ended the call.

I sat in my chair overlooking the park and my mind was going over the hall grounds as best I could remember them. I was willing my mind to find something, but alas, it drew a blank. Just then, Tuppence entered the room and broke my train of thought.

'Everything set with Sergeant Brown?' I put to her.

'Yes. Chief Constable Mondell has set him up in an office just down the corridor from his office, so he can work with more confidence and not look over his shoulder from prying eyes.'

'Both Chief Constables are from the same tribe. Chief Constable Gregg has set our station incident room just down the corridor from his office.'

We both laughed.

'We will go to Cromley Hall. However, we will go to Cromley station first.'

'Why?'

'I want to drive into the car park, walk across to the door and then to our incident room. I want Sue Bentley, SIO DI Grainger and his team to see me, and see that I am fit and well and carrying on. I especially want SIO DI Grainger to see that I am determined as ever to crack this case, so when we get out of the car we will walk with authority and purpose. I will probably ache when I get to the room, but they will not know it.'

Tuppence laughed.

We set off and I walked gingerly down the stairs to the car park. I eased into the car seat. The drive to the station was uneventful and eventually we arrived at the station and parked up. We got out of the car and we walked with authority and purpose, as we arranged. I did not need to look, as I could feel Sue Bentley and SIO DI Grainger both burning their eyes into me with intensity.

It made me feel good. We walked to the desk and signed in. Sergeant Phillips was on duty and spoke.

'How are you, DS Blackmore?' he asked, with little emotion.

'I have never felt better, Sergeant Phillips. Thank you for your concern,' I replied, without looking up. 'Such a fine day, do you not think?' I said as I walked away, not waiting for a reply.

Tuppence and I arrived at the incident room. I was glad to sit down. I had been discharged from the hospital and they had told me time would be the healer.

The phone rang and Tuppence answered, put the phone down and spoke. 'Chief Constable Gregg wants you to go and see him.'

I stood up and made my way to his office. I knocked and waited for the call that came after a few seconds.

'Please sit down.'

He pointed to a chair. I duly carried out his instruction.

'Why didn't you tell me you were returning to work? I was expecting you to be off for at least a week,' he said, with a level of concern.

'I will be perfectly honest, sir. I have never taken time off, so to say to you I would be returning never occurred to me and I do not mean that in a disrespectful way.'

'Are you fit enough to return? It was a nasty injury you received.'

'Yes, sir, I do feel fit to return and, yes, I am a little stiff, but walking helps me, sitting around does me no good at all. I also have Tuppence there to keep an eye on me,' I said, laughing.

'So, what are your plans for today?'

'We are going to Cromley Hall, so I can speak with John Holmes. Tuppence has spoken with Sergeant Brown at Mortley station. We are carrying out background checks on the Cromley Hall staff,' I answered with assurance.

'Very well. Keep me informed of developments.'

I rose from the chair and walked with a purpose from the chair to the door. I could feel him watching me closely for any signs of a grimace, but I was making sure that never was going to happen.

I made my way to the incident room, I could hear Tuppence singing *Bibbledee, babbled and bobbledee doo*. I knew she was not alone. I reached the door and saw the grotesque shape of SIO DI Grainger.

'Is there something I can do for you, Inspector Grainger?' I said in an aggressive manner.

'I popped along to see how you are, DS Blackmore,' he said, with no level of concern in his voice.

'It is not like you to show concern for anyone,' I said, looking him directly in the eye.

Just then, Chief Constable Gregg came walking down the corridor; he had obviously heard our voices.

'Is there a problem?' he said.

'No, sir. Inspector Grainger was just leaving.'

'Yes, I was.'

With that he left the incident room and scuttled off to his office. Chief Constable Gregg, assured nothing further was going to happen, went back to his office. All this left me a little late for the hall, so I said to Tuppence, 'Come on, we are going.'

Tuppence saved her work to a memory stick and shut down the computer. She grabbed her coat and we headed off to Cromley Hall. We walked again with purpose to the car and again I could feel those eyes on my neck.

We made our way to the hall, then Tuppence said, 'You certainly got your intentions across. That creep was surprised to see you and thought you were badly hurt and would be off work for a few weeks,' she said, in a light-hearted manner.

'Good. My message was clear: I am back and raring to go.'

TWELVE

We arrived at the Cromley Hall security gate; the gorgeous soft Irish voice greeted me when I pressed the intercom.

'Hello, can I help you?'

'DS Blackmore to see John Holmes.'

'Yes, he did tell us to expect you. You know where to park and which door to go to?' she said efficiently.

'I certainly do,' I replied, in a cheerful voice.

The barrier opened and I drove to the car park. We made our way to Blaggards' Door and Tuppence rang the bell. The door was opened by Cynthia Holmes. I apologised for being a little late and after the usual greetings she escorted us to the library.

'John will be with you shortly.'

She made her way from the library, and I sat looking at all the books. A lot of the books were certainly many years old, and I wondered if they have all been read at some stage over the years or were just for show. There was a section of military books and a section of children's books. The children's books looked more modern, so I know they have been read. I noticed Tuppence looking around, so I guess she was doing the same as me. I was brought back to the present when John Holmes entered the room.

'DS Blackmore,' he said, with his hand extended.

'Thank you for waiting.'

He was in a relaxed mood and less burdened than the last time I had seen him.

'How can I help you?' he said with great sincerity.

'Besides the usual doors and windows, are there any other entry points to the hall? If I can be perfectly blunt, are there any secret passages, doors, etc, that no one knows about. Do you have a drawing of the hall buildings?'

'There have been rumours of secret passages relating to the hall for years, but never found. As for a drawing of the hall, all drawings and paperwork pre the Civil War were destroyed, as well as chunks off the hall. The door you entered today is known as Blaggards' Door as a reminder to those days.'

'Wow,' I said, stunned. 'The problem I have is there are no physical signs of forced entry to the hall, so if the crime was committed by an outsider, how did he or she get in?'

'Yes, I am aware of this,' he replied solemnly.

I asked him if I could look around the hall and he agreed so we left him to his thoughts in the study.

'Let us go to the dining room,' I suggested to Tuppence, and she readily agreed.

'The plan, as you would have figured out,' I said as I looked at her, 'is to see if there any secret passages. I do not want to start banging about and risk damaging anything. I would say almost all the items in this room have been here for several years. I would say a good cleaner would put things back exactly on the same spot, so we look for tidemarks of items that look to have been moved.'

We set about our task and started with the fire and mantelpiece. Tuppence gently lifted the ornaments, clocks, pictures, etc. I gently felt around the fire and pulled the mantelpiece, but everything appeared to be sound in their fittings and placements.

We moved to the window, more specifically the panel boards. The walls of the hall were quite deep, so in my mind it was feasible, although highly unlikely, that a person could squeeze between them. I checked the panels; they were all secure in their fittings.

Tuppence also said, 'It's unlikely anyone would have come through here as there would be a bit of a mess. The person would be covered in dust and trailed it through the house,' she offered.

I had to concede her point. We moved to the exceptionally large dresser unit.

'I don't think we need to move any of the items off the shelves or empty the cupboards, as once more, entry and exit would not be easy and would be time-consuming,' Tuppence said, with a good level of sound mind. I had to concede to her point.

We set about feeling around the large unit. One of the hall staff walked through the room and looked at us with a quizzical look as we stood by the unit. She knew who we were so carried on walking. We pulled gently on each side, but this old unit was not going anywhere. After a good look around the rest of the dining room, there was not anything else of any real interest, so we crossed this off the list.

'I am feeling hungry,' I said to her.

'So am I,' she readily replied.

We made our way to the café by the lawn and purchased some lunch.

'As we are working, I will break my rule and discuss the case, and it will be good to talk as we eat.'

Tuppence agreed.

'Your point on not moving things off shelves is a very valid one. It would be entirely impractical to do this; it would be noisy and messy for the murderer to enter by these routes.'

I looked at Tuppence, giving her space for a comment, but none came. I continued, 'I am more and more convinced the murderer came across an access point and decided to use it to his or her advantage. I do not believe the murders were intentional, but the whole process went horribly wrong, so let me put forward a scenario.

'The murderer knew of the access point to the hall from previous visits. He or she decides to come back at a later date to steal the heirlooms. He enters the building and makes his way through the rooms. He hears voices in the Grand Hall but knows the heirlooms he is looking for are not in that room. He feels safe, as the family are all in one room and all the staff have the night off, as the family will look after themselves. He makes his way to the main corridor that links the dining room and the library. The heirlooms are housed in the main hall in glass cabinets. As the murderer is putting the heirlooms in a bag, Jake and Arthur Holmes stumble across and challenge him. It is my opinion that the brothers tackled the murderer, the murderer panicked, and he killed both of them.'

I looked at Tuppence and raised an eyebrow. Tuppence took this as a cue to say something.

'A good theory and I can't disagree with it, so as I see from that, the entry point has to be found. Do you think you will have to bring in a few people to search for it?'

'If I do that then it will be known to all of my intentions. It is important to keep everything under wraps for now; but if I have to, I will.'

We walked around the outside of the hall and down the steps to the church. Mr Holloway was sitting waiting for me. He offered his hand in a warm handshake and a smile. He looked as if the world has been taken off his shoulders. There were visitors in the church, so I asked him if there was somewhere we could talk privately. He led the way to the vestry; we entered and shut the door behind us.

'I have searched every conceivable place for a passage entry point, but I could not find anything,' he said.

'To be honest, I would have been surprised if you

had. It was a childhood dream of mine to find a secret passage from the church to the hall. I am still convinced there is a secret entry point to the hall, but I no longer believe it is down here. If you think about it, the hall is on a much higher level than the church and the church is a fair distance from the hall, so I think it would be impractical,' I offered.

'I agree,' said Mr Holloway.

'I think we need to look closer to the hall. However, it would look odd for the verger to be inspecting the outside perimeter of the hall, as it will raise a lot of questions about your motives. I will have to ask you to not get involved anymore. I thank you very sincerely for your help and I will always be grateful for your help and support,' I reluctantly put to him.

Mr Holloway agreed. I told him I would come back and see him once all this was over. We parted our ways on good terms.

'It is sad for him,' Tuppence said sympathetically.

'Yes, it is. However, I cannot let sentimentality get in the way,' I said with a heavy heart. 'Come on, let us go up to the hall.'

We grabbed a coffee from the café in the grounds and sat down near the north wall. We watched all the visitors chatting and looking at the hall programme, their children happily playing on the lawn. I was looking closely at the walls of the building, carefully looking for any possible points of entry. We finished our coffees and went for a walk. The hall is a large building with lots of walls jotting out and reflects extensions over the years.

'Come on, we will go for a walk down Peasants Walk.'

'Peasants' what?' she said.

'Yes, it is a cobbled walkway between the inner hall wall and the outer wall. It is hundreds of years old, so it is protected. They open it three times a year: Easter, Halloween and Christmas. I will ask permission to gain access. I do not want to show my badge and go all gung-ho up the Peasants' Walk. I will ring John Holmes and return tomorrow morning.'

We walked over to the north wall, I pointed out the bordering counties and the River Sorrow that flows across the valley on the way to the sea. Cromley Hall, with high walls, is situated on a higher level in the valley. This made it easier to defend for hundreds of years.

'Why is it called the River Sorrow?' asked Tuppence.

'It is not the river's real name, I believe it goes back to the Civil War where it is said the blood from the fighting flowed down to the river; I believe it has been known as the River Sorrow since that time,' I offered.

I pointed out the villages we could see and told her of the good pubs that serve great food in said villages. I suggested to Tuppence we would go to one when we left here. There is one I am greatly fond of so we will go there. The pub is called The Scythe in the village of Carewell.

The food is freshly cooked to order, so none of this ready-to-heat or hours-under-a-heat-cabinet stuff, and you also get plenty of it. I was starting to salivate, so I turned to Tuppence.

'I am starving.'

Tuppence laughed and we set off.

We got to the car, and I decided to ring John Holmes. He answered in a lighter voice than earlier, which caught me by surprise. I explained to him what I wanted to do tomorrow morning and he readily gave permission; he would personally give me the key to the gate. I thanked him and asked him to exercise discretion. He agreed and I ended the call.

We arrived at The Scythe in a short time as it was only a couple of miles down the hill. We walked in and were greeted by the owner and hosts Tom and Jenny Woods. They have been running this pub for twenty years and are one of the most popular hosts in the area.

'Hello, Paul,' he called out, with hand extended. I happily shook it.

'Jenny,' he called out. 'Come and see who's here.'

Jenny Woods came in from the kitchen with a warm wide smile when she saw me.

'Good to see you again, Paul,' she said warmly.

I introduced Tuppence as a colleague, and said she was assisting me in the case. We talked about families and the years until eventually Tuppence and I sat at a table. I said to Tom,

'I know what is on your mind, but I cannot discuss the events at Cromley Hall.'

He nodded his head and handed us our menus.

Our food duly arrived, and it was as fantastic as ever. Tuppence was suitably impressed, desserts were ordered, and washed down with soft drinks for me, of course. We made our thanks to Tom and sent our compliments to Jenny, who was busy in the kitchen.

We took a walk around the village and Tuppence loved the stone cottages and how quaint the village was with stone buildings and years of history. It looked like a setting out of an Agatha Christie novel.

We made our way back to the car and headed off back to the apartment. I stopped about a half mile up the road and Tuppence looked at me with a quizzical look in her eye.

'Why have we stopped?' she asked.

'I am glad you asked. The building across the road was once Carewell railway station, but was closed in June 1966. The butchering of the rail network and stations was in the long term a great mistake; the writing was on the wall in October 1959 when the M1 motorway was opened. The then Transport Secretary, Ernest Marple's said, "The M1 will set the pattern here for the next fifty years." The priority, to them, in my opinion, was the road network. I guess there would be more revenue from cars than trains, and now our road network is overloaded. We had the opportunity to have the greatest rail system in the world, but they screwed it good and proper.'

'Wow!' said Tuppence. 'You are really angry about that. My dad would enjoy talking to you, as he loves trains as well. He has set up a track with stations in one of the back bedrooms and has been adding bits and bobs over the years. My mum rarely goes in there in fear of breaking something, as there is so little room.'

'I will talk to him one day and I would love to see it,' I replied.

We spent about half an hour with me giving Tuppence a local history lesson and she seemed to enjoy the area. Then I eventually said to her, 'Come on, let us get back to the apartment.'

We set off and after about half a mile I noticed in my rear-view mirror a car approaching very quickly. About a hundred yards from me blue lights started flashing, along with a siren. I thought maybe it would overtake us on the way to some incident. The car, however, came right up behind us, so I pulled over in a safe spot. The unmarked police car stopped right behind us. I sat and waited for the police officer to come to the car. I was not getting out of the car and leaving Tuppence on her own. The officer walked to the car. I lowered the window and I said, 'Can I help you?'

'Is this your car?'

'No, it is a hire car from Cromley police station,' I put to him.

'Do you have your driving licence?'

'Yes.' I handed it to him.

'Have you been drinking?'

'No,' I replied.

'It was reported you were eating and drinking in The Scythe pub in Carewell.'

'Yes, we were in the pub and had something to eat, but no alcohol was consumed by me,' I replied.

'Then you will not object to taking a breathalyser test?'

'I do not have a problem with that,' I agreed.

The test was duly carried out and the result was clear. I said to him, 'If you are finished, we will be on our way.'

He said nothing and went back to his car. I started my car whilst watching in my mirrors and drove off. The officer started following us a distance behind. I had noted his number and I would check it out. I decided to take an elongated route and he continued to follow me. I noted a layby coming up, so I pulled over. I decided it was time to ring Chief Constable Gregg. He answered in a concerned voice.

'DS Blackmore, if you are ringing me then it means you have a problem,' he stated.

'You could say that, sir.'

I told him of the events from The Scythe pub to now in a shortened version. I said I would come in to see him early tomorrow morning.

'Leave it with me,' he said in an angry voice.

During this time, the unmarked police car had stopped and parked up further down the road. I set off and passed slowly and the car pulled out behind me. After a couple of minutes, the police car suddenly turned off, so I headed for the apartment. I parked up when we arrived, and I had a good look round. Satisfied all was good, we made our way to the apartment.

I ran a bath, so I could bathe my aching side. Tuppence decided to speak with her daughter. The hot water felt good on my body.

Later on, we sat on the sofa to relax and discuss the day's events. Tuppence told me she recorded the events with the unmarked police car on her phone and I was pleased with that. I poured Tuppence a drink, but I decided not to have one. I then set out to Tuppence:

• Someone - I believe it was the murderer - tried to take me out, but failed. He will be permanently stressed, so I do not want to spook him at this time.

• The police car incident has SIO DI Grainger written all over it. He will want to discredit me and have me bombed out of the force. I was obviously followed and set up because how else would they know where I was. He is convinced he has the killer and the thought of losing face would not go down well with him. I do not expect any further incidents like this.

• We have to find that hidden entry point to the hall, so we will head back there tomorrow after I have spoken with Chief Constable Gregg.

Tuppence sat listening and agreed with my reasoning. I said to her,

'The stakes are getting higher and with that the danger levels are also rising. I have to be careful of your involvement; I cannot risk you getting hurt in any way,' I said to her directly.

Tuppence agreed and curled up on the sofa.

'How is your daughter?' I asked her.

'She is good and doing really well in New York. She shares an apartment now and they are furnishing it to their own taste,' she said excitedly.

'You know, you speak of your daughter, but I have never asked you her name.'

'It's Georgia.'

I looked at her and we both laughed.

THIRTEEN

I slept well and woke early, as I usually did. My injuries were becoming easier every day.

'Don't make breakfast just yet. I have to pop over to the shop to get a couple of things,' said Tuppence.

I decided to have a shower, shave, etc, whilst she was out. I put on the television to the news channel, but nothing regarding the case was highlighted. Just the usual nonsense of a Member of Parliament telling everyone who cares to listen how wonderful he is.

Tuppence appeared presently with her shopping and a copy of the Cromley Echo. She pointed out a small heading on the bottom corner of the paper where Sue Bentley highlighted that the investigation had widened to London.

'What do you think of that?' she asked.

'It looks to me Chief Constable Gregg is flushing out the mole by feeding some misinformation. He will flush him or her out. Chief Constable Gregg is not the type to get the wrong side of and he will succeed. I will just leave it with him.'

We collected our things and headed for Cromley police station. It was a sunny morning, and the town was waking up as we drove the route. We duly arrived at the station parked up and walked across the car park. I looked to my left and caught sight of Sue Bentley standing by her office window. She looked expressionless; the smugness she had the last time I seen her was gone.

We entered the reception and signed in; Sergeant Phillips was on duty, but said nothing today. Since the incident where I was almost taken out and being stopped by a squad car, I sensed a change in mood and temperature in the station. I felt my decision to work independently and from an apartment was the right one. It was good to be away from it all.

We made our way to our incident room, I left Tuppence there and I made my way to the office of Chief Constable Gregg. I knocked on the door and shortly I was summoned into his office.

'Good morning, DS Blackmore. Please sit down.'

I duly carried out his request.

'I am personally investigating the incident when you were stopped, so we will say no more about it.'

I got the message.

'Update me with your investigation,' he said firmly.

'The recent incidents, especially the first one, have convinced me Roderick Holmes did not carry out the crime. Sergeant Brown and Tuppence are carrying out background checks on the staff family members. I will be going back to the hall this morning; I am convinced there is another access to the hall and confident of finding it.'

'Have you requested any help in finding it?'

'It may come to that, but for now I would like to carry on as I am.'

'Very well. You need to make progress as questions are being asked.'

'Sir, I know I am making progress, but it is not visible at the moment, but bear with me,' I stated with confidence.

'Very well, but keep me informed.'

I left his office and again heard voices coming from my incident room. Tuppence was talking with one of the office girls, but this time it was just girlie talk. She left soon after.

'Come on, let us go to Cromley Hall,' I said.

With that, we set off to the car with the usual feeling of eyes burning the back of our necks. We laughed when we got in the car.

We set off for the hall and I casually said to her, 'You seemed to have found a friend in the station.'

'Not really. She asked me if you were married or had a girlfriend,' she said, laughing.

'Like hell she did,' I said, laughing back.

We arrived at the hall and once again I looked forward to hearing that soft Irish voice. I was greatly disappointed when a gruff voice answered. He duly opened the gate. Tuppence laughed her head off as we headed to the car park.

We made our way to the main entrance and past the two large oak doors and on to the lawn. I said to Tuppence to wait there whilst I went to the office to collect the key for access to the Peasants' Walk. On my return she was talking to one of the hall staff. The girl left as I approached them, so I carried on walking and Tuppence joined me.

I said to Tuppence, 'We have been here a few times now and the hall staff are getting to know us, so word will be getting around. I am determined to find the entrance today. The reason I want to start on Peasants' Walk is due to a higher level of buildings, so it would seem more likely it will be there.'

Tuppence smiled in acceptance.

We got to the gate and let ourselves in to the walk. I have never in all my years visited this part of the hall. The hall is a magnificent building with high walls and rich in character and Peasants' Walk is one of the oldest parts of the hall and generally closed to the public. I was excited to be in this part of the hall and would look with great interest to all the nooks and crannies.

John Holmes joined us from a side door and pointed out what each building was used for. There was the laundry, bakery and servants' quarters for the women. The male quarters were in a separate part of the hall. Interaction was never encouraged. There was the coal shed, wood shed and wool shed. I said to Tuppence we would inspect them together as I could not risk her getting injured. My side was aching a little, but it was not going to stop me.

John Holmes supplied us with a rough sketched lay out of the hall and Peasants' Walk buildings. We studied them and planned our order. The plan was to look for fresh signs of something being recently moved. This would save a lot of time. By the look of the buildings, their contents had been there for a long time.

We started with the wool shed, but bar a few incidental bits, it was clear. There was a bicycle in the shed belonging, I guess, to someone of the family or staff; it was of no interest to me. I checked the externals of the building, but there were no signs of a recent disturbance.

Next was the wood shed and it was almost full to the top. I rang John Holmes and asked him when it was last filled, and he informed me it was a couple of months ago. It was obvious it was filled before the crime took place. We searched, however, around the externals of the building, but found nothing that had been disturbed. Next was the coal shed; I looked at Tuppence in her white trousers and laughed.

I volunteered to check the coal shed and she stood outside. The building was full to the roof, but I would not assume it was filled at the same time as the wood shed. One of the estate staff walked by so I asked him when the shed was filled, and he told me the same time as the wood shed; I rang John Holmes just to check and he confirmed it was. It was clear, after inspection, nothing had been disturbed around the outside of the shed.

There was a general use shed that held estate tools and other bits. There were signs of movement, so I set about inspecting the shed. Again, I told Tuppence to stay outside, not because of her white trousers, but more so she did not get injured. It took a while to move the tools and carry out an inspection, but nothing was found. I checked the outside and signs of any movement. My side ached every time I bent down, but I had no choice but ignore it.

The buildings were on the left-hand side of the walk and attached to the main outer wall. I thought it would be a good time to stop and have a break, much to the delight of Tuppence. We made our way to the café and purchased our coffees. It was a nice day, so we sat outside and chatted.

I said to her, 'John Holmes said the male and female quarters were kept apart from each other. Men being men and women being women, even in those days, they would want to meet each other.'

I placed the sketch that John Holmes prepared for me on the table. The female quarters were on the extreme left side of the building above the wool shed that was next on my list to inspect. The male quarters were at the other side of the hall. There was only one route through the hall and that was the main passageway, but that would take them past the butler and housekeeper's rooms. It was highly unlikely they would risk it as it would certainly lead to them losing their jobs and that would be a big thing in those days. The female and male quarters were attached to the rear wall of the buildings, so I thought I would concentrate around that area.

I had noticed it was a long walk from the female quarters to the servants' door at the left-hand side of the building as they walked towards it. People being what they are would find a shorter route to the hall by whatever means they could find or make. The female servants' quarters were the furthest away from the hall, so they would pass the laundry room and kitchen on the way.

We set about inspecting every bit of the wall and yard, but we could not find anything.

I said to Tuppence, 'Looking at the female servants' quarters, I noticed it is possible to walk along the top of the wall to the other side to the rear of the kitchen. I need to check that out.'

We made our way up the stairway to the door. The door was not locked; every other door was locked. I carefully opened the door in case there were fingerprints on the handle. I stood at the entrance and carefully looked around the interior. The room had not been used for several years. However, there were signs that someone had been in the room.

'Before we go any further,' I said to Tuppence. 'I need to get forensics in here. There are signs, as you can see, of someone having been in here and I do not want to damage any possible evidence. It is time to ring Chief Constable Gregg.'

I carefully closed the door and we made our way down the stairway. I thought of ringing John Holmes, but it might be a risk and give false hope for now and it was obvious to me the room was never used. We made our way to the café and locked the door to the yard behind me. I rang Chief Constable Gregg.

'DS Blackmore, what can I do for you?' His tone was calm.

'Sir, I need a forensics team.'

'That means you have found something,' His tone was now more serious.

'Possibly, sir. Tuppence and I have been checking down the Peasants' Walk for an entrance to the hall. When we reached the servants' quarters situated above the wool store, it was clear the building had not been used for a number of years. There is evidence that items have been moved recently and before I go blundering in, I felt it would be wise to have some forensics carried out. The door was also unlocked, but all the other buildings were locked. The other buildings appeared to be in their natural order,' I put to him.

'Very well, I will arrange it.'

'Thank you, sir. Will you arrange for discretion? I feel if they come during normal visiting times they will blend in naturally and not stick out. They can slip in by the side door.'

'Very well. I will arrange for them to contact you.'

I found Tuppence sitting at a table next to the north wall and I approached with a smile on my face.

'Chief Constable Gregg is arranging the forensics team to contact me shortly. You know, I believe we are now on the right track. I need to speak with John Holmes.'

With that I rang him, and he came outside.

'What can I do for you, DS Blackmore?' he asked, puzzled.

'I am arranging for a forensics team to carry out an investigation in the Peasants' Walk area possibly tomorrow morning. In the meantime, I will declare the area out of bounds to all the family and staff; I will also retain the keys.'

'Does that mean you have found something?' he asked.

'I cannot answer that just now; and can I also ask you keep all this to yourself? It will be extremely helpful to us.'

He nodded agreement and returned indoors.

'Come on, let us go to The Lodge for some food.'

She agreed and we headed back to the car. We drove from the hall grounds in a good positive spirit. I was confident we were on the right track; I could feel it in my aching side. I would now have to wait for the forensics team to contact me.

We had just arrived at The Lodge when my mobile rang. I answered and an unknown voice said to me,

'DS Blackmore, this is Graham Coleman, Crime Scene Manager. Chief Constable Gregg asked me to give you a call in all confidence,' he asked in a quizzical voice.

'Thank you for your call. It concerns the events at Cromley Hall and an area of the hall I want you to look at,' I said with confidence.

'Could I have some information?' he requested.

'I am not prepared to discuss it over the phone, so can I suggest we meet at the hall at nine o'clock tomorrow morning?' I said with authority.

Graham Coleman agreed to meet me at that time.

Tuppence and I entered The Lodge with great appetites, sat down and duly ordered from the menu. We were in good spirits, with Tuppence telling me how much she liked this part of the world.

'Are you mad?' I said, laughingly.

'Because you are from here you do not appreciate what is around you. I, on the other hand, like what I see,' she said with definition.

We watched the local news, but there was nothing of great interest, so we headed back to the apartment.

We arrived at the apartment with no incident and no police or unmarked police cars to be seen. Tuppence made us some coffees and I stood by the window overlooking the park. Tuppence came over with the coffees and spoke.

'What are you looking intently at?'

'The girl running down the park on the left is Amber.'

'Pretty girl, but I would not expect anything less,' she said, looking at me.

'She sure is, but as usual she is never on her own. She attracts guys like a fly strip.'

Tuppence laughed at my description of her.

'As long as I have known her, there has never been a guy very far from her. She likes the attention.'

'Do you want me to pop out and get you some shorts, top and trainers?' she said, laughing.

'In my condition, no way. I can honestly say there is no spark there that is luring me out there. I guess it was the schoolboy crush that was always there, but is now diminishing.'

We headed to our incident room, and I spoke to where we are so far.

'We have found the start, I believe, of the entry point to the hall. I believe he/she went to the female servants' quarters and through to the far-right hand corner. In the corner is large wardrobe and behind that I believe we will find an exit point to the rear of the room and access along the top of the outer wall. The murderer walked along the top of the wall and followed it around the corner and somewhere up there is access down to the kitchen. The crime scene team will have to go carefully over each step of the way, so I have to be patient. The risk now is as more people are involved then the likelihood of it coming out will increase.'

I looked at Tuppence and she nodded agreement, so I continued.

'Chief Constable Gregg is up to date with proceedings. The area is cordoned off and I have the keys. We have John Holmes handwritten plan of the area for the investigation team.

'We have carried out interviews with all the family

members and the estate staff and are all duly recorded. Tomorrow morning you will liaise with Sergeant Brown regarding the background checks he has been working on. You can do this while I make my phone calls.

'Any questions?' I asked.

Tuppence shook her head, so we called it a night at that. I went and ran myself a bath to soak my weary side, but it is improving all the time and I have more mobility. Tuppence went to speak with her daughter. I soaked in the bath feeling satisfied at a fruitful day. I got out and sat in the chair by the window just chilling and going over the events of the day when Tuppence appeared and spoke.

'You did well today, kid.'

'Thank you, my good lady,' I replied with equal humour.

I just wanted to relax for the remainder of the evening, so I switched on the TV and found, yes, *Midsomer Murders*. Tuppence raised her head in disgust and decided to go to bed.

FOURTEEN

The new days brought fresh optimism. I headed to the shower and enjoyed the hot water running down my side. I was stirred back to reality when Tuppence walked into the bathroom – topless!

'What the hell are you doing?' I asked in astonishment.

'Well, I thought I might find somewhere to hang my towel,' she said, directly.

We stood looking at each other and then burst out laughing.

'OK, I get the point. I will sort out my things in the bathroom when we return later today,' I replied. 'Get your top on.'

I put on the news, and besides Chief Constable Gregg stating the investigation was still ongoing, there was nothing else of interest to me. I noticed Sue Bentley was not at the briefing, in fact she had been incredibly quiet lately, not that I was complaining.

My phone rang and it was Chief Constable Gregg.

'Good morning, sir.'

'Will you come in and see me as soon as you can?'

'I will be with you in thirty minutes, sir.'

'Change of plan. I have been summoned by Chief Constable Gregg, so I will go straight away. Will you ring

Sergeant Brown to see where he has got to and brief me when I get back?'

Tuppence nodded in agreement.

I arrived at the station in good time, parked up and walked across the car park and, yes, I could feel the eyes boring into me. I glanced to the left and saw Sue Bentley standing at the usual window and I assume it is her office. She looked stern-faced with arms folded. Wow, I thought. What is going on?

I went to the reception and signed in. Sergeant Phillips was not behind the desk. It was manned by a female officer I did not know. I said good morning and made my way to my incident room. As I was walking down the corridor, the officer who had pulled me over was coming towards me. He almost froze when he saw me and his body language revealed his awkwardness. As I got nearer, I smiled and said, 'Good morning.'

I knocked on the door to Chief Constable Gregg's office and the call to enter came.

'Sit down,' he ordered. I duly obliged.

'Did Graham Coleman get in contact with you?'

'Yes he did, sir.'

'And what have you arranged?'

'I have arranged to meet him at Cromley Hall at nine o'clock this morning.'

'Good, now take me through your thoughts of events,' he asked, whilst sitting at his desk and looking thoughtful.

'My belief, as you know, is the murderer – or

murderers – knew of another entry point to Cromley Hall. I believe I am getting nearer to that point. My belief is the murderer or murderers entered the hall via the rear of the kitchen or the scullery next to it. There was no obvious access point in the wall, so I entered the servants' quarters. There is evidence someone had been in the old servants' quarters. It appeared furniture at the far end of the building had been moved and they left the building by an exit point behind the wardrobe at the far end, walked along the top wall and exited at some point before the laundry room attached behind the kitchen. I want Graham Coleman's team to test for evidence before we enter and then every step of the way in front of us,' I concluded.

'Very well, I am prepared to support you with this,' he said.

'Thank you, sir,' I said with gratitude.

'I have found the source of the leaks to the press and it is being dealt with. I do not want you involved with it, as it will be a distraction you don't need right now. Your gut feeling was right about it, as your gut feeling is now regarding Cromley Hall, so keep me informed,' he finished off.

I left his office feeling so high I could have flown to Cromley Hall on his support. I rang Tuppence to tell her I was going straight to Cromley Hall.

'How did you get on with Chief Constable Gregg?' she asked.

'I have received a great vote of confidence. I now

have to earn that confidence and deliver.'

'I know you will deliver,' she said with assurance.

'Chief Constable Gregg has sourced the leak from the station to the press. However, he does not want me involved and to just concentrate on Cromley Hall.'

'Has he said who it is?'

'No, but Sergeant Phillips was not behind the reception desk this morning. I am not saying it is Sergeant Phillips, but time will tell. Change of mind: if you are ready, I will swing round and pick you up.'

We headed for the hall in good spirits with the radio on and the song playing was very appropriate: The Herman's Hermits 'I'm Into Something Good'. Yes, that is the way I feel.

We arrived at Cromley Hall gates and to brighten my day even further, the gorgeous Irish voice spoke to me, and I melted. She opened the gate and we made our way to the car park.

'You will have an orgasm one of these days,' Tuppence laughed.

We got out of the car and made our way under the arched entrance. I approached an impeccably dressed gentleman who had a great air of authority. He reminded me of my school English teacher who dressed in a similar fashion from an old English world. His hair was well gelled. He wore a grey, three-piece suit with elegant brown brogue shoes. He wore a cravat instead of a tie.

'Good morning, Mr Coleman,' I said, extending my hand. He looked bemused that I knew it was him.

'Good morning, DS Blackmore. Please call me Graham and how can I help you?' he replied.

'I am following a different line of investigation from SOI Grainger. No entry point has been discovered to Cromley Hall, so I believe the assumption has been made it was an inside job. This does not sit right with me. I believe there is an alternative entry to the hall and with this sketch, drawn for me by John Holmes, I will outline my thoughts.

'I have looked over the area around Peasants' Walk and everything is as it should be, except the female servants' door was unlocked, with signs that someone has been in there. It is my belief this is the start of the entry to the hall. It is logical to me; the female quarters are furthest from the hall and human nature will find a shorter route in. It is possible there may be an exit point at the back of the female quarters, the murderer or murderers walked along the top of the wall and around to the other side and made their way to the back of the kitchen. I would like you and your team to check every step for forensic evidence.'

'OK, we will make a start.'

He introduced me to the two members of his team he brought along. I introduced Tuppence, and pointed out she was a civilian and there to take notes for me, and would not be involved with any investigative aspects of the case. It was important I made that clear to them.

We reached the door to the Peasants' Walk, and we duly entered the area. I pointed out the old servants' quarters and the route I wanted them to check. They set to work, and I asked Graham to keep me informed of his progress, to which he agreed.

'Come on, Tuppence, let us go to the kitchen.'

We set off to the kitchen and blended in with the paying visitors. There was no point in closing this area off, as there had been so many people through there the area would have been compromised or contaminated.

We walked around slowly looking at every detail, but nothing was obvious to the eye. I suggested to Tuppence we go outside.

We walked around the lawn and I said to her, 'I do not think we will find anything as there is too much human traffic. I believe it will be apparent the entry point will be from the other side.'

We made our way over to a table by the north wall and waited.

I received a call from Graham to say they had finished in the servants' quarters. Tuppence and I made our way back to the building. We walked up the steps and stopped at the door. Graham told me they had taken some swabs and taken some photographs and footprints in the dust. I suggested to him my fingerprints would be on the door handle at the lower end, but not the main handle part. Graham said there were no fingerprints, so it was probable gloves were worn. We made our way to the far end of the building where a large cupboard was standing.

'OK, if you guys will give me a hand, we will move

this wardrobe out of the way. It is my belief there will be an exit point behind it.'

We moved the unit easily and then removed a large brown sheet off the wall. To my delight and the crime team's surprise, there was a hole in the wall large enough for someone just to get through. We discussed the exit point and I thought it was too narrow to use on a regular basis. Graham pointed out servants at this level of the staff would usually be young girls and they would get through there quite easily. I think he had a point.

I stood back as the team carried out their checks on the exit point and across the top of the wall. The team set about examining across the top of the wall. Footprints were found and they looked recent. The team set about making a cast of the prints and took some photographs. They slowly made their way across the wall and then turned right and made their way along to a point where the footprints stopped. There was a gap in the vegetation big enough for someone to go through.

The team slowly and painstakingly made their way through the vegetation and arrived at the back of the kitchen. There were a lot of footprints, so the team once again made casts and took more photographs. We were faced with the rear of the hall building.

I walked slowly back and forth, inspecting every part of the wall without success. I figured the entry point would be accessible from the ground level, so I slowly ran my hands over the wall, feeling between the stones and mortar. I felt a small indent and ran my fingers along it until I found a slightly larger indent. I could get my four fingers into it and slowly pulled; a section started to open. My heart rate started to rise; I could feel the adrenalin flowing through me. I opened it about six inches when I heard voices from within, so I slowly closed it again. I turned to the team smiling and they stood in disbelief.

I said to them, 'There are voices from within. It will be the guide with a party, so I do not want to startle them. The last tour party will be through in twenty minutes, so we will have to work quietly. I do not want to spook them.'

There was agreement all round. Graham gave me a set of overalls, boot covers, gloves and a mask to put on and I duly complied. I very slowly opened the access door; the door was very well balanced and opened easily. The internal view showed a passageway approximately six feet high, four feet wide and twenty feet long. There was a musty odour from within and I guess it was to be expected after years of being closed up. Graham and I shone our torches inside and we could see a wooden panel at the end of the passageway.

Graham carefully started to inspect the entry point and more footprints, followed by more casts and photographs. We very slowly entered the passageway, shining our torches everywhere. The torchlight picked up a recess in the wall on the left side; we slowly made our way towards it. We looked inside and we stopped when we saw the missing heirlooms standing inside. I pointed to Graham to retreat outside. We removed our masks and gloves and stood for a moment in disbelief when Graham spoke.

'We need to go in and do our forensic analysis, so I suggest you remain here, DS Blackmore.'

I duly complied.

I sent a message to Tuppence to check she was OK. She said Cynthia Holmes had invited her in to the hall and she was in the library reading up on the hall's history.

Graham and his team exited the passageway with the heirlooms in sealed bags and he told me he had removed what appeared to be phlegm from the wall next to the heirlooms. He would inspect it and have a DNA analysis carried out.

I put on a fresh mask and gloves. Graham Coleman and I re-entered the passageway. We slowly made our way to the far end until we reached a wooden panel. I believe the good side is on the passageway by the kitchen. Graham carried out checks on the panel and gave me the go-ahead to proceed. The panel on one side was held closed by a wooden latch. I carefully lifted it and the panel opened inward to the internal corridor between the kitchen and the scullery. We now had our entry point.

We left the building and made our way back to the female servants' quarters. We removed our overalls etc and made our way back to the main yard. I thanked Graham and his team for their detailed work and bade them farewell. Graham would inform me when he had completed his analysis and report. I went to find

Tuppence.

I walked to the library. I found Tuppence reading studiously a book on the history of the hall.

She looked up at me and said, 'What a fascinating place this is. I really want to come and do a tour. How did you get on?'

'I need a drink, so let us head for The Lodge.'

'We will leave the car at the apartment, and I will tell you all about it over a bit of alcohol.'

We found Cynthia Holmes and said our farewells and headed to the car.

We dropped the car off and duly walked to The Lodge. We found a table, sat down and the first pint went down very well.

'Easy!' said Tuppence. 'So how did you get on?' she asked again, impatiently.

'We have found the entry point.'

'Wow, that is brilliant!' she said with a smile.

I told her how the events unrolled over the course of the day and that Graham Coleman had the heirlooms, plus the footprint castings and photographs.

'I am just popping outside to ring Chief Constable Gregg; he needs to know,' I put to her.

The phone rang for what seemed like an eternity and he eventually answered.

'DS Blackmore,' he said rather breathlessly.

'Hello, sir. I have some great news. we have found the entry point to the hall, and we found the missing heirlooms hidden in the passageway,' I said with a high level of satisfaction.

'Hold it there. Come in and see me at eight o'clock tomorrow morning. I was on my way to next year's budget meeting; it will go late into the evening.'

I could sense his frustration.

'Sure, sir. I will be there.'

We arrived back at the apartment, so we headed for our incident room. I suggested we have our briefing now and she agreed.

'OK, it is safe to say we have had a good day. The access point has been found and as a bonus the heirlooms have been found and are in the safe hands of Graham Coleman. How are you getting along with the case notes?' I asked her.

'My handwritten notes are up to date.'

'I have to go in to see Chief Constable Gregg at eight o'clock tomorrow morning, so you can start then. We need to concentrate on Cromley Hall staff, so we will speak with Sergeant Brown when I come back.'

Tuppence agreed. We called it a night and I went to soak my body in some hot water, but first I had to tidy up and make some room in the bathroom.

FIFTEEN

I woke up early as usual and I was feeling good within myself. I was still a bit stiff from my injuries, but I can work through that. Tuppence finally decided to make an appearance.

'Good morning,' I said with positivity.

'Why are you so cheerful every morning?' she said with a level of sarcasm.

'Life is good and should be embraced.'

'Does the high profile of the case not get to you?' she asked with concern.

'To me it proves nothing by being pressurised. People demand answers, but if I do not have them, I will not bullshit them. I keep a cool head, I have my theories and put them in place. I am controlled by my instincts, the forensics and interviews and they take their course. As each result comes in, it fits into the overall jigsaw and to a final result. Life in other ways has to go on. You cannot be totally consumed by a case, as it clouds the mind and impairs judgement.'

She just looked at me, nodded, but said nothing. I turned on the television, but there was nothing of interest, so I turned it off and turned on the radio. A song called 'Leap Up and Down (Wave Your Knickers in the Air)' was playing. I looked at Tuppence and laughed and she said, 'Go to hell,' and laughed.

We set off for the police station.

I arrived and parked up as normal and again I felt the eyes boring into the back of my neck as I walked across the yard, but had become bored with it. Sergeant Phillips was not behind the reception desk and again it was manned by an unknown officer. I signed in and made my way to my incident room. At eight o'clock I made my way to Chief Constable Gregg's office. I knocked on the door.

'Come in!' shouted the booming voice.

I made my way in and sat in my usual seat.

'Don't get too comfortable. We are going to one of the meeting rooms for a conference call.'

I got up and followed him down the corridor to the incident room. He asked me how Tuppence was, and I told him she was busy typing up her notes. We entered the room and Chief Constable Gregg turned on a TV monitor and we waited for a connection. The familiar face of Chief Constable Mondell appeared.

'Good morning,' said Chief Constable Gregg.

'Good morning,' said Chief Constable Mondell.

'Good morning, sir,' I chipped in.

'Good morning, DS Blackmore.'

It was all very formal, but I expected that, and then Chief Constable Gregg spoke.

'DS Blackmore, I have given a small briefing to Chief Constable Mondell, so could you go into more detail?'

'I inspected the walls around the outside of Cromley Hall and got to the Peasants' Walk. Inspection of the outer wall revealed no possible points of entry. The female servants' quarters are above the wool store, so I believed the murderer could go through the quarters, out through an exit point at the back. He would go along the wall and round to the side wall. An exit point was found from the wall down to the rear area of the kitchen. On inspection, I found an entry point to the back of the kitchen. We opened an access door to reveal a passageway. We found the heirlooms in an alcove in the passageway wall. The passageway led to a wooden panel at the end. I pushed the panel and it opened to the corridor between the kitchen and the scullery room. The crime team have taken the heirlooms back to the laboratory for inspection. They have taken swabs, impressions of footprints, fingerprints, etc. I have informed John Holmes the area is still out of bounds, but I have not told him of our findings. I have also asked Graham Coleman and his team for strict confidentiality.'

'What is your next step?' asked Chief Constable Mondell.

'We will be working with Sergeant Brown regarding the background checks on members of the hall staff families or someone familiar with Cromley Hall. I believe the answer is in there somewhere. I do not believe at this point I have enough evidence to release Roderick Holmes, as it could be said he used this route.'

Both Chiefs agreed.

'Very well,' said Chief Constable Gregg. 'Thank you and you may go now.'

I made my way out and decided to go back to the apartment. I found Tuppence typing with her notebook open.

'I had a positive meeting with Chief Constable Gregg and Chief Constable Mondell, and they are fully up to date with events. I want to think, so I will go out for a while to take in some fresh air. I am going to West Cromley Park to have a walk round. It will give you time to do your notes and we will have a video call with Sergeant Brown when I return.'

Tuppence nodded in agreement.

'I know a good café, so I will call in and get us a sandwich and cake with our coffees when I return. By the way, Chief Constable Gregg was asking after you,' I said, with a level of mischief.

I made my way to the car and drove at a leisurely pace through the town. I would be passing awfully close to my parent's house, but I would leave that for another day. The roads were fairly quiet, but it was that time of the morning when people were at work and children were at school. I arrived at the park and parked up. I parked just inside the gate, as this would give me a longer walk down the park road. I set off on the path between the trees, with the sun dancing on the leaves.

My mind was going over the previous day and the progress I was making. I was thinking of the possible finds by the forensics team, the secret passage I am dying to tell John Holmes about and to show him, and the positive meeting I'd had with both Chief Constables. I was by now passing the mini lake housing a raft of ducks, so I was approximately three-quarters of the way around the park. I decided to go to the café, get a coffee and sit on the bench just off the path just up from the mini lake.

The café was busy, so I took my turn in the queue and looked around. I recognised a couple of female staff members of Cromley Hall and they were looking at me. Not to be seen as ignorant, I nodded to them both. They both looked away, I think more through embarrassment at being recognised. My turn duly came, and I purchased my goods and made my way to the bench I had seen earlier. It was also the bench I used to use a lot when I was studying, and I guess in a way I still was. The park is popular with visitors from all around the county and beyond. There is a heritage centre where a display of the town's history can be seen and preserved for the children of the future, which was especially important in my eyes. The sun was disappearing behind a cloud and…

'Paul Blackmore?'

A familiar voice broke my chain of thought. I looked up to see Amber standing in front of me.

'Amber!' I said politely. 'How are you?'

'I am good.' She was standing there smiling.

'Please, sit down.'

I motioned to the bench. She duly sat down.

'I am going to get another coffee, so would you like one?' I asked politely. The reality was I just needed a little time to get my thoughts together.

'Yes, I would love one,' she said, smiling.

I headed to the café looking around as I walked. There is never a guy very far away, but none was to be seen. I purchased the coffees and headed back. I sat down and handed her one.

'You have changed quite a bit since I last saw you,' she said. 'You are a lot more assured, and you have become quite the talk of the town.'

'I am just in town to assist with the case regarding the events at Cromley Hall,' I said matter-of-factly. 'How is your life?' I asked, changing the subject.

'It's OK,' she said. 'I have a little boy who is now three years old.'

'Wow.'

'Yes. It was not planned, but I make the best of it. There was no way I would consider an abortion.'

Admirable, I thought. She is softer in personality and demeanour. I guess motherhood has brought out another side of her I have never seen.

'Are you here on your own?' I asked.

'No, I am with my mother and son. He is playing in the park just behind us.'

I did not look round as I would not recognise them.

We chatted generally about our younger days in Cromley, and we laughed; she seemed to enjoy talking about them. Alas, time was moving on and I had to get back to the apartment. I made my apologies, as I had to go.

'Listen, would you like to go out for a drink and catch up a bit more?' she asked with a smile.

It caught me out as she, as far as I know, never asked any guy out; it was always the other way round.

'Sure. I have no idea when that will be; I am fairly preoccupied just now.'

'That's fine,' she said and gave me her mobile number.

We walked up the path and then she turned and went through the gate to the children's park. I bade my farewells and made my way to the car. I sat for a moment going over the last half hour and how I felt. My heart was not dancing and turning in circles; I was quite calm. A few years ago, I would be tongue-tied and in knots. I laughed to myself and headed back to the apartment.

I made a slight detour to a fabulous café where the owner uses good beans for coffee and bakes fantastic cakes and makes fantastic sandwiches. I went inside and the familiar voice shouted, 'Paul!'

The café owner Bridie came over and gave me a massive hug and smile.

'It's great to see you after all this time. There is no need to ask you what you are in town for; it's all over the media. What can I get you?'

'I would like two slices of your fabulous cappuccino cake and two coffees to take away, please.'

'How are you? I heard about your recent incident,' she said with concern.

'I am fine and nothing to worry about,' I reassured her.

She gave me one of those knowing mother looks, but did not pursue the point. I went to pay, but she refused payment and said they were on her. I thanked her and promised I would come back soon.

I arrived back at the apartment and put the cake box on the table.

'What cakes are these? They look great,' said a surprised Tuppence.

'I popped into a very good café where the owner bakes all her own cakes and they are all great. These are slices of a cappuccino cake and I absolutely love them.'

We had our coffees and cake and I promised to take Tuppence there soon.

Tuppence had caught up with all her work and it was now time to speak with Sergeant Brown at Mortley police station. We went to our incident room and Tuppence set up the video call. Sergeant Brown duly answered and after the exchanges we cracked on.

'What have you, if anything?' I asked.

'I have fifteen lines of enquiry so far for you to follow up. I have looked at the last five years, so I will email them to you individually to look at. It will be better this way, rather than me reading through each one.'

'I am happy with that.'

'Off the record, Paul, how are you? I heard about the incident the other night and it sounded serious,' he said, with concern.

'I am good. A little stiff, but it is easing every day. I will not go into detail, but I will tell you over a pint when I return to Mortley.'

'He is one of life's good guys,' I said to Tuppence. She nodded her head in agreement.

'Listen, before we go any further, I suggest we stop for a while. I want to go for a walk in the park out there to get some fresh air,' said Tuppence.

'Do you mind if I join you?' I asked.

'Sure, it will be good.'

We grabbed our jackets and set off the short distance to the park. There is a path that runs all the way around the park, so we set off to walk it. I pointed out the football pitches and changing block with a clubhouse the lads and I used when we were much younger. There are tennis courts, but it was not one sport I was into, although Tuppence said she was a handy tennis player when she was younger. She said she had not played for a few years, as the courts in Mortley were in a poor condition and the local council do not really bother with supporting sports. She did say the courts here are in good condition and the park is generally well looked after and she was tempted to play.

There were the usual runners and joggers in the park, as there are most of the time. I needed to get back to a fitness regime, as it had been greatly lacking. We both decided we would start a fitness programme to get back to a level of fitness.

Whilst we were walking, I decided to tell her about

my encounter with Amber.

'When I was at West Cromley Park I met Amber, or should I say she met me. She sat with me, and we talked for a while mostly about our younger days, which are obvious, as I have been away for a while.'

'How did you feel about it?'

'Years ago, I would have been tongued tied and wound up, but I never felt that way today. I guess the pent-up feelings I had were from our younger days when I was intimidated by her.'

'How was she towards you?'

'She was a lot softer in her personality and was quite relaxed, but still self-assured. She was not spending time looking around her whilst we spoke and gave me her full attention. That did surprise me, as there was never another guy far from her. I guess motherhood and maturity have changed her into a more normal human being.'

Tuppence looked at me and we both laughed.

'How did you leave it when you left the park?'

'She asked me if I would like to go for a drink. I have never known her to ask any guy out. She never needed to; they were around her in droves,' I laughed.

'And will you?'

'I do not know; it is not a priority just now.'

'That tells me a lot,' she said knowingly.

Before we knew it, we had arrived back at the apartment and were ready for work.

We went to the incident room and Tuppence

printed off the files that Sergeant Brown had sent to us. We went into the lounge where it was more comfortable to sit and read.

I said to Tuppence, 'We might as well go through these together as you might pick up on something I might miss.'

Tuppence agreed.

'I will read through them and make two piles: Possible and Unpossible.'

'There is no such word as unpossible,' she said as a matter of fact.

'There is now.'

I laughed and so did she.

I opened the first file, and it was the daughter of the cook, Mrs Wilmslow. Her daughter was fined for shoplifting four years ago with some other girls. This was a teenage thing to do, that bit of devilment and defiance. There was no way I felt she was capable of the murders.

Tuppence agreed. 'The unpossible pile?' she offered.

The second file was the brother of one of the estate workers, Mike Foster. He had been charged and fined for possessing a small amount of marijuana. This was two years ago, of no concern to us, so it went on the unpossible pile.

The third file was one of the hall staff who found herself pregnant five years ago. She was young, alone and had to fend for herself with no job and on benefits. She sought extra money from doing favours for some men; she was caught and feared she would lose her baby.

However, Cynthia Holmes, as a member of a local social group, became a mentor for her. Cynthia Holmes gave her a job and one of the estate cottages, and by all accounts she is now established and doing very well at the hall. There was no way she carried out the crime at the hall, so it was placed on the unpossible pile.

The fourth file was more interesting. The son of a former employee was arrested three years ago for burglary and threatening behaviour. His name was John Grant, so he was definitely on the possible pile.

The fifth, sixth and seventh files were motoring offences, so put on the unpossible pile.

The eighth file was of interest. A former employee Phillip Smith was sacked for stealing, prosecuted and was fined. It is possible he could hold a grudge against Cromley Hall. This was put on the possible pile.

File nine was a former employee who was sacked for insulting and shouting at some visitors. The visitors reported the incident to the hall staff, where an investigation took place, and she was sacked. The employee's name was Helen Green. There was a possible motive; she was put on the possible file.

I opened files ten, eleven and twelve and again they were minor motoring offences, so went on the unpossible pile.

File thirteen was an estate worker's son, Peter Franks, who was involved in a brawl in a nightclub. The police were called and the club pressed charges, so he received a fine. We put it on the possible pile.

File fourteen was again a motoring offence, so was put on the unpossible pile.

File fifteen was again a son of one of the estate workers and his name was Mark Curtis, known to everyone as in the notes as Piss, apparently because he was always on it. He was charged with drunken behaviour in a public place. He was aggressive when he was arrested, so he was of interest, so went on the possible file.

So, my possible file was completed so time now to go into more detail.

'Which file do you want to start with?' asked Tuppence.

'Take your pick,' I answered.

Tuppence laughed, closed her eyes, shuffled the pack and chose one; it was file eight.

File eight was former employee Phillip Smith, who had been sacked for stealing. The police were brought in and he was charged, prosecuted and fined. There was sufficient motive against the family for me to speak to him, so we cracked on.

I rang John Holmes for the last known address of Phillip Smith. He duly obliged. The address was not too far away. I would take Tuppence with me; she could sit in the car whilst I spoke with him.

We duly arrived at the address. I turned to look at Tuppence and spoke. 'Well, here goes.'

I made my way up the path to the house. I knocked on the door; it was answered by an elderly lady.

'I am DS Blackmore of Cromley Police.' I showed her my warrant card. 'I would like to speak with Phillip Smith,' I said with a level of assertion.

'He doesn't live here and hasn't lived here for the last year.'

'Do you have an address for him?'

'No. We haven't seen him for many months and neither do we want to see him,' she said, with an air of defiance.

I thanked her and headed back to the car.

'How did you get on?' asked Tuppence.

'He does not live there; she has not seen him for a few months,' I put to her.

'Do you believe her?'

'Yes, I do. The look on her face was genuine to me.'

'What will you do now?'

'I need to find him.' 'How will you do that?'

'We will go back to the apartment and do a search.'

With that, we set off for the apartment, with Tuppence again taking an interest in the town along the route. We arrived and went straight to our incident room. The checks revealed an address not too far away, so once again we set off.

We arrived at the address, so I duly made my way up the path. I noticed the curtains twitch. I knocked on the door, but got no answer, so I knocked again and there was still no answer. I leaned down and shouted through the letterbox.

'DS Blackmore of Cromley Police. I know you are

in there, so either you open the door or I will make a call and get a squad down here to break it down,' I shouted with menace.

I could hear movement inside and a woman came to the door; why do they always send a woman? The door opened and she looked defiant. I showed my warrant card and spoke.

'DS Blackmore of Cromley Police, I want to speak to Phillip Smith and do not tell me he is not here, as I know he is,' I said with a level of menace.

A shabbily dressed guy came to the door and he looked dishevelled.

'Are you Phillip Smith?'

'Yes. What do you want me for? I ain't done wrong,' he said in a confused way.

'I want to speak with you regarding the murders at Cromley Hall,' I deliberately directed at him.

'What? That's got nothing to do with me. What makes you think it has?' he said, even more confused.

'Where were you on Saturday 6th June evening?'

'That's easy. I were in hospital. I went in on the Thursday and was released on the Monday.'

'What were you in for? I will check,' I said with a level of sarcasm.

'I were knocked off me bike by the library and were taken to hospital in an ambulance,' he said in a confident manner.

'There is a strong odour coming from your house. I recognise it, so I will send a team around to check it out,'

I said to him.

I turned and made my way down the path with a wry smile on my face and Tuppence looking at me with a quizzical look on her face.

I got in the car, and she spoke. 'OK, what's going on?'

'We can put him on the unpossible list, as he did not do it. He says he was in hospital and I believe him. However, we will check anyway, but we will do it in the morning.'

'So, what were you laughing at when you were walking down the footpath?'

'I told him there was a strong odour coming from the house and I would send a team round to check it out. I know the odour of marijuana, so I guess the house will be the cleanest it has been for a long time.'

Tuppence just laughed and said, 'Will you really send a team to that house?'

'No, I would not waste their time.'

We set off back to the apartment and I refused to give a guided tour but drove slowly as she looked out of the window. It had been a long day.

SIXTEEN

A new dawn and a new day were upon me. I felt fresh. I went for a shower and started singing.

'Why are you so jovial in the mornings? It drives me round the bend,' Tuppence said with great annoyance.

'Embrace life and all it brings.'

'Yes, I get that, but not this time of the morning!'

She brightened up and it was not long before she was back to normal, if that is how I could describe her.

'What's on the agenda today? We didn't have a briefing last night,' she said.

'I will go to the hospital to check Phillip Smith was telling the truth. I believe he is. You could catch up with your notes.'

'Yes sir!' she said and saluted.

I left her to it and headed to the car. I drove the route that I have done so many times over the years. I duly arrived and parked up. I walked into the reception, I walked straight into my sister.

'Paul!' she said excitedly, giving me a massive hug. I winced when my ribs squashed. 'What a great surprise to see you!' she said, standing back and looking at me. 'What are you doing here?'

'I am following up an enquiry.'

'What sort of enquiry?'

'I interviewed a suspect and he said he was in this hospital on the night of the crime.'

'Come with me,' she said.

We walked down some corridors and chatted generally, and we eventually arrived in some sort of official room.

'What dates are we talking about?' she asked.

'Saturday 6th June.'

'What is the name you are looking for?'

'Phillip Smith. He said he was knocked off his bike and an ambulance brought him here on Thursday 4th and he was released on Monday 8th June.'

'Here we are and, yes, the details are correct. I can confirm the dates.'

'Thank you. That is one more off the list.'

'How are your injuries? I was aware of your incident; I knew you were being treated well, so I kept my distance.'

'They are OK. I am just a little stiff now, but it does get better each day.'

There was no point in saying anything else; she would have seen right through me.

'You should really be resting.'

'I find it easier if I move about. Sitting around makes me feel uncomfortable.'

She smiled as we chatted some more as she walked out with me to my car. I promised her we would meet up soon.

I made my way back to the apartment when my

mobile started ringing. I pulled into a layby and parked up. I duly called back, and it was Graham Coleman.

'Good morning, DS Blackmore. I have completed my examination of the heirlooms so do you want me to tell you over the phone or will you come to the station?'

'Do you know the coffee stand in Cromley Park?'

'Yes, I do. I use it frequently.'

'I will meet you there in fifteen minutes.'

I arrived, parked up and made my way purposefully to the coffee stand. Graham Coleman was already there. We took our coffees and made for one of the benches.

'What have you to tell me?' I asked.

'The heirlooms were wiped clean and there were no fingerprints at the access to the passage or the panel door to the interior corridor. It was the same in the servants' quarters; it confirms my view that gloves were worn. All we have are the casts of the footprints. I can confirm the footprints are off one person. It is clear the murderer was incredibly careful and went to great lengths to conceal himself. I am still waiting for the DNA results. Hopefully this will throw up better news.'

I thanked him and we left with a handshake. I made my way back to the car and as I was about to open the door a familiar voice called out.

'DS Blackmore, how are you?'

I looked up and saw Sue Bentley of the Cromley Echo walking purposely towards me with a smile on her face. Her features were softer than I have seen her before, and she was a lot more relaxed.

'I am very good,' I said non-committedly.

'Glad to hear it. It was quite a knock you had.'

'It was not as bad as reported,' I said. As I was standing bolt upright, there was no way she was going to see anything in my eyes.

She changed tack. 'Are you making any progress?'

'The team is working on the case,' I offered.

'I was asking about your progress. I know you are working on a different angle from SIO DI Grainger,' she said in a more aggressive manner.

'I have given you an answer, so if you do not mind...'

I opened the car door and got in, closing the door behind me. I did not wait for her response and drove off.

I drove the very short distance to the apartment, carefully checking my mirrors for any sign of her, but she was nowhere to be seen. I entered the apartment and found Tuppence was up to date with her notes and had selected the next file to look at.

'How did you get on at the hospital?' she asked.

'Really good. I was walking to the reception when I literally walked into my sister, who is a senior nurse. She took me to a records room and confirmed Phillip Smith was in the hospital at the dates he said he was.'

'That's handy,' said Tuppence.

'As I was making my way back to the apartment, Graham Coleman called me, so I met him in Cromley Park. The report was disappointing, as the only thing recoverable was the footprints. Just as I was getting in the car, Sue Bentley collared me with a nice starter and then tried to extract information from me.'

'What did you do?'

'I left her in the car park.'

'You sure know how to treat a girl,' she said, laughing.

'You know, my view on this case has changed.'

'In what way?'

'The fact that the heirlooms had been wiped clean and the culprit was very careful not to leave fingerprints. The case has taken on a new level, from an opportunist to a planned crime.'

'Wow!' said Tuppence.

'Come on, we will head to the station.'

We arrived at the station and once again walked the gauntlet of eyes. Sergeant Phillips was once again not at the desk, but an unknown officer was. We signed in and made our way to the squad room. I picked up the phone and rang Chief Constable Gregg.

'Sir, do you have time for a chat?'

'Come and see me at two o'clock,' he said directly.

'I will be seeing the Chief Constable Gregg at two o'clock, so I will go for a walk to the car. I will be interested to see who will come and see you while I am gone!'

I headed for the car and went into it. I pretended to look for something in the glove box. I sat for a few minutes looking at the car user manual for the tyre pressures. I made my way back to the room and heard voices. As I made my way down the corridor Chief Constable Gregg was just leaving the room.

'Ah, DS Blackmore! I was coming to let you know I am available now, so come on to my office.'

I looked at Tuppence and smiled, duly followed him and sat in my now familiar seat.

'Sir, I believe the case has now taken another turn. Graham Coleman has told me the heirlooms have been wiped clean; there are no fingerprints on the entry to the passageway, in the passageway or exit point to an internal corridor. It is the same with the servants' quarters. The only thing he has is a cast of some footprints made by the same person and DNA results. I was of the view the crime was opportunist, but now it shows that it has been well planned and carried out. I do not think the murders were planned, because the party was on the other side of the hall; so how would he or she know the brothers would be there? I feel the thefts were planned.'

Chief Constable Gregg agreed, and I returned to our incident room.

Surprisingly, Tuppence was sitting by herself; she had received no visitors.

'OK, who is next on the list?' I asked her.

'That is number four. His name is John Grant. He was arrested and charged with burglary and threatening behaviour. He was fined and received a suspended sentence three years ago. His whereabouts are unknown.'

'Well, he is someone I definitely want to talk to. I will ring John Holmes and see if he can help.'

I dialled the number.

'DS Blackmore,' said the now familiar voice. 'How can I help you?'

'I am looking at a former employee with the surname of Grant or more specifically his son, by the name of John Grant,' I requested.

'Yes! I remember him well. His father died around a year ago and the last I heard of his son he moved to Aberdeen in the north of Scotland, just after the funeral. I believe he has some relatives living up there; it was reported the opportunity would give him the chance to start afresh and leave his past behind him. That is all I know of him.'

'Thank you. I greatly appreciate your help and I will follow this up.'

'If it helps my family, I am more than happy to help,' he said, like a man who had the weight of the world on his shoulders.

He really is a decent guy, along with the rest of his family, and I know Roderick Holmes is innocent. I must prove it.

There was no way I was going to go to Scotland, so I would ring the Aberdeen police. I found and rang the number. The call was answered by DI Fraser Robertson.

'DI Robertson, this is DS Blackmore of Cromley Police, based in Northamptonshire.'

'Hello and whit canna do for you?'

'I am investigating a crime at Cromley Hall where two elderly members of the Holmes family, Jake and

Arthur Holmes, were murdered. I am interested in a suspect who has previous for burglary and threatening behaviour. He moved to Aberdeen around a year ago and I want to know if he was in Aberdeen from 4th to 8th June. I would be grateful for your help with this. His name is John Grant, and he was reported to be staying with family in Aberdeen.'

'Aye, I will see what I can do.'

We chatted for a few minutes regarding the case, as he was genuinely interested. He said he would ring me as soon as he had something for me.

'Right Tuppence, we can check another one whilst we wait for DI Robertson. Who is next?'

'The next one is number nine, who is Helen Green, who was sacked for insulting and shouting at a group of visitors. I have her address on the file.'

I left Tuppence in the squad room and headed for the address she gave to me. It was on an estate on the edge of the town, that I knew, and as I approached the place looked rather run down. I parked up and walked up the path to the house and noticed the missing gate lying on the lawn with the grass growing through it. I knocked on the door.

'Who are you and what do you want?' she yelled.

'DS Blackmore of Cromley police,' I said.

She opened the door and I showed her my warrant card. 'I want to speak with Helen Green.'

'Why? What am I supposed to have done?' she said, with a great level of agitation.

'Will you confirm you are Helen Green?'

'Yes,' she replied with aggression.

'Would you mind telling me where you were on Saturday 6th June?'

'I was here with my boyfriend all day and night.'

'Is your boyfriend here to verify this?'

'Yes, he is.'

She called out to him.

A guy a little older than her came to the door and looked a bit embarrassed.

'Can you verify you were both here on Saturday 6th June through the day and night?'

'Yes, I can,' he replied with hesitation.

'And your name is?'

'Bryan Gates,' he said reluctantly.

'And is this your permanent address?'

'No, I stay here when I am in town,' he said, with an uncomfortable air.

'Fine, then you will not mind giving me your permanent address,' I said, looking him straight in the eye.

He duly supplied the address.

'What's this all about? I will get my solicitor on to you for harassment,' she said in her aggressive manner.

'Go ahead,' I replied, as I looked and smiled at the guy. I turned and walked down the path. She is his bit on the side when he is in town. I do not think he wants his wife to know what he gets up to when he is out of town.

I made my way back to the station and followed up

the address I was given. Both the name and address checked out. He was a rep for an out-of-town food company specialising in food ingredients.

'OK,' I said to Tuppence. 'We can move her to the unpossible side. I think we have done enough for today. We can drop the car off and go to the lodge for some food,' I said with a smile.

'Yes, that's a fabulous suggestion, DS Blackmore,' she said with a fair amount of joviality.

We made our way to the car, I noticed Sue Bentley was not at her usual window.

We arrived at the apartment, parked up and headed for The Lodge; it was a lovely time of the day to walk. The pub was quiet, so we took our seats and placed our orders.

I looked around and noticed Sue Bentley on the opposite side of the pub. She was sitting with a group of girls, so it was obviously a girls' outing. She had not, as yet, noticed us. I moved my position to restrict her view of us and fortunately a party of four arrived and sat at a table directly between us. I was safe for now.

Our meal went without incident. I paid the bill, and we left the pub. A voiced called out as we were leaving.

'Goodnight, DS Blackmore,' shouted Sue Bentley, who was walking towards the ladies' room.

We ignored her and laughed as we walked back to the apartment. When we arrived, I said to Tuppence, 'We will have a relaxing evening with no catchup.'

SEVENTEEN

I woke early as normal and sat by the window. The usual people were out doing their thing in the park. There was no sign of Amber, but then again, I was not really looking for her.

I could hear Tuppence in her room moving about. She had no cause for complaint this morning, as I made no noise. She appeared and sat beside me at the window, taking in the waking world.

'Why do you rise so early in the morning?' she asked.

'It is something I have always done for as long as I can remember. My mother never had to get me up for school, I was always the first up in the morning,' I said with a smile.

We got ourselves ready and headed to the station.

'OK, out of the five possible people to interview, I have spoken with two and one is pending with DI Robertson. Who is next?'

'File thirteen and he is Peter Franks. He is the son of the present kitchen manager. There was a fracas at a nightclub and the police were called. The club pressed charges. He was fined for his troubles,' she offered.

'I will call John Holmes.'

'Hello again, DS Blackmore,' he answered in a cheerier tone.

'I need another address from you, please, for a Peter Franks, who is the son of your kitchen manager. I do not think he is involved, but I need to check him out.'

'I will save you the trouble; he is a good lad and just got caught up in the altercation at the nightclub. He is living in Cornwall. He was there when the terrible events happened at the hall. His mother had the weekend off and she went down to see him,' he said with assurance.

'That is good news and thank you for that.'

Just then, my mobile rang, and it was DI Robertson of the Aberdeen police force.

'Hello, DS Blackmore, I have news for you regarding John Grant. I can confirm he was in Aberdeen on the dates given. He works on a fishing trawler, so I checked with the company and they confirmed he was at sea at that time,' he said with confidence.

'Wow, you do not hang about,' I said with gratitude.

'Aye, happy to help,' he replied.

We spoke in civil terms for a few minutes as he was interested in what happened at Cromley Hall. We finished our conversation and I focussed on the case again.

'Right Tuppence, there is only one left from the possible file, and he is…?'

'File fifteen and he is Mark Curtis, known generally as Piss, as he is always on it, i.e., drinking. He was charged with drunken behaviour in a public place. He was aggressive when he was arrested, put on file but not charged.'

'I am not going to ring John Holmes again, so I will do some checks myself.'

'It's about time you did,' she said, with a level of sarcasm.

I just looked at her and laughed.

I decided to check the registrar's office; I do not know why, just an instinct. I checked the deaths section and found his name; he had died two years ago.

'OK, we have now gone through the possible list and moved them to the unpossible list, so that avenue is closed,' I said with a level of deflation.

'Well, any inspiration?'

'I need to go to Cromley Hall. The answer is there, I just need to feel it. Grab your jacket and we will go there, sit on the lawn, have a coffee and absorb.'

We headed to the car and made our way to the hall. I was looking forward to the soft Irish voice at the gate and I was not disappointed. The gate was duly opened and I drove to the car park.

We purchased our goods and sat by the north wall and scanned my eyes around the building. I became restless and motioned to Tuppence I was going to stretch my legs, and she smiled her approval.

I walked the outer wall to the rear gardens and looked over the valley. I was thinking back to my younger years and the antics the lads and I would get up to - and then it hit me like a thunderbolt. I quickly turned round and made my way back to Tuppence.

'Well, something has certainly sparked you into life,'

she said, bemused.

'Yes! I was walking around the rear garden when I started thinking about the times the lads and myself were messing around looking for secret passages or tunnels and the time when BJ and I were thrown out of the church by Mr Holloway. What if that happened to some other kid doing the things we were doing?'

'An interesting thought,' she said.

'Yes, and I need to speak with John Holmes.'

I duly rang the number and the familiar voice answered.

'DS Blackmore, you ring me more than my dear wife,' he said, with a level of humour.

'I need to speak with you. I am sitting by the north wall, if you would like to join us.'

'I will be with you presently.'

We did not have to wait too long when he emerged from the house and strode across the lawn and sat at the table with us.

'Thank you for your time again and your patience; I appreciate it is a difficult time for you and your family, as it is indeed for Cromley Police.'

He nodded to me.

'When I was twelve years old, some of my friends and I used to search around the church for secret passages or tunnels into the hall. One day, Mr Holloway caught us in the church and sent us packing with a clip round the ear,' I said smiling, but John Holmes looked bemused.

'Have you, over the last five years, caught anyone doing exactly the same thing as my friends and I, and evicted them from the hall?' I put to him.

'This happens all the time. The hall is a haven for explorative excitement to young people.'

'I was thinking in any one individual who was persistent, rather than generally.'

'I will check with the staff,' he offered and headed back to the hall.

'Come on, we will go for a walk around West Cromley Park. It is just around the corner by car,' I put to Tuppence, who nodded in agreement.

It was a good day for a stroll around the park and good to take in some fresh air to the lethargic brain cells. The park was busy with dog walkers, couples, etc. I showed Tuppence my favourite bench and we sat for a while.

'How tranquil. I could sit here for hours looking over the valley,' she said, with a smile on her face.

'I have sat here for hours on end while I was studying and generally just had time to myself.'

'I like what I have seen so far of Cromley. It is so much better than Mortley. I find the people a lot friendlier and good to talk to,' she said, happily.

'Steady, it may be difficult getting you back to Mortley,' I laughed.

Just then my phone rang; it was John Holmes.

'DS Blackmore, I have news for you. There was one particular individual who attracted attention and he was evicted a few times until he was permanently banned from the hall. This was around three years ago; he has not been seen since. He was not related to anyone working at the hall and no one can recall his name,' he offered with a resigned tone.

'That is unfortunate. Is it possible you may have some video footage from that time?'

'It may be possible. However, our head of security is on holiday and is due to return to the hall tomorrow. I will arrange for him to start that process then.'

'Can you get him to come in and start now?' I requested.

'Alas, no. He is due to arrive home late this evening after a long flight. I feel it will be in everyone's interest for him to start tomorrow morning after a night's rest.'

I reluctantly agreed. We headed back to the apartment, feeling it was a good day and progress was being made. We headed to the incident room for a recap.

'OK,' I said to Tuppence. 'We have eliminated all the possible to the unpossible file, so we can close that. We have a potential suspect that must be identified, so hopefully tomorrow will bring some good news.'

I went to my seat by the window to think and watch Amber jog around the park with a usual companion.

EIGHTEEN

I woke early as usual and hoping for some good news for the forthcoming day so I could move forward. My gut feeling, and what I had so far, was telling me I was going in the right direction. I was focused and ready to move on.

I turned on the television for the early morning news. I was stopped in my tracks when it was announced that Roderick Holmes would make his first appearance in court. Just then Tuppence appeared by my side, and she had just caught the bulletin. I turned to her.

'I was so focused on my own investigation I forgot about Roderick Holmes. That guy and his family must be going through hell.'

'It's not your fault. His best defence is for you to focus on your work, I know you will solve the case,' she said with a smile.

'Thank you; that is just what I needed.'

I have not as yet fully read the pathologist's report on the deaths of the two elderly Holmes brothers and now would be a good time to do this. I was struck by the lack of detail and basically it said the deaths were caused by a blow to the head of each brother. The report looked very amateurish; I needed to speak with the pathologist who carried out the autopsy. This was not a job for the phone, so a visit was required.

'Tuppence, grab your jacket and pad, we are going out. I will explain on the way to the hospital.'

We set off and made our way through the morning traffic, and I said to her, 'I was reading the pathologist's report and I was alarmed at the lack of detail and basically put the deaths down to blows to their heads; it does not sit right with me.'

'Is that why you are going to see the pathologist?'

'Yes, I want to know why.'

We arrived at the hospital and enquired at the desk for the duty pathologist. The desk clerk duly made a phone call and presently he arrived.

'Hello, I am Gordon Black. What can I do for you?' he asked in a civil manner.

'DS Blackmore of Cromley Police.' I showed him my warrant card. 'This is Tuppence. She is a civilian working with me taking notes, etc. Is there somewhere we can talk privately?'

'Yes, of course. Come with me.'

We followed him down a few corridors to an office at the end of one of them. He invited us in and pointed to some chairs for us to sit on.

'I am investigating the deaths of Jake and Arthur Holmes who were murdered at Cromley Hall on Saturday June 6th.'

'Yes, I am aware of the events, but I was not directly involved in the case. I was in New Zealand for a three-week vacation over that period. The autopsy was supposed to be carried out by a locum who was to stand in for me. However, he unfortunately fell ill. The autopsy was carried out by someone brought in at very short notice. What is it that is a cause for concern to you regarding the report?'

'Have you read the report?' I asked with surprise.

'No, it is not normal practice. You can appreciate the volume of cases that pass through this hospital would create a lot of work.'

'Will you please have a look at my copy of the autopsy report?'

I handed it to him.

'It appears to me an open and shut case where they were hit over the head and that was it,' I put to him.

He sat and read the report, he read it again and then said to me, 'Yes, I see what you mean.'

'I take it the bodies are still here, as I am not aware of any funeral arrangements, so I would like another autopsy carried out.'

'You will need a formal request for me to do that.'

'If I can have your details and email address, Tuppence will set up a direct link between us. I want to see the bodies with you present; in the meantime, I will seek the permission you require.'

With that we parted on good terms. I pointed Tuppence in the direction of the hospital café. We collected our purchases and I saw a familiar face, so I steered Tuppence in her direction and sat down beside her. She looked up and a large smile spread across her face and gave me a hug.

'Tuppence, this is my sister Helen; and Helen, this is Tuppence, who is working with me on the case I am involved in.'

'It's nice to meet you,' said Helen. 'My mother says a lot of good things about you.'

'She is very kind.'

'What are you doing at the hospital?' Helen asked.

'Following up some leads and that is about as much as I can tell you.'

We talked generally, then Helen had to return to work and so did we.

We returned to the car, then Tuppence asked, 'Where to now?'

'To Cromley police station. I need to speak with Chief Constable Gregg.'

I pulled into the station entrance, parked up and we made our way across the car park, signed in and headed for our incident room. I rang Chief Constable Gregg and we arranged to meet in thirty minutes.

The time came and I made my way to Chief Constable Gregg's office. I knocked on the door and waited for the call.

'Come in, DS Blackmore,' his booming voice called out.

I made my way in and sat on my usual chair.

'I hope you have some news for me as I could use it right now,' he said with resignation.

'I believe I am going in the right direction, sir; I

have a potential suspect that we are in the process of tracking down. He was ejected from Cromley Hall and then eventually banned on a permanent basis three years ago due to constantly being found in various rooms in the hall. I do not have a name for him, but John Holmes will be checking security videos with the hope he will be on one of them. I am interested in his whereabouts in the three-year period up to the crime at the hall.

'Sir, I am greatly concerned at the lack of detail in the autopsy report; it is as if the deaths were passed off as blows to the head and signed off. I have spoken to Gordon Black, the pathologist at the hospital, and he shares my concerns. He was on holiday in New Zealand at the time of the murders; his holiday cover unfortunately fell ill, so a locum came in at very short notice and subsequently carried out the autopsy. It was the last one before the return of Gordon Black. I also want to speak with the pathologist who carried out the autopsy. The bodies of Jake and Arthur Holmes are still held at the hospital, so I would like another autopsy carried out on them. However, Gordon Black requires an official request for this, so will you please authorise my request?'

'Do you have the report with you?'

'Yes, I do.' I passed it to him.

He sat and read through it very quickly; it would be quick as there was not a lot in it.

'I see your concern; I will authorise your request and you will hear shortly.'

I made my way from Chief Constable Gregg's office and headed to my incident room. I could hear voices and recognised the voice of DC Harrow; he was talking to Tuppence. I walked in and startled DC Harrow.

'Another visit, DC Harrow? Shall we set up a desk with all the trimmings for you here or a satnav for you to find your way back to your office?' I said with a high level of sarcasm.

I could see Tuppence out of the corner of my eye supressing laughter. He got up and made his way out of the office.

'What was he after?'

'He was fishing for how you were progressing in your investigation.'

'What did you tell him?'

'I did the movie thing where I looked around to check no one could hear me and said to him you were hitting dead-ends and you were not getting very far, then you came into the room.'

'I am teaching you well.'

My mobile phone rang, and it was John Holmes. I answered.

'DS Blackmore, I have news for you. We have managed to find an image of the person we spoke about. However, the image is very grainy.'

'That is fantastic news. I will be right over. Come on, we are going to Cromley Hall,' I said, with intent to Tuppence.

'Yes sir,' she said and saluted.

'Normal walking; best not let anything show to our observers,' I said, laughing.

We made our way through the reception and the driver of the police car that stopped me that night was behind the desk. I duly signed us both out and we went our way.

We walked across the car park to the car. I shifted my head slightly and I could see Sue Bentley standing at her office window. She was expressionless, but she was looking directly at me.

We made our way to Cromley Hall and once again I gave Tuppence a running commentary on the route, so I took a detour past the water treatment works. The odour was very pungent today, so I laughed my head off.

We duly arrived at the hall, but the lovely soft Irish voice was not on duty. The gate opened and I drove to the car park, parked up and made our way to Blaggards' Door. I rang the old bell; an elderly gentleman opened the door and invited us in. He escorted us to the security office where I found John Holmes with a member of his staff.

'DS Blackmore, this is Joe Williams, head of Cromley Hall security. Some time ago we bought a new security surveillance system to enable us to record images with a greater degree of clarity. We only keep the recordings for one month so your person of interest will not be on them. However, Joe pulled out the old system we had stored away with the discs, and he has managed to find a clip of the individual we were discussing. As I said to you it is grainy, but you may be able to get some sort of a description. Unfortunately, there is no more footage of him.'

'Can I see the video?'

Joe Williams put the disc in the machine and put it on fast-forward and then put it on normal speed. After a few seconds I saw an individual walking across the yard towards the main gate.

'Is that him?' I directed at John Holmes.

'Yes. As you can see, it is very grainy and it is difficult to obtain a clear image.'

'I will need to take the disc with me,' I said directly.

'Of course; it's no longer useful to us,' he said as he handed it over.

'DS Blackmore, can I have Peasants' Walk returned to us? It is causing a great inconvenience to the daily running of the hall.'

'Of course.' I reached into my pocket and handed him the key to the gate. 'Will you please reduce the need to visit the area to a minimum for now and ensure the door is locked at all times?'

He agreed and we bade our farewells and took our leave.

'Where to now?' Tuppence asked.

'Back to the apartment. We can study the disc in more detail.'

We arrived back and I went straight to the video machine. I watched the disc all the way through. The only sighting of the suspect was the original twenty-second segment I watched.

I grabbed a pad and started to write down a description. He was medium to large build; unkempt mop of curly fairish hair; he was wearing large, round glasses, blue denim jeans, a plain white T-shirt and scruffy white trainers with laces dragging along the ground. He looked clean shaven, but it was difficult to tell.

I removed the disc from the machine and put it in my case and locked it away. I had something to work on and I needed to find him.

'Your day is getting better. Your request for another autopsy has been granted and Gordon Black will be doing it tomorrow morning at nine o'clock,' said Tuppence.

'That is fantastic news. Tell him I will be there at eight thirty. I want to speak with him and see the bodies before he starts.'

She duly sent off the email and my attendance was confirmed straight away.

'This has been a very good day and I really feel we are getting somewhere. Come on, let us go to The Scythe for something to eat and chill out,' I said with a smile on my face, and we headed off.

NINETEEN

The new day had me looking forward to me going to the hospital and inspecting the bodies of Jake and Arthur Holmes. I am keen to see if any marks on the bodies that are not recorded. I will not be present when Gordon Black does his investigation; however, I will return to discuss his findings.

'How do you feel this morning?' Tuppence asked.

'I feel good, I knew that I would.'

'How do you feel about going to see Gordon Black?' she asked.

'I am fine with that. I do not have an issue looking at the bodies; I am keen to see if there is anything that might be missing on the report. I will not be there when Gordon Black carries out his examination, but I will discuss with him his findings.'

'Rather you than me, I couldn't look at them!' she said with a grimace.

We headed to the hospital. We were met by Gordon Black in the reception area, and he escorted us to his office. After checking Tuppence would be all right, I left her in the office, and Gordon Black and I headed for the post-mortem examination room. We walked in and both brothers were on the examination tables, covered up.

'I want to inspect the bodies with you and

crosscheck against the official report,' I put to him.

'That's fine,' he replied.

Upon looking at the bodies, the two obvious external signs were the blows to the back of the head to both Holmes brothers. Everything else appeared as the report, except I noticed some discolouration under the nose and around the mouth of one of the brothers. I looked at the other brother and I saw the same discolouration.

I turned to Gordon Black and enquired, 'There is discolouration on the mouths of both brothers; what do you think that is?'

'It looks like bruising to me,' he said, looking closely.

'They are not recorded on the report,' I put to him.

I picked up a small torch that was lying on the instrument tray and looked more closely around the faces of each brother.

'There is the same discolouration on the sides of the brothers' noses so I take it that will be bruising as well. That is not recorded on the report.'

'Yes, I would say it is,' he replied, a bit bemused.

We carried out a further detailed examination of the bodies and agreed there was nothing else that was missing off the report. I started looking at the pictures that were taken at the scene of the crime and the one thing that was apparent to me was the small amount of blood around the heads of the brothers.

I called Gordon Black over and said to him, 'Look at this photograph. There is a small amount of blood around the heads of each brother. I was of the opinion a head would bleed quite a bit after a blow.'

He looked at the photograph and a pained expression grew across his face.

'Look, I will let you get on with your examination. We can discuss your findings once you have finished, but please do not discuss it with anyone else.'

He agreed. I left him to it and went back to his office, where Tuppence was still sitting patiently.

'Hi.'

'Hi to you,' she said. 'How did you get on?'

'Come on, we will go down the corridor and I will tell you.'

We got to the café, grabbed our purchases and sat down. I looked around but there was no sign of my sister.

'Look, if you feel a bit squeamish then just say and I will stop. There is nothing really gory. There was discolouration around the nose and mouth of each brother; it was bruising as identified by Gordon Black. It was not recorded on the report. There was, in my opinion, a lack of blood around the heads of the brothers and again Gordon Black agrees with me. I have left him to focus on his examinations, but there are answers to the questions that must be found. That is it, in a nutshell.'

Tuppence just sat and nodded her head, but said nothing.

'Come on, we will go back to the apartment. I feel I can work better from there.'

Tuppence smiled in agreement.

Back at the apartment, we set to work.

'I feel I am getting closer; I no longer feel the deaths were unintentional, but deliberate murders. I think they were murdered independently; one brother came in and came across the murderer and he was killed. The other brother unfortunately entered the room and suffered the same fate. I do not think the original intention was to kill them, as how would the murderer know they would be there? But he could not care less if he had to kill them; I think he sincerely thought he would get away with it. The autopsy, in my opinion, was a botched, amateurish job. I now have to focus on finding the face on the video, but with no name, address, DNA, fingerprints, etc., it will not be easy,' I said firmly. 'But I will find him.'

I looked at Tuppence with an intensity she had never seen before. I went over and sat in my chair by the window with my mind swimming over the park. It was like a kaleidoscope of thoughts bouncing around the clouds. I could see Amber like an oasis in the centre of it all as she was running around the park. I was brought back to earth when Tuppence appeared and spoke.

'Why don't you ring her and invite her out for a drink? It will do you a lot of good to have a distraction for a while. It's not a commitment.'

She was standing behind me looking over my shoulder at Amber as she neared the bottom end of the park where our apartment is. I thought for a few moments and spoke.

'Yes, I think you are right.'

I picked up my phone and dialled the number and watched as Amber stopped and looked at it for a couple of seconds then answered.

'Hi,' I said.

'Paul, I'm surprised to hear from you!'

She was leaning against the park fence, running her hand through her blonde hair.

'I thought you might like to go out for a drink tonight and catch up on the years,' I said with confidence.

'Yes, I would love that. It will be nice to see you.'

'I will pick you up at seven thirty, so text me your address.'

'I will do that and see you later.'

I could see her still leaning against the fence for a minute and then she did not finish her run, but left the park and I guess for home.

I returned my mind to the case and said to Tuppence, 'Gordon Black is carrying out his autopsy on the Holmes brothers, so we wait for his report. I must now focus on the unidentified suspect from the video. We have a brief description of him but no name or any identification. We have footprints, but no person to match them up to. So how do we find him? He was banned three years ago from the hall, so where has he been since that time? I have a hunch that he was in prison and is obviously now out of jail; he knows what valuables are displayed at the hall and would have a grudge against the family. I agree with Graham Coleman that it was one individual working alone, so it will now be a person of interest.'

'It sounds feasible, so are you going to find that person of interest?'

'For that we need to go to the police station and go through records for the last three years.'

We grabbed our jackets and headed for the car. I took another route pointing out the fabulous local sights on the route to the station. There was the local recycling centre and food waste plant. Tuppence turned to me and spoke.

'You're a sarcastic bastard,' she said, with a disgusted look on her face.

We arrived at the station, parked up, signed in and made our way to our incident room and turned everything on.

'Everyone who is brought in and charged will be photographed and filed so we will start with that,' I said to her.

I brought up the archive file and went back three years and we set about our task. There were quite a lot over the three years, so we went about it methodically. We worked steadily into the afternoon; I called a halt.

'We will resume tomorrow morning,' I said, with relief. We shut everything down and made our way from the building. We went past Chief Constable Gregg's office, and the door was open. I told Tuppence to go on and sign us out. I knocked on his door and he invited me in.

'What can I do for you, DS Blackmore?'

'Sir, I am going out this evening and I cannot take Tuppence with me. Would you arrange for someone to keep an eye on the apartment until I return?'

'Yes, I will arrange it,' he said, quite readily.

I thanked him and headed for the reception, where I found Tuppence waiting for me. She joined me as we made our way to the car and then on to the apartment; I took the direct route this time.

'I have arranged, through Chief Constable Gregg, to have the apartment under observation whilst I am out tonight. I do not think there will be a problem; it is for me really,' I said with assurance.

We arrived at the apartment and decided to have fish and chips with mushy peas for dinner tonight. It is not mine or Tuppence's usual meal, but a change they say is as good as a rest. We headed across the road to the chip shop and purchased our goods.

'Go and have yourself a shower and get ready for tonight; I will bring you in a coffee,' she said directly. 'How do you feel about tonight?'

'I have not really thought about it. She may change her mind as she has not sent me her address. I just plan to take her for a drink and a catchup and nothing else.'

'I am going to call my daughter. I plan to have an early night,' she said with a smile.

I duly carried on getting myself ready and I was ready in plenty of time. I went to the lounge and sat in my chair by the window and looked out over the park. It was noticeably clear to me how many people revolve their lives around a strict routine and in six months I guess they will know exactly what they will be doing. I guess I could say that as well, as I go to the gym every morning before I go to Mortley police station.

Tuppence appeared from her bedroom and disappeared to the bathroom. I put on the local radio. It was a Tamla Motown soul show and I love that music.

I rang the radio station and requested 'Midnight Train to Georgia' by Gladys Knight and the Pips. I asked them to play it at seven fifteen as I knew Tuppence would be out of the bathroom and would be sitting at the table doing her hair. Just before seven fifteen I turned up the volume and Tuppence looked at me bemused. Bang on seven fifteen the song was duly played; Tuppence turned to look at me and spoke.

'You asshole.'

She threw her brush at me.

I started laughing and Tuppence also started to laugh, as she saw the funny side. It was, however, time for me to leave.

I sent a text to Amber to say I was just leaving, and she replied with her address straight away.

I was wearing a pair of fresh blue jeans, a white shirt, brown jacket and brown shoes. I went back into the lounge area and Tuppence was standing looking at me.

'You look and smell nice.'

I bade my farewells and headed for the car. I noticed the unmarked police car that stopped me recently, with the same crew parked close by. I looked at them and nodded and they looked at me impassively.

I got in the car and headed for Amber's house, her house was on the other side of the town close to the area where I grew up. The satnav in this case was not required; she lived not too far from BJ's house and was in an area I knew well. I arrived at the house and parked outside and sat for a moment. I was just about to get out and go and knock on the door when the door opened, and she appeared.

She locked her door and turned around. My God, she looked stunning. In fact, she looked awesome; she was dressed to kill. She was dressed in a white dress that flared out slightly at the bottom with two thin straps at the top. It sat about three inches above her knees, and it buttoned right down the front. The dress sat great on the fantastic curves of her body. The top couple of buttons were undone down to her cleavage. She wore high heels that perfectly showed off her toned legs. Her blonde hair was bouncing on her shoulders as she walked and showed off her great looks. She walked in her confident, assured way. She had little makeup on, but in my opinion she did not need it; she was naturally beautiful. She got in the car and spoke.

'Hi,' she said, with a smile.

'Hi to you.'

'Where are we going?' she asked, as she got in the car and put on her seat belt.

'I thought we could go to the Arms by the stream in

Milden.'

'Good choice and it will be nice; it is a glorious evening to sit outside.'

She is softer in nature than the girl I knew ten years ago; she is still assured within herself.

We chatted generally as we drove the route and we eventually reached the pub and parked up. We walked across the bridge that straddles the stream and Amber selected a table. I went to the bar to order our drinks; the pub was busy. I could see all the guys looking at her. Yes, she has that effect. I was used to this. I smiled inwardly. Amber was on gin and tonic and me, just bottled water. Yes, exciting, but I was driving.

'Aren't you having a drink?'

'No, not whilst I am driving.'

'Can you talk about the events at Cromley Hall?'

'In a nutshell, no, that will not be possible.'

'That's fine. We will have plenty of other things to catch up with.'

The evening went well and the conversation flowed. We talked about the past years and where we are now. She told me she fell pregnant because for one time she was careless, but there was no way she would abort her child and she was hell bent he will not miss out on anything and do her best for him. (Similarities to Tuppence here.) She is training in law to be a solicitor. Her parents help her with her son, and he is with them now.

'Tell me,' she said. 'Why did you leave Cromley?

One minute you were there and then you were gone.'

'I felt I had to leave. I was too cocooned and suffering from claustrophobia in Cromley and it was time to make my own mark in life. A promotion came up in the force for the position of Detective Sergeant in Mortley. My exam results for the grade were very good and after a series of interviews I was offered the position and I gladly accepted. It meant, however, I had to leave straight away. I did not tell anyone about my application or interviews. I told my parents the day before I left.'

'What about your buddies? Didn't you tell them?'

'I rang them the night before and they were all in favour. They have been to Mortley on a few occasions for a lads' night out.'

'Hmm, I'm sure they were interesting nights out. You have certainly changed. Gone is the shy and unsure boy and replaced with a mature assured man. I find it hard to put the two together,' she said, leaning forward and looking into my eyes.

'That was the reason I had to leave Cromley. I had to leave that boy behind, and it has been good for me.'

'You have succeeded; you have made your mark since you have returned. I know Sue Bentley and she is convinced something is in the air, but she can't put her finger on it. She is convinced you are at the heart of whatever is happening, and it will come out soon. Don't worry, I have not told her I know you; that would not be fair on you, as she would pester me for anything I know of you,' she said, with sincerity.

'Thank you, I appreciate that.'

I thought, wow! She had noticed I had left the town. I guess if she really wanted to find me it would not be hard. She knows where my parents' house is and she lives very close to BJ. She is clearly a discreet woman and I am grateful for that.

Soon it was time to go as I did not want a late night. Amber did not have any objections, so we headed off. I drove steadily and we chatted some more. I never mentioned I saw her running around the park, as it would lead to questions about where I was living. Soon we were back at her house. I had just intended to drop her off.

'Come in and we can have a coffee,' she said, softly, and again looking into my eyes.

'Why not.' I could not see what harm it could do.

Amber showed me into her lounge and pointed to the sofa, I sat where she indicated. The lounge was tastefully furnished with soft lighting that presented, shall I say, a sensual atmosphere; she had set the mood before she left. She was confident I would accept her invitation.

Amber walked over to her music system and turned it on. She turned and walked slowly to her kitchen. She was looking at me as she slowly left the room, not intently, but with a soft smile and again deep into my eyes. The music was set as well. I was intrigued.

I recognised the tune as it played. I have played it myself a few times over the years. I was first aware of it as my dad played it a lot in his workshop; he would plane a piece of wood and the tempo of his work changed with the oscillations in the music, I would laugh as he exaggerated the movements, I grew to love it: 'Tubular Bells' by Mike Oldfield. The tune is approximately twenty-five minutes long, so I was intrigued what the twenty-five minutes would bring.

After approximately six minutes, Amber duly arrived with the coffees and sat beside me. I could feel her body and the aroma of her perfume as she sat close to me and, to be honest, she felt good. It has been a while since I have been this close to a woman. Tuppence is a whole different scenario, a platonic relationship you have with a friend.

I drank some of my coffee and put it on the side table, I went to speak to her, but she put her right index finger very gently on my lips to silence me and smiled. Amber put her coffee on her table and she turned to face me. All the time she was seated on the sofa she looked intently into my eyes. I feel she was searching for a reaction, but I remained passive. There was no way I was going to back out, not on her turf.

She moved her right hand to my hair and started to run her fingers slowly through it all the time looking into my eyes. I was conscious of the music and her hand movements and how they synchronised together. She started to undo the buttons on my shirt and removed it. She ran her hand slowly over my chest, to my face, hair and back to my chest. All the time she was looking deep into my eyes. I returned the look. The tune was building in intensity and so was Amber.

She moved and straddled across me with her legs either side of me. We started kissing slowly and gently, becoming more passionate, Amber was moving around me and, wow, it was intense. I realised then that she was dancing in a choreographed movement, with the music, around me and it felt good.

I moved my hands to her back and the curves of her body felt good as she was moving around me. She was breathing deeply, but controlled. I started to undo the buttons of her dress. She pulled her arms out wide and the dress fell to the floor. She was not wearing a bra. Her breasts felt good, they were firm and felt good in my hands. She threw her head back, opening herself up to me. Her breathing became deeper, breathing deeply, but still she was in control.

The music changed after approximately fourteen minutes, when she moved her legs between mine forcing them apart. She slid down between them on to her knees on the floor. She started to undo my trousers and stripped me. I could feel her deep breathing on me. She touched me, and it felt like a bolt of lightning hit me as she went down on me. She was blowing my mind and in control. She was running her hands over me and kissing me gently, passionately and now intently. The finale of the tune was now close, so she moved and pulled me to the floor. She got on top of me as the finale started. The pulsating guitar that runs through the finale was having an effect as she became more intense and passionate.

Her body movements were controlled and synchronised with the music. She was dancing with me at the same time; she is something else. She had been in control from the moment I set foot in her house and had a hold over me since I first set eyes on her all those years ago. I could not leave her house with Amber still in full control.

I put my hands up and pulled her down to me, I held her tight and rolled her over on to her back. She started to resist me, wanting to get back on top of me again, but I pinned her arms to the floor and she started to relax. For the first time she went with me. I decided to go with the music as well; she opened her eyes and looked at me, smiled and closed her eyes again.

She put her hands on my back and started to run her nails up and down my back and occasionally dig them in to me. I could feel the sweat off my back stinging the marks she was making. I stopped and told her to turn over on to her knees and she did so. She was lying face down on the couch, she grabbed a cushion in each hand digging her nails in to each one. The finale was building, our movements were going with it. The vocal introduction to each instrument was adding to the atmosphere as we got more intense. I could feel her body dancing with me and now she was breathing deeply and noisily. The tune was moving to its climax and so were we. The sound of the 'Tubular Bells' and the choir arrived like an emotive crescendo over us, it felt like all the stars in the sky had lit up all at once.

We lay there as the music started to gradually fade

out getting our breath and senses back. My back was stinging like hell, but I will deal with that back at the apartment.

I had never known a woman with so much physical passion and want to control, but I could not let her control to the end. I felt I had broken a spell she had over me and I could now move forward.

I got up and she put on her dressing gown. She picked up her coffee, sat on the sofa and watched as I dressed. She looked relaxed and she was looking deep into my eyes for what I do not know, but I stayed impassive throughout. We hardly said a word whilst I dressed, but I guess there were no words that needed to be said. I picked up my jacket and decided to carry it and I spoke.

'I have to go.'

'I know. I was not expecting you to stay the night.'

She opened the door, and I made my way down the drive to the car. I opened the car door when she said, 'I enjoyed tonight, and it was good to see you, perhaps again in the future.'

'Perhaps,' I replied and got in the car.

I drove back to the apartment reflecting on the night. I guess I now know why she is so popular with the guys. Amber is very sexually charged. I like sex like most guys, but a relationship is more important to me and the sex that goes with it.

I arrived back at car park at the apartment block. The unmarked police car was still there, so I gave them the thumbs up; they drove off as I entered the apartment. I went to my room to remove my shirt; it was sticking to my back through the sweat and going by the inside back of my jacket, blood as well. My shirt had adhered to my wounds. I decided to have a shower with my shirt on so the water could loosen it from my back; it did the trick. I looked in the mirror as best I could; she had made a good job of digging her nails in, but there was nothing I could do tonight, and I would deal with it in the morning.

TWENTY

I woke early as normal and sat by the window taking in the new day. My back was sore; it felt on fire, so I did not lean back. Tuppence came into the lounge. She came and sat beside me and spoke.

'I wasn't expecting you back last night.'

'There was no way I was staying overnight; it never crossed my mind to do so.'

'So how did your night go?'

'Let us say a ghost was laid to rest!' I said, looking directly at her, and then smiled.

'How was Chief Constable Gregg?' I asked.

'He is fine!' she answered, with a shocked expression on her face. 'Did the officers in the car tell you he was here?'

'No,' I answered, with a teasing smile.

'Then how the hell did you know he was here?' she said, with a level of frustration.

'You are the budding detective, work it out,' I said, laughing.

She stormed off to the kitchen and I headed to my bedroom.

'Come here!' she yelled.

I stopped in my tracks and went back to the lounge.

'Take your top off.'

'What?'

'Take your top off,' she ordered.

I duly removed it. She went around to my back and spoke.

'What the hell! I know you said a ghost was laid, but she didn't go quietly, going by the state of your back. Sit there and I will pop over to the chemist to get some cream.'

I sat overlooking the park and Tuppence returned in good time.

I stood up and she stood behind me and started to apply it over my back. She pressed quite hard, to the point where I said, 'Easy!'

'Then tell me how you know Chief Constable Gregg was here, you shit bag,' she said firmly.

'He wears a distinctive aftershave, and I could smell it when I came in last night,' I said, laughing in agony.

She eased off and I could feel my back start to cool down.

'I suggest you throw your shirt out as it is badly marked with blood and sweat. You would have been better off putting it in the bin rather than the wash basket.'

Just then I received a call from Gordon Black.

'Good morning, DS Blackmore. I have the results of the autopsy if you would like to come over.'

'Good morning and, yes, I will come over in an hour.'

We grabbed our gear and headed for the hospital.

My daily running commentary was coming to an end as I had covered all the routes now, so we just listened to the radio. We duly arrived and parked up and made our way to Gordon Black's office. His office door was open, so we walked in.

'DS Blackmore and Tuppence, good morning, and please sit down. I have completed the autopsy.' He handed me a copy. 'A lot of my findings were as the original autopsy, except for two key points I will go through. First, you were right regarding the lack of blood; they were both dead before they received the blows to their heads but not long before. They were asphyxiated. Second, the marks to their noses and under their mouths were indeed bruising, but what caused them I don't know.'

'Thank you. I would be grateful for you to keep this under wraps for now.'

'Consider it done,' he replied.

'What are you thinking from Gordon Black's report?' Tuppence asked with concern as we left his office.

'It confirms to me that Roderick Holmes did not kill his uncles, but as yet I cannot prove it. I do believe I am narrowing it down and I fully believe the unknown guy on the video is my man. I just have to get him,' I said with a great level of defiance. 'Come on, we will go back to the station and continue through the court files.'

I pushed the exit doors open and stopped halfway and winced.

'What's wrong?' Tuppence asked.

'Just a sharp pain in my chest. I guess my injuries are not fully healed from the incident with the car.'

'Last night wouldn't help either,' she said with a high level of sarcasm.

We headed for the station, parked up and after signing in we made our way to our incident room. I rang Chief Constable Gregg to request to see him and I was duly invited to his office.

'Good morning, DS Blackmore. What have you got for me?'

'I have come with the autopsy report into the deaths of Jake and Arthur Holmes. The report is as the original except for two key points. Both Jake and Arthur Holmes died from asphyxiation. They were dead before they received the blows to their heads. I was suspicious when I saw the lack of blood on the ground around their heads. There is bruising on the nose and mouth of each brother that is not recorded on the report. I have yet to identify the cause of why they are there. I have asked for the name of the person who carried out the original autopsy as to how that conclusion was made.

'I have a face and description of an individual that has been identified from a Cromley Hall video. The person in question was banned from the hall due to being caught consistently in various parts of the hall. Tuppence and I are going through cases from the last three years to see if the individual shows up, and he may have been in prison and has been released.

'I found the heirlooms in an alcove in the secret entrance. Why would Roderick Holmes use a secret entrance? It does not make sense. It is my view Roderick Holmes did not murder his two elderly great uncles; the evidence against him is very circumstantial and now incorrect. Any one of the family or staff could be charged on that evidence as the heirlooms are moved around on a regular basis. How it ever got through the CPS is beyond me, I believe it will be thrown out of court,' I said, with total belief in my investigation so far.

Chief Constable Gregg was silent and was sitting contemplating what I had just reported, before he finally said, 'Speak with the pathologist who carried out the original autopsy as a matter of urgency, then come and see me afterwards.'

'Yes, sir. I will do it straight away.'

I got up and left his office and returned to my incident room to find Tuppence writing up her notes. She went to speak, but I put my hand up to stop her and pointed to my phone. She looked at me and nodded.

I rang the number of Gordon Black and he duly answered.

'DS Blackmore?'

'I need the name of the pathologist, along with the phone number, who carried out the original autopsy, and where he or she is now, I want that information   right now.'

'OK, I will find that and get back to you.'

I hung up and sat down just as Tuppence returned

to the room with two welcome coffees. I had no sooner taken a sip when Gordon Black rang back.

'DS Blackmore, her name is Aimee Lloyd. She is based in Oxford. I have emailed all the details to you; you should have them.'

I thanked him for his prompt reply. I asked Tuppence to check the emails and it was there, so she printed it out. I duly rang the number and a soft female voice answered.

'Good morning, this is DS Blackmore of Cromley Police. I am investigating the murders of Jake and Arthur Holmes, the two elderly brothers at Cromley Hall. I believe you were the pathologist who carried out the autopsy on the bodies of the brothers?'

'Yes, I did carry out the autopsies.'

'I want to come and see you to discuss your report.'

'I am due to travel down to Cornwall in a couple of hours.'

'Sorry, but you are going nowhere for now. I will travel down to see you and I will be there in two hours,' I said to her strongly.

'Very well,' she said.

'Good. Please text me your postcode. I will see you in two hours.'

'What's happened?' Tuppence asked.

'Come on, grab your stuff. We are going to Oxford right now; I will tell you on the way.'

We made our way from the building, signed out and made our way to the car. We headed out and I headed for Oxford. The postcode was on my phone, so Tuppence set the course on the satnav. I told Tuppence of my conversation with Chief Constable Gregg and how I was going to speak with the original pathologist. He advised I do that as a matter of urgency. I decided to strike whilst the iron is hot, so the phrase goes.

We made our way listening to the radio and me pointing out various places en route. I pointed out we were not far from Blenheim Palace, the birthplace of Winston Churchill. He is buried, with other members of the family, close by near the palace. I have never visited Blenheim Palace, but I will one day.

Soon we were in Oxford and the satnav negotiated the route to the meeting place. I rang Aimee Lloyd to inform her of our arrival and she came out to meet us.

'Hello, DS Blackmore. This is Tuppence. She is a civilian working with me purely to take notes on my behalf, if you have no objections,' I offered.

'None at all. I have arranged a room for you to use, so if you'd like to follow me.'

We followed her down a few corridors, and I was thinking how young she was. We arrived at a small meeting room where we sat.

'How can I help you?' she asked.

'I am investigating the break-in and murders of Jake and Arthur Holmes at Cromley Hall. There are two points from the autopsy that I would like to clarify with you.'

I leaned forward speaking directly to her.

'The first point is from the photographs taken at the crime scene, which show extraordinarily little blood around the areas of their heads as they lay on the ground. It indicated to me they were dead before they received the blows to their heads. A second autopsy I had requested revealed they died of asphyxiation. Your autopsy recorded they had died of blunt force trauma blows to their heads.

The second point, from the second autopsy, showed bruising around the mouth and nose of each Holmes brother but not recorded on your original autopsy. I would be grateful if you could explain both of these points.'

I looked at her and she was looking down at the table with her hands tightly clamped together and then she said, 'I was asked to go to Cromley to do the autopsies, but I refused as I had just qualified and had no experience. The normal pathologist was on holiday and his stand-in took ill. I was told it was an open and shut case and I would be back in no time. I reluctantly accepted and drove to Cromley the next morning and went straight to the examination room. I was looking at the bodies when a policeman came in and he said, very abruptly, it was straightforward, and the cause of death was from the blows to the head. I will be honest and say I was intimidated by him.'

'What was the policeman's name?'

She opened her bag and pulled out a diary and opened it. She went through the pages and eventually stopped.

'His name was SIO DI Grainger. I remember he was very abrupt; he was right up against my face. He said it was obvious they were killed by the blows to the head and if I recorded it at that we could all get on.'

'What about the discolouration to their noses and under their chins?' I put to her.

'I did not see them, as I was not looking for them. I was being pressurised for a report,' she said with honesty.

'Thank you. You have been very helpful.'

'What happens now? Will I be reported?'

'Not as far as I am concerned. I will not be making any sort of complaint. I just wanted to know how you achieved your results and I am happy with that.'

'Thank you. I am grateful to you,' she said, with a look of relief on her face.

With that we said our goodbyes and headed for the car.

'Where to now?' asked Tuppence.

'Back to Cromley station.'

'You were really good with her. She looked very scared.'

'She was petrified, doing a high-profile autopsy, under pressure, fresh out of college and with SIO Grainger in her face. I think she was so scared she just wanted out of there. She has a long, good career ahead of her and she will learn from it. I have no intention of screwing it up for her.'

We got back in the car and headed for Cromley

station and arrived back in the car park and parked up. We made our way across the yard with the usual eyes staring at us. I noticed Sue Bentley was not at her window, but I was past caring. We headed for our incident room. I rang Chief Constable Gregg, and I was summoned straight away. I knocked on the door; I was called in immediately. I entered his office and sat in my usual seat.

'What do you have for me?'

'Sir, the autopsy was carried out by a fresh-faced graduate on her first case. The present pathologist was on holiday and his cover took ill. She did not want to do it, but was told it was an open and shut case and she would be home in no time. She arrived and went straight to the examination room and was confronted by SIO DI Grainger, who went right up to her face and told her it would be straightforward as they were killed by blows to the head. In my view, she was scared out of her wits and greatly intimidated by SIO DI Grainger and just wanted out of there. I do not apportion any blame on her. She was seriously out of her depth and scared witless. I believe taking any action on her would be grossly unfair and ruin a young pathologist's career. She did not let us down, the system let her down,' I said with controlled anger.

Chief Constable Gregg sat there deep in thought and finally he said, 'Thank you and leave it with me.'

I returned to my incident room and found Tuppence catching up with her notes. I phoned Gordon

Black.

'DS Blackmore, you are a very busy man. Did you manage to talk to Aimee Lloyd?'

'Yes, I did. I have been to Oxford, spoken to her and now I am back in Cromley station. I have found out all I need to know. I am happy with that. Thank you for your help and patience.'

'I'm always happy to help to achieve the truth.'

'Come on,' I said to Tuppence. 'I am starving and you must be, too, so we will go to The Lodge for some food.'

'Yes, of course.'

I dropped the car at the apartment, and we walked to The Lodge. It was a beautiful evening to walk and take in some fresh air. We both developed a habit of looking for cars coming at us unexpectedly. We arrived at The Lodge and sat outside and ordered our food.

'How is your back?' she asked.

'It has been niggling me, but I have been on such a high I have pushed it aside. The cream you put on me has certainly worked. I think on Saturday night, if events allow us, we will have a small party at the apartment. It will be something different for us. I will invite the lads and their partners round. I think it is something we both need right now,' I offered.

'Oh yes,' she yelled out loud and then noticed everyone turn to look at her. We both laughed. We had our meals and headed back to the apartment.

I soaked my sore body in the bath and my back

stung as the hot water washed over it, but it did feel good. I got out, put my shorts on but left my top off. Tuppence called me over and told me to turn round.

'I am going to clean your back with some lotion, so it will sting a little, but must be done to reduce the risk of infection,' she said, with a hint of menace.

I winced as she slowly and gently cleaned my back. I was not going to show her I was a wuss. She allowed my back to dry and then put on the cream she applied in the morning. My back started to cool down and I left my T-shirt off.

I picked up my phone and made the calls to the lads and thankfully they were all up for it, so it was set. Tuppence was pleased.

TWENTY-ONE

The new day arrived and Tuppence as usual was still asleep, so I was as quiet as possible, although according to Tuppence that was impossible.

My injuries from the car incident were improving every day to where they were now just more of a nuisance than pain. The painful marks left by Amber's nails had settled down.

'Good morning,' shouted Tuppence as she made her way to the shower.

'Hi,' I replied.

I turned the radio on, and the local station plays a lot of Tamla Motown, soul music and Northern soul; I had to explain Northern soul to her. I did not mind, as I like that type of music with the feel-good factor and it's great to dance to. It is played a lot in Cromley.

Tuppence emerged from the bathroom. She was in good humour I thought the forthcoming party would have lifted her spirits. I said to her, 'When we are ready, we will head to the station and go through the rest of the files.'

She nodded agreement and headed to her room to get ready.

We set off for the station at a leisurely pace and eventually arrived, parked up, signed in and made our way to our incident room. We started the computer engines and slowly, but methodically started to go through the files of the last five years.

So far nothing remotely close was coming up, but we carried on. After an hour or so, a possibility popped up, so I printed it out and put it to one side. I felt a sense of relief that I have something. Tuppence also printed off another possibility, so at the end of it all we had two. I compared both files, two was better than nothing and better than a lot.

It was time for a break, so I said would take Tuppence to The Bean, a café I like and use when I am in Cromley. We did the usual as we left the building. I glanced to the side and there was no sign of Sue Bentley at her usual window. She had been very quiet, and I guessed that was down to Chief Constable Gregg cutting off her source, but she was not the type of person to go quietly. I believed she would be on to something. I would hear soon enough.

We arrived at The Bean, and we received a warm welcome from Bridie.

'Paul, good to see you again,' she said, with a smile and looking at Tuppence.

'Bridie, this is Tuppence. She is working with me for a while. I have been praising you and your wonderful café to her, so I thought it was time I brought her here.'

'Thank you,' beamed Bridie. 'Welcome to you both.'

We sat down by the window and ordered our goods and Bridie was a great host, but alas, we had to get back to the station.

'I really like this town and especially the people,' Tuppence stated. 'The more I learn, the more I would like to live here rather than Mortley. Bridie makes amazing sandwiches; cakes and she is fun and intelligent to talk to.'

We arrived back at the station, and I formulated my plan to investigate both guys of interest. The names of the two persons of interest were Graham Pope and Scott McKay, both sentenced at the same time but not related in any way.

Graham Pope was an opportunist and persistent burglar who walked around looking for silly people who left their house doors unlocked, their windows open and the numpty car owners who left their cars unlocked and at times with the keys in the ignition. Cromley Hall did not really fit his profile. He had no history of violence in any shape or form, so my gut feeling he was not my man; I would look anyway.

Scott McKay had a history of drugs, car theft and breaking and entering. He was extremely high on my radar as a person of interest, especially the car theft, to interview. I would be speaking with him. In the meantime, I would be speaking with Graham Pope.

Graham Pope was released from prison two weeks prior to the crime at Cromley Hall, a couple of phone calls revealed he was wearing an ankle tag, so it should have been straightforward speaking with him. I got his address from his police file and set off. I left Tuppence to catch up with writing her notes.

Graham Pope lived in one of the villages on the outskirts of Cromley, so it was easy to follow the satnav to take me to the address. I walked up the path to the front door and I duly knocked. The door was opened by an elderly lady. I took out my warrant card and showed it to her.

'Good morning, I am Detective Sergeant Blackmore of Cromley Police. I am looking for Graham Pope,' I said politely.

'Come in,' invited the lady.

I followed her into a small, modest sitting room and sat down. The lady left the room and returned with a man I took to be Graham Pope. He sat down and spoke.

'I'm Graham Pope and why do you wanna talk with me? I ain't done nothing.'

He had fairish hair, but that was about all he had in common with the video. He was small in stature, scruffy and feeble in nature.

'I do not recall accusing you of anything, I am investigating the murders of Jake and Arthur Holmes at Cromley Hall. A video showed a man looking like you at the hall. I want to establish your whereabouts on Saturday 6th June.'

'I was here with me nan; I can't go out at weekends as part of me parole.'

His nan cut in and spoke. 'Yes, he was here from five o'clock Friday evening to eight o'clock on Monday morning, as he is every weekend.'

I stood up to leave and the elderly lady showed me out.

I walked down the path to my car, thinking this guy was not responsible for the murders, but I would check his alibi with the probation service when I got back to the station.

The drive back was uneventful, and I eventually arrived back in my incident room. Tuppence's new friend from the Cromley pool was sitting with her. I made my way to the kitchen and made myself a coffee and made my way back. When I got there the lady had left. Tuppence looked at me and said, 'She has the hots for you,' she laughed.

'Did you check her nails?' I said, looking all serious.

'Sod off, you asshole,' she responded whilst laughing. We both burst out laughing.

'Listen, SIO DI Grainger has not been seen at the station today and he is not answering his phone and there are all sorts of rumours going around. What do you think it is?' she said, with great sincerity.

'I have no idea. It could mean anything: he is ill, has a family problem or a short-notice holiday. I am sure it will all come out soon enough.'

I would be lying if I said I was not intrigued. I looked up the phone number for the probation office and they confirmed Graham Pope has been observing his movement restrictions and he was at his nan's over that weekend. I could now focus fully on Scott McKay.

'Can we go for lunch now?' pleaded Tuppence.

'Of course, sorry. I have lost track of time. As it is a nice day, we can walk across to Queens Park and get something to eat from the café,' I offered.

'Yes, I am happy with that.'

She had been in very great spirits since I returned but held off mentioning Chief Constable Gregg. It would not be a good move for now.

We strolled across to the park and purchased our food and drinks from the café and sat at one of the benches. We talked about the party tomorrow night and how she was looking forward to it, and when we finished tonight we would go to the supermarket to get the goods. We made our way back to the station to start on the file for Scott McKay.

We looked at the video again from Cromley Hall, but it was very grainy; it was difficult to be completely sure it was Scott McKay; the technical guys had a look at it but could do nothing with it. I looked through all the files we had but nothing, except Scott McKay, was outstanding.

'OK, let us have an update. We have a very grainy image of the person of interest. We have footprints with a cast of each trainer. There is a small notch on the outside of the right trainer near the little toe that will help when we find him, as long as he is wearing them or has them in his possession. There is a person of interest who was jailed three years ago, Scott McKay, who roughly fits the grainy image. I am convinced he is my man and everything fits around him.

'There is no address for him, so it will be difficult to find him as he will be holed up somewhere. I believe he is living with someone who may know or not know what he has done.

'He will not know we have the heirlooms, as it will be too dangerous for him to surface. He will be secure in that he thinks they are still in the passageway at Cromley Hall.

'I think now I will need some more hands on this case to find him. I will speak with Chief Constable Gregg on Monday morning, but for today that will do us.'

We headed off, signed out and made our way to the car. I looked up, but there were no faces at the windows. Odd I thought. Sue Bentley was not the only one who is curious to what is going on.

'We will start the weekend in good vogue and head to The Lodge,' I said in a theatrical manner and bowed to Tuppence.

'You asshole. Let's go,' she said as she curtsied.

We walked in good humour to The Lodge and the pub was busy when we arrived; well, it was a Friday. We sat outside, ordered our food and sat taking in the sun. Well, that is not strictly true; Tuppence likes to take in as much sun as possible sitting directly into it; as for me, I sit with my back to it, table canopy fully up and avoid it as much as possible. I am the guy, who whilst on holiday, will sit in the shade, T-shirt and hat on, avoiding the sun. I am quite happy to accept the strange looks from other holidaymakers who think, *crazy Englishman.*

We talked about the party on Saturday night and how the change in people and conversation would be good for the both of us. It is not good to fully focus on the case; there has to be a release from it. It would be good for Tuppence to know the lads and their partners. We finished our meal and drinks and walked slowly back to the apartment. Tuppence is always nervous of the route due to the previous incident. I was confident it was a one-off incident and would not happen again. We arrived back at the apartment and chilled out. Tuppence went to her room to chat with her daughter.

Saturday morning came and I was up early as usual and feeling fresh. I showered and my back had stopped stinging and my ribs were now a whole lot better.

I did some work to locate Scott McKay, but I came up blank. I had an address for when he was arrested, so I would pay a visit. Since he was released from prison there had been no sign of him.

I got dressed and headed off to the address I had. When I arrived, the house was completely empty, and speaking with the neighbours, it had been empty for some time; they were not familiar with the McKay name. I headed back to the apartment to go over everything I had for now. After a while I stopped as the evening was ever closer; it was time to get ready to greet our guests.

BJ was the first to arrive with his partner Evet. I introduced him to Tuppence as George. Yamma followed soon after with his partner Lucy. I introduced him as Richard. Last to arrive was Yak with his wife

Shirley. I introduced him as John.

After the usual pleasantries, I suggested we drop the nicknames and revert to our proper Christian names; there was agreement all round followed by a lot of laughter. We spent a fair bit of the evening talking about our younger days and how we acquired our nicknames, much to the amusement of the girls. We regaled over the time George and I were thrown out of Cromley Hall church, how we chased sheep and they turned the tables with me ending up in the nettles. I did not lie to my mother; I was, as the Irish would say, economical with the truth. I had made a point to the guys the Cromley Hall investigation was off the agenda, and they had happily agreed.

The evening went well with plenty of laughter; the food was good and Tuppence was a perfect hostess. Sadly, all things come to an end. It was really great to catch up with them all and get to know their wives and partners. Tuppence really enjoyed the night and I feel it did us both the power of good.

'What wonderful friends you have, and their partners are delightful; it was so good to meet them,' she said, with the biggest smile I have ever seen.

TWENTY-TWO

Monday morning came soon enough and after the usual morning activities we headed to Cromley police station in a vibrant mood. I had spent Sunday going over and over what I had so far; I still felt I was on the right track. I was ready for the day and looking forward to the work ahead. Saturday night certainly did us the power of good.

I parked up as usual and we made our way across the car park and noticed no eyes boring into us, not even from Sue Bentley. I was thinking about it when we entered our incident room.

Tuppence spoke. 'You are very quiet. Is it because there were no eyes at the windows?' she said observingly.

'Exactly that. Something is amiss, but I dare guess we will find out soon enough,' I said, with finality.

I had hardly sat down when I heard footsteps coming down the corridor; they were recognisable. Tuppence and I looked at each other and mouthed, 'The Chief!'

Chief Constable Gregg walked into the incident and spoke. 'DS Blackmore, come to my office at nine o'clock!' he said with a level of seriousness.

'Yes, sir!' I replied and nodded.

He left and I said to Tuppence, 'I guess I will find out what is going on.'

She looked at me with a serious expression on her face and just nodded.

It was just before nine o'clock and I made my way to Chief Constable Gregg's office. I do not normally suffer from nerves, but I will be honest and say I was nervous then. There had been a different atmosphere in the station since last week and somehow, I knew I would be in the centre of it. I knocked on the door and the familiar voice called out, 'Come in.'

I entered Chief Constable Gregg's office, and he was standing by his office window looking out over Queens Park. He turned and said, 'Please sit down.'

I duly sat down.

'I have been unhappy and dissatisfied in the way the events at Cromley Hall have been handled and all the flak that has come with it, and it can't continue. I have been hounded by the press and television companies and from above. I have held off with the daily news briefs. I have spent the weekend going over all the case notes and pathologist reports and spoken with the prosecution office. Taking them all in, I have decided to take decisive action; I have to do this to move the case forward.'

He paused for a moment to take in some deep breaths. I sat there stunned and the atmosphere in his office was electric.

'SIO DI Grainger has been put on garden leave until this case is resolved and his team have been stood down. So where does this leave you, DS Blackmore? Your investigation so far has been thorough and your reports are logical with a clear direction. I have decided a new team is required and I want you to head that team. This will give you all the resources and manpower you will need,' he said whilst looking directly at me.

My insides were turning over at a rate of knots, but my mind was clear.

'Sir, it would be an honour for me and I am ready for the challenge,' I said with a positive outlook.

'Good. That's just the positive reply I was looking for. I have put all my trust in you to solve this case as quickly as possible,' he said, again looking directly at me.

'I will not let you down, sir,' I said with great enthusiasm.

'Good. We will go to the squad room to break the news and there will be a news briefing tomorrow morning; you will need to be there. There is one other thing. I have promoted you to Acting Detective Inspector Blackmore on a temporary basis. You have the exam results for that rank and you will need that rank.'

'Thank you, sir, for the vote of confidence; but can we defer until two o'clock? I need to go to Cromley Hall and speak with John Holmes.'

'Very well, two o'clock it is.'

I left his office and headed back to Tuppence.

'My God, what the hell has happened?'

'Grab your jacket and I will explain on the way.'

'Where are we going?'

'To Cromley Hall to speak with John Holmes.'

We made our way with purpose to the car, and we

were soon on our way to Cromley Hall.

'Come on, the suspense is killing me.'

'Chief Constable Gregg has put SIO DI Grainger on garden leave and stood down his team. He wants a new team formed and he wants me to lead it. I have been temporarily promoted to Acting Detective Inspector. I must be in the squad room for two o'clock this afternoon to start forming a new team. There will be a press conference tomorrow morning which I have to attend. That is it in a nutshell,' I put to her.

'Bloody hell!' she said. 'I'm gobsmacked.'

'I had planned to speak with Chief Constable Gregg this morning for extra resources, but I now have the authority for everything I need. But look, we will park it up for now and discuss it back at the apartment tonight. I have a lot to do and think about today and my priority is John Holmes.'

I passed Tuppence my phone and asked her to ring John Holmes as I need to talk to him urgently and to meet us at the garden table. Tuppence duly carried out the request and the meeting was set up. We duly arrived at the hall and when I pressed the intercom the gorgeous Irish accent replied.

'Hello, can I help you?'

'Hello, it is DS Blackmore to see John Holmes.'

'Yes, he is expecting you,' she replied and opened the gate.

I drove to what is now my usual parking spot and we made our way across the driveway and walked under the archway to the garden area. The hall had just opened to the public, so a small number of visitors were already purchasing their tickets. We made our way to the table we normally use by the north wall, then we sat and waited for John Holmes.

I was sitting looking around when I spotted a female face I was familiar with. It was the face of Helen Green, the sacked former estate worker I recently interviewed and revealed she had a good alibi.

I leaned over to Tuppence and said to her, 'That woman across the other side of the yard, she is Helen Green, the former estate worker who was sacked from her post. I am interested as to why she is here, because she looks agitated and is not acting like a visitor,' I put to her. 'Take this pamphlet, walk round casually like a tourist and at the same time keep an eye on her and note what she is doing.'

'Yeah,' she said, with a smile. 'Real detective work.'

I could not help but smile. As she left the table, I caught sight of John Holmes exiting the hall and making his way over to me. I had turned my chair so I was a bit more obscured from Helen Green, but I could see her in the reflection of the café windows. I stood up as John Holmes approached the table. Before he sat down, he beckoned one of the staff over.

'DS Blackmore, how can I be of help to you this morning?

Before I could answer a member of the café team approached and we gave our orders.

'There has been a major development in the case where SIO DI Grainger and the original investigation team have been stood down,' I paused slightly and watched as his eyebrows raised and his mouth opened. 'A new team has been put in place and will be led by me. This will be a formality from two o'clock this afternoon, with an official press conference tomorrow morning. I have been promoted to the rank of Acting Detective Inspector. I wanted to come and tell you personally rather than you find out through the normal media outlets.'

Whilst I was talking to John Holmes, I noticed Helen Green heading towards Peasants' Walk, but I knew the access to it would be locked. Tuppence was not far from her and she was playing her part well; she was talking casually to another visitor whilst watching Helen Green.

'Where does that leave Roderick?' John Holmes enquired.

At that moment Helen Green clocked me and she froze. She turned quickly and made her way out of the grounds via the archway. I knew then she was tangled up with this somehow. Tuppence made her way back to our table.

'I will be very honest with you in telling you, in my opinion, he had nothing whatsoever to do with the murders of his great uncles. However, at the moment I cannot release him until I have the evidence to prove it. Please, it is not for general knowledge until tomorrow when the new team will be revealed. There will no doubt be questions asked regarding Roderick, so I will deal with them as they arise,' I put to him.

'Absolutely, as requested.'

We left John Holmes and headed back to the station. We had enough time to stop for some lunch, so I suggested we go back to the apartment and have it there. Tuppence agreed. Whilst we had our lunch, Tuppence threw a question at me I had not considered.

'What happens to me now? Does it mean I go back to Mortley?'

'What on earth makes you think along those lines?'

'Well, you will be heading a team now, so I guess I will be surplus to requirements,' she said, with a sad look on her face.

'No way. We started this journey together and we will finish it together.'

She looked at me directly and she burst into one of her brilliant wide smiles that just lights up a room.

'Come on, we have to get back to the station.'

TWENTY-THREE

The journey was good; Tuppence was buzzing and looking forward to what was to come and so was I.

We arrived at the station and duly parked up. We walked across the yard and this time there were a few sets of eyes looking down on us. For the first time I returned the gaze to all of them, and they backed away from the window. They know there is change in the air and I am involved in it somewhere. Well, good people, that time is soon. I looked to the left, but there was no sign of Sue Bentley at her office window.

We signed in and headed to our incident room; the time was one fifty pm. I left Tuppence in the incident room and headed to Chief Constable Gregg's office. I knocked on the door and he called me in.

'Are you ready for this?' he asked directly.

'Absolutely, sir.'

'Well, let's get on with it. I have arranged for the squad team to be in the main incident room at two o'clock sharp.'

We made our way along the staircase and corridors; I could hear the voices getting louder as we approached the main incident room. Chief Constable Gregg opened the door, a silence descended the room immediately.

'Good afternoon,' Chief Constable Gregg said

strongly. 'I have not been happy with the way the investigation has been going regarding the events at Cromley Hall, and after spending the weekend reviewing all the reports and evidence, I believe a completely fresh outlook is required. SIO DI Grainger has been taken off the case and a new investigating team will be formed and headed by Acting Detective Inspector Paul Blackmore.'

All the eyes turned and looked directly at me.

'Acting Detective Inspector Blackmore will be known to some of you and as a local lad he is familiar with the layout of Cromley Hall. I believe this is a great advantage to the investigation. Now, does anyone have any questions?' he asked, but was met with silence as he looked around. 'Good, I will leave you with Acting Detective Inspector Blackmore and I expect complete cooperation and for you all to apply your expertise, as I know you will.'

With that he turned and left the room and closed the door behind him, his statement was very short and very much to the point.

I left a few moments of silence to let his words sink in. I looked around and a lot of eyes were looking at the floor. I caught site of Tuppence standing in the corner alongside the new female friend she had made. She winked at me and I smiled inside.

'OK,' I said finally. 'Let me have your comments.'

'Why do we need a new investigation? We have the bastard who killed his great uncles. He has been charged and is waiting for trial,' piped up one of the team.

'And you are?' I asked directly.

'DC Derek Callaghan.' I glared at him.

'Sir.'

'So as far as you are concerned, the case is cut and dry?'

'Yes, it is.'

'Does anyone else agree with the guilt of Roderick Holmes?' I asked as I looked around. 'Let there be a show of hands.'

There were seventeen people in the room and ten agreed with DC Callaghan.

'Interesting,' I said to them. 'This investigating team is too large for what I have so far, so I will spend the afternoon putting a new team together,' I said to them, directly.

'What will happen to officers who will not be part of the investigation?' enquired DC Callaghan.

'I am sure Chief Constable Gregg will have something interesting for them to do. However, it will not be my concern.'

I looked at them directly; I could feel their eyes boring into me. It had the desired effect, but really, I could not give a damn. I had a job to do.

'DC Callaghan, go with Tuppence to my incident room and help them bring our equipment up here and set it up in that office.'

'That is SIO DI Grainger's office,' he offered with attitude.

'Correction; the word you are missing is "was". It

will now be where the two admin support staff will set up and compile all the files, reports, etc, in one central point. Tuppence, will you and this lady arrange this? I will be based in this room as part of the team, so we will rearrange the room.'

I looked at DC Callaghan and he sloped off behind them. I decided my decision to shorten the investigation squad would be easier if I would remove the guys who voted with the current view that Roderick Holmes was the murderer; their minds were set, so it would be easier to work with more open minds.

I looked around and a familiar face was sitting in the corner of the room. He was the officer who pulled me over and breathalysed me so I will start with him. I went over to him and spoke.

'Come on, let us have a chat.'

We made our way over to a corner of the room and sat down.

'Tell me about you and your views on the case so far.'

'I am DC Stephen Taylor. I have been at Cromley station for three months and I was assigned to the investigation squad. However, I have not really been involved as the view was it was an inside job, but I did not agree with that. I felt the arrest and charge of Roderick Holmes was a desperate move by SIO DI Grainger and other members of the squad. If I can further say, that particular night I was driving back to Cromley when I received a call to say a drink-driver was leaving The Scythe pub and would I investigate. I had no idea who you were. However, checking the number plate revealed it was a hire car assigned to Cromley station, having stopped you I was duty bound to go through the system of checks. I received a call for the results and I reported a negative. I was asked to follow you to see where you were going and then a further call to back off. I believe SIO DI Grainger was behind the calls.'

'Thank you for your honesty and I am pleased you followed through with your checks. That to me shows commitment and I like that in my team; I like that strength of character. Unless you hear from me, report to this room at nine o'clock tomorrow morning.'

'Thank you, sir, I will be more than willing to be a part of the squad,' he said with belief. I liked this guy.

I spent the next couple of hours chatting to the other squad members and I had formulated my team and I was more than happy. It was time to see Chief Constable Gregg and put my plans to him. I walked the stairs and corridors to his office and knocked on the door and was invited in.

'Tell me your plans.'

'I have shortened the investigating team as it is far too large for what I need. Most of them are entrenched in SIO DI Grainger's camp and they feel Roderick Holmes is the murderer. I have shortened the investigation team to a team of seven: DC Taylor, DC Sharp, DC Kumar and DC Kelly. Two admin girls and myself. That is enough to have an effective investigation,'

I put to him directly.

'Very well. Give me the names of the officers you don't want and I will arrange for them to be allocated to other duties.'

I left his office in a positive mood and headed to Queens Park. I needed time to think about my new team. I made my way back to the squad room and announced my new team. There were a few if-looks-could-kill moments, but I just smiled at them. I sent them all home to start afresh tomorrow morning. That just left me Tuppence and Tuppence's new friend.

'I am sorry, I do not know your name,' I said.

'It's Lena,' she said in slightly broken English.

'Lena, you might as well go home and ready to start afresh tomorrow.'

We chatted for a minute and then she headed off into the afternoon sun.

'I need a drink,' I put to Tuppence.

'Amen to that.'

We headed back to the apartment to drop off the car and then took a leisurely walk to The Lodge. We sat outside and decided we would eat as well.

'It has been an eventful day,' Tuppence stated.

'It sure has and bring on tomorrow morning.'

We had our food, so we headed back to the apartment. Tuppence, as is now her habit, was constantly looking for speeding cars along the route. Chief Constable Gregg rang me just as we entered the apartment, so I took the call.

'Sir.'

'I was interested in the reaction when you announced your team.'

'There were a few raised eyebrows sir, but generally it was accepted.'

We talked about a few other details and then ended the call.

I went to run a bath, but Tuppence had sneaked in and beat me to it.

'You bitch!'

'Tough.'

I walked into the bathroom, and I started to strip off.

'What the hell are you doing?' she yelled.

'I am getting in.'

'No, you're not, I'm getting out, so get out!' she yelled.

I left the bathroom laughing my head off and she appeared in a couple of minutes wrapped in a towel and headed for her room, muttering as she walked.

Tuppence stayed in her room and spoke with her daughter. As for me, I sat down and turned on the TV and watched the news. The only item I was interested in was a reference to Roderick Holmes' appearance in court on the following morning, but there was nothing.

The new day arrived, and I felt fit to see the job through.

'Are you all right now, grumpy?' I shouted to Tuppence.

She just looked at me and stuck her middle finger up; such charm, I thought, and laughed.

We arrived at the station and parked up. There were no eyes at the windows. We signed in and made our way to the squad room. The team I had selected were all there and they appeared relaxed, so I set to work.

'Good morning. Today is the start of a new investigation into the crime at Cromley Hall. I want you all to clear your minds of the previous investigation and I will replace it with my thoughts and findings. Any questions so far?' I asked as I looked around.

There was a silence and that was good.

'To start, I want you to clear the boards and store all paperwork, pictures, etc into boxes and put them in the corner of the room.'

They carried out my request with good humour and enthusiasm, and I liked their positivity. It took about an hour to clear the boards and generally tidy up the room.

'OK, guys, we look more organised and ready for work.'

I went to the board and picked up a marker pen.

'First of all, the word "Squad" will be removed and replaced with "Team" because that is how we will crack the case, together.

'Tuppence and Lena will be based in the office, where they will collate all the information to store, file, etc. The rest of us will be based in the team room and work together, share information and work in an open atmosphere. Everyone will be heard, no matter how daft it may appear. It is important we discuss all aspects, because that is how gems come out, so never be frightened to say anything you think could be relevant. Any questions?' I asked.

There were no questions, but the body language told me I was hitting the right notes. I stood up and walked over to the marker boards and spoke as I picked up one of the pens.

'I will share with you what I have discovered so far in my time here. Please bear with me and we will have an open discussion when I have finished. Everything we find or discuss remains within the team and must not be discussed with any other parties. Are we clear on that?'

There was agreement all round.

'It is without doubt Jake and Arthur Holmes were murdered inside Cromley Hall. There were no signs of forced entry, so the assumption was made it had to be a member of the family. To me there was no logic to this. Why would Roderick Holmes kill his great uncles and steal valuable heirlooms? It makes no sense at all. I was convinced there was an alternative entry point to the hall and after spending some time at the hall, the entry point was discovered. At this point I will not reveal where it is.'

There was a stunned silence whilst looking at each other.

'The missing heirlooms were found in an alcove in the passageway of the entry point. They had been wiped clean with no fingerprints. A sample of what looks like phlegm has been taken and it is with the forensics team.

I'm waiting for the results.

'We found some recent shoe imprints in the soft earth. They were the soles of trainer-type shoes; one had a small defect.

'We have a very grainy video of a person of interest who was thrown out of the hall three years ago. Investigations revealed a person matching the description was sent down for robbery around that time and was released three months ago. It is my opinion he is the person who tried to run me down. However, I cannot prove it or waste time trying to prove it, as it will be a distraction. I believe he is in hiding somewhere, as there has been no sign of him.

'Former employees at the hall were spoken to and all have alibis. However, a former female employee was at the hall yesterday morning and she was acting suspiciously. She almost freaked out when she saw me and left the premises straight away. She had an alibi on the night of the crime, but I am now very suspicious of that. I believe she and the person of interest are linked in some way and it is an avenue I want to investigate.

'The Holmes brothers did not die of blows to their heads; they were asphyxiated first and then clubbed over the head after. That was clearly evident by the lack of blood, as seen in the police photographs.

'When I looked at the bodies of the Holmes brothers, there was bruising on their noses and around their mouths. These injuries were not recorded on the report. The autopsy was carried out by someone who was fresh out of university and through unfortunate circumstances was asked to do the autopsy. There is no way blame could be put on that person, as pressure was applied for a quick report.

'OK, I will now throw it open for discussion.'

There was a short silence, then DC Taylor broke the silence.

'Bloody hell. That's amazing. It makes a lot more sense, so where do we go from here?' he asked.

Before I could answer, I received a call from Chief Constable Gregg to go and see him.

'Excuse me guys, I have to go and see Chief Constable Gregg. Make yourselves a coffee and think about what I have just disclosed. We will discuss your views when I come back.'

I set off for Chief Constable Gregg's office, knocked on the door and waited.

'Come in, ADI Blackmore.'

I entered his office and duly sat down.

'How is your morning going so far?'

'I have just briefed the team on what I have so far and left them to think about it until I return, when we will discuss the next moves.'

'Then don't let me detain you. Keep me informed of your progress.'

The shortest visit to date.

I entered the incident room to find the atmosphere to be positive and the body language was good, and they were drinking coffee. Before I could say anything about my coffee, Tuppence put one in my hand.

'OK,' I said. 'We will go through the points one at a time and have a general discussion.'

They all agreed.

'The hall. Entry was made through the old servants' quarters, along the back wall and down to the rear of the kitchen area. There is a cleverly concealed door cut into the building with a passageway down to the corridor between the kitchen and the scullery. The missing heirlooms were in an alcove that had been cut into the wall of the passageway some years ago. It was on the top of the wall between the old servants' quarters and the kitchen the footprints were found. So, any comments?' I put to them.

'Is the only evidence the footprints?' asked DC Taylor.

'Yes,' I said. 'The shoe size is a size nine. We believe he is around five feet eleven and from the pressure in the soil he is around fourteen stone. The person of interest was incredibly careful to cover his tracks except where he was walking.

'The heirlooms. Both were cleaned very well, with no fingerprints or DNA. They were not used to hit Jake and Arthur Holmes. Phlegm was discovered on the wall next to the heirlooms and it is with the forensics team. We are waiting on results.'

There were no comments, but there was not really a lot to say. I set up the video machine and played the short clip.

'The video. As you can see it is very grainy. I had the technical guys look at it and they cannot clean it up anymore, so it is all we have. I am convinced he is the person of interest I want to talk to. He has disappeared off the radar. However, my gut feeling is he is linked to Helen Green, the woman I have interviewed and saw at the hall yesterday. She was very agitated and left when she saw me.

'Autopsy. I have explained about the autopsy, so I feel there is nothing left to say, but I am confused with the bruising around the nose and under the chin.'

'I believe they may have been "Burked",' said DC Taylor.

There was a stunned silence as everyone looked at him.

'They have been what?' said a baffled DC Kumar.

'Explain,' I said to DC Taylor.

'Burke and Hare were two body-snatchers in the early eighteen hundreds who lived in Edinburgh. They stole bodies, removed bodies from their graves, murdered weak and ill people with the purpose of selling them for students to practise on in an Edinburgh hospital. Burke was a large man and I believe he would put his thumb and index finger around their nose and suffocate them with something in his hand across their mouths,' he concluded.

'That would fit nicely with the bruising on their faces,' I added.

There was a temporary silence in the room, when

Tuppence piped up: 'Bloody hell, how barbaric!'

There was general agreement in the team.

'OK, I know you are all a little stunned by my revelations as it is a completely different line from the one you worked on previously. We now have the opportunity to work together going forward, so here is how we will kick it off.

'I believe Helen Green and Scott McKay are involved in some way and I suspect together. At this moment in time, Scott McKay is invisible, but Helen Green is very visible. Helen Green has an alibi for the night of the murders, but I am not convinced by that, so we should focus on her.

'I want to set up an observation point of her house and movements. I want this to be around the clock and working in pairs in twelve-hour shifts. We will start this tomorrow morning at seven o'clock.

'DC Sharp and DC Taylor will work the day shift; DC Kelly and DC Kumar you will do the night shift. I have obtained use of an observation van we can use. You will have videos to record all comings and goings and if she leaves the house. We cannot take our eyes off the house. If a guy who looks like Scott McKay appears, do not approach him, as he may be very agitated and dangerous. Call me straight away.

'We will be checking all the usual social media outlets, etc. Guys, we have a lot of work to do, so any questions?' I finally concluded. No questions were raised.

We broke for lunch, so Tuppence, Lena and my

good self walked down to the café in Queens Park to grab a sandwich and coffee. It was quite busy today, but the familiar face of Sue Bentley was sitting at a table, and she waved to me when I clocked her. There was no way I was going to acknowledge her, as I might just as well leave the door to my incident open, so I just ignored her, much to her indignation.

After lunch we made our way back to the incident room. The rest of the team were waiting for us on our return.

We sat and discussed the work ahead and the detailed log I expected. They were all full of enthusiasm for the work ahead. I sent both teams home to prepare for their shifts.

Tuppence and Lena had rearranged the room and cleaned up a bit and were busy catching up on the case notes so far. I sat at a table going over the last few hours; I was feeling good and felt we were on the right road.

Just then my mobile phone rang. It was Graham Coleman.

'ADI Blackmore, I have the DNA results for you from the phlegm we removed from the wall. We found traces of nasal hair in the phlegm; I can confirm it belongs to Scott McKay.'

'Thank you. It only proves he was at the hall, but does not prove he killed Jake and Arthur Holmes.'

TWENTY-FOUR

I woke to the new day with great vigour and a sense of excitement; every bone in my body told me I was on the right track. I went over to Tuppence's bedroom door, banged on it quite loudly and shouted out, 'Get up, you lazy git!'

'Clear off, you asshole!' she shouted.

I turned on the TV and put on the local news and headed to the kitchen. I had just filled the kettle and turned it on when a mention of Roderick Holmes caught my attention. I walked into the lounge and met Tuppence, who was already there standing watching the screen. I stood beside her and we listened to the report.

'There has been a major development in the murders of Jake and Arthur Holmes at Cromley Hall. It has been reported the Senior Investigating Officer Cornelius Grainger has been taken off the case and his investigating squad has been disbanded. I also understand Detective Sergeant Paul Blackmore, a local man who has been drafted in to assist on the case through his local knowledge, has been given the task of solving the crime and a new team to work with. There will be a news briefing at nine o'clock this morning, where I believe all this will be confirmed.'

I turned to Tuppence and spoke. 'This morning's

news briefing will be very interesting, and Sue Bentley will be all over me like a rash,' I laughed.

'Does it not bother you, being under the spotlight?' she asked with concern.

'Actually, no; it comes with the territory, I have to deal with it. I will focus fully on the case and ignore everything else. I have a good man in Chief Constable Gregg beside me.'

Seven o'clock soon came around, so I rang DC Sharp.

'Good morning. Are you in place?' I asked.

'Yes, we are in place and ready for action,' he replied.

'This is a patience game, so bear that in mind and concentration is of the utmost importance. Something important will come up and that will be the key point we are looking for. I do not know the time limit, but I feel it will not be too long. I have the DNA results we have been waiting for and it confirms it is that of Scott McKay. The only thing it proves is that he was at the hall; it does not prove he carried out the murders.'

'It proves progress is being made,' he said, with a positive tone in his voice.

'There will be a news briefing this morning where the changes to the team will be announced. I feel the agitation levels will rise with our suspects, so be wary of that,' I said, with purpose.

'We sure will and good luck at the briefing,' he said in good humour.

We made our way to the station and arrived in the

incident room at eight o'clock, where Lena was waiting for us. 'Sorry we are late, but I could not get Tuppence out of bed this morning,' I laughed.

Tuppence glared at me, but there was a hint of a smile and Lena did not know what to make of it, so I just laughed. I sat down and the office phone rang. Tuppence took the call.

'Chief Constable Gregg wants you in his office at eight forty-five!'

I nodded. I duly arrived at the appointed time and knocked on the door and was called in immediately. I entered and took my usual seat.

'Good morning, ADI Blackmore. Did you see the report on the local news this morning?' he enquired.

'Yes sir, I watched with interest.'

'I deliberately had it leaked about SIO DI Grainger as I felt it would be better if all were prepared, rather than just throw it at them with the resulting flak.'

'I can understand that, sir, and it is not a problem to me.'

'Good,' he said. 'OK, let's get this over with.'

He led the way out of his office, with me following closely behind. We entered the briefing room bang on nine o'clock. The room was packed, with Sue Bentley right at the front with her eyes firmly fixed on me. We sat down and the questions started straight away, with everyone trying to be heard. It was, hilarious so I just sat back looking and laughing internally. Chief Constable Gregg stood up and shouted for order. (He would be good as Speaker in the House of Commons.) He had his hands in the air.

'This behaviour is not acceptable,' he said in his authoritative and commanding voice.

He has a way about him that commands respect and the room calmed down immediately.

'Sue Bentley?' he asked.

Sue Bentley was on her feet in a flash. 'Where is SIO DI Grainger? Has he been put on garden leave? Is DS Blackmore now leading the case?' she spouted off like a machine-gun.

'I felt the investigation into the crime at Cromley Hall needed a new direction,' Chief Constable Gregg replied calmly.

'Has SIO DI Grainger screwed up and been put out to grass?' asked the reporter from the television news programme I'd watched this morning.

'No, SIO DI Grainger will be working on other cases. As I said, I felt the case needed a new direction,' he said, calmly.

'DS Blackmore, isn't your rank too low to lead this investigation?' Sue Bentley asked aggressively.

'I am Acting Detective Inspector,' I said impassively. 'I have put a team together and we are working on the case.'

'ADI Blackmore, what is your enquiry taking that is different from SIO DI Grainger's?' Sue Bentley asked.

'Sorry, I cannot reveal any details of the investigation as it may compromise events. You are experienced enough to know that,' I put directly to her.

'Do you have a suspect in mind and, if so, will you share that information with us?' requested Sue Bentley.

'As I have just said, I cannot reveal any details of the investigation and when we can you will all be informed.'

'How do you feel returning to Cromley?' asked a new face.

'It is not an issue; I am here to do a job,' I answered.

'Right, time is up, we have answered all your questions,' said Chief Constable Gregg with authority. 'We will have another briefing on Friday morning at the same time, so until then, thank you,' he said with finality.

We stood up and left the room with a barrage of questions bombing our ears. We got back to his office, shut the door and he burst out laughing.

'I loved the way you answered the newspaper reporter,' he said, laughing his head off.

'Somehow I do not think she will give up that easily,' I replied, laughing.

I left his office and made my way to the incident room and sat down.

'You look as if you need a coffee,' said Tuppence.

'I would love one.'

I rang DC Sharp, and all was well so far. I told them about the briefing, and how everything is now out in the open and to be watchful.

I sat thinking about the comment made by DC Taylor regarding the Burke and Hare characters. I was intrigued and needed to find out more. The internet is a great modern invention for finding out information without getting off one's arse, so I typed in Burke and Hare in a search engine and the information appeared. I started reading and I was intrigued.

I learned that Burke and Hare operated in Edinburgh in 1828. They stole corpses and murdered to sell bodies to Robert Knox for dissection at his anatomy lectures at the Edinburgh hospital. The hospital was a leader in anatomical study in the early nineteenth century. The demand for bodies for research led to a shortfall in supply.

Scottish law states that corpses used at that time for medical research should only come from those who died in prison, suicide or from foundlings and orphans. The lack of bodies led to body snatching by what was to become known as 'resurrection men'.

Burke and Hare were well paid for their efforts, but they were eventually caught. It was reported their victims were suffocated, but this was not proved. Also, there were no reports of bruising on their faces. They were a nasty pair of dudes who truly deserved their fate.

'It's lunchtime,' Tuppence said with enthusiasm. 'Are you coming with us?'

'No, I want to do a bit more research.'

'We are going to The Bean, so we will bring you back something.'

I sat thinking about what DC Taylor said about Burke and Hare and I felt there might be more to it. Scott McKay was in prison, so I was curious as to how he spent his time in there. I thought a visit to the prison would be in order. It was too late to go there this afternoon. I looked up the prison phone number and duly rang the number and I eventually spoke with the Assistant Governor. After the usual formalities, it was agreed I could visit the prison tomorrow morning. The prison was about an hour and a half drive, so easily manageable.

The girls returned in good humour and Tuppence has found a great friend with Lena that pleased me immensely. I dread the day when we will go back to Mortley, as I know she is not looking forward to it. I enjoyed the lunch they brought back for me.

'I really like Bridie,' Tuppence said. 'She is fun, intelligent with a wicked sense of humour and runs a fabulous café.'

I decided to pay the lads a visit at the van, so I made my way to the car and slowly drove out of the car park. I was looking over to the window of Sue Bentley; sure enough, there she was, standing there.

I decided to do a random route to the van to check I was not being followed. The guys were in good humour, despite the restrictions of the room in terms of what they could do. We talked about their day so far. Helen Green had left the house once to visit the convenience store to buy some milk and a loaf of bread. She left the house again to visit the store and returned with a copy of the Cromley Echo.

'That is interesting. She is very keen to get a copy of

the local paper,' I said.

Both guys agreed. I bade them farewell and I drove slowly back to the station, feeling a good vibe about how things are going.

The rest of the afternoon was going over everything we have so far, and when our day was complete, we made our way back to the apartment. We stopped off for Tuppence to pop out to buy a copy of the Cromley Echo. We sat and looked at the headline and it read:

CROMLEY HALL

There have been further developments in the case of Jake and Arthur Holmes where the Senior Investigating Officer Cornelius Grainger has been taken off the case and replaced with a rookie officer DS Blackmore. DS Blackmore is a local man brought in to assist on the case. A new investigation team has been put together; so does that mean Roderick Holmes is believed to be innocent of the crimes? If he didn't do it, then who did?

'Cheeky cow,' said Tuppence. 'Rookie, indeed.'

I just laughed. 'I was expecting something from her, but that is quite polite. Perhaps that is why she is still working at the local paper,' I responded.

We both laughed all the way back to the apartment. I would, however, remember that comment.

Later that evening, I rang the two lads on the evening duty, they reported all had been quiet. There had been no further sightings of Helen Green.

After dinner we sat for a while, then I said to

Tuppence, 'How is it going with Chief Constable Gregg?'

She looked at me, and after a moment or two and a smile spread across her face.

'He asked me if I would I like to go out for dinner with him.'

'And you said yes?'

'Yes, I did. You know, behind Chief Constable Gregg's persona is a great guy. I like him, I like him a lot. He has a great heart and is very courteous and also very funny. I feel really good in his company. I feel very drawn to him,' she said with a smile.

'I think you are both very well suited and I hope it works out for you,' I said with heartfelt sincerity.

She reached over and gave me a big hug.

'Of course, he is no patch on me,' I said, laughing.

'You asshole,' she laughed.

TWENTY-FIVE

I was awake the next morning very early as usual. I sat and watched the local news on the television. The main points were the removal of SOI DI Grainger to be replaced by me, and a piece on Roderick Holmes.

There were no further points of interest from the day before. I picked up the Cromley Echo and generally there is nothing in it except a lot of advertising and a story of a missing cat. I rang the night crew, and they reported no sightings.

Tuppence appeared and when we were both ready, we made our way to the station. We got in the car, and I said to her, 'I am going to Braford Prison to have a look at what Scott McKay was up to while he was detained there. I want you to stay at the station with Lena to finish organising the room,' I said to her.

'That's fine and I have no problem with that,' she said, smiling.

I think she would rather be near Chief Constable Gregg, as I smiled inwardly. I dropped Tuppence at the station and I headed for Braford Prison.

The journey was uneventful and I duly arrived at the gate. Could I dare to dream of a sexy, soft Irish voice would greet me? Hell, no, it was a gruff deep voice.

'Can I help you?' he boomed.

'Acting Detective Inspector Paul Blackmore of Cromley Police to see Assistant Governor Adam Poole,' I replied.

I sat for a couple of minutes when the voice replied, and the gate opened.

'Please drive to the visitors' car park to the left and then report to the visitors' door,' he ordered.

I duly obliged and rang the bell and waited. A side door opened and I was met by a couple of prison officers.

'Can we see your warrant card?' I was asked. I duly obliged.

I was invited in and escorted to the Assistant Governor's office; the two officers remained with me. The Assistant Governor arrived within a few minutes.

'ADI Blackmore,' he extended his hand out. 'You are interested in a former inmate by the name of Scott McKay?'

'Yes. A crime has been committed at Cromley Hall where the elderly brothers Jake and Arthur Holmes were brutally murdered, and valuable heirlooms were stolen. I believe Scott McKay was thrown out of Cromley Hall due to persistently snooping about and the crime happened after he was released from this prison. He was in this prison between the two events mentioned. I believe he is a person of great interest to me; I am interested in what he did in his time here.'

'The two officers here, Brian James and Nick Douglas, oversaw the wing Scott McKay was allocated to.

They will be happy to help you in any way they can, so I will leave you in their capable hands.'

With that, we shook hands and he left the room.

'Could you tell me how he spent his time here? Did he have a job?' I asked.

'He kept very much to himself, and he was well behaved,' answered Brian James. 'He worked in the kitchen and served meals to the inmates,' he added.

'What did he spend his free time doing?' I asked.

'He would read a lot and was a regular visitor to the library,' answered Nick Douglas.

'Do you record what books are taken from the library, and can we go there?' I requested.

'I will make a call,' said Nick Douglas.

I sat whilst the phone call was made. Clearance was finally given and both officers escorted me to the library.

I entered and Scott McKay's library record was ready for me to inspect. I sat and read through, and I instantly stopped at a book about body-snatching. I made a note of it, and I told the two officers I had what I was looking for. We made our way back through the prison and eventually to the exit gate. I shook hands with Nick Douglas and Brian James and thanked them for their help. I walked back to my car feeling incredibly positive and that my trip was worthwhile. I would have to get this book and read it. I drove back to the station.

I walked in and briefed the girls on my morning's work. I told them about the body-snatchers book and Lena said she would get it for me.

I rang the guys at the observation van whilst Lena sourced the book. They had nothing to report, and Helen Green had not left the apartment all day. Lena quickly sourced the book from a local shop. I sat and read.

I did some speed reading as I was not particularly interested in the details, just the modes of death. It mentioned death by suffocation a few times and compressions on the chest, but no concrete proof they were the cause of death. I think this will be the way with this case.

I received a call from DC Taylor to say Helen Green had paid a visit to the shop, but she left with her purchases in a bag, so he did not know what she bought. I thanked him.

The day was long, but fruitful, so we called it a day and headed back to the apartment. After dinner we sat down with a drink. I was staring at the wall ignoring the television.

'What's on your mind?' Tuppence asked.

'At this time, I have a lot of ideas and circumstantial evidence, but no hard evidence. There was some good news when DC Taylor rang me to tell me Helen Green had left the house to buy what looked like a bag of groceries from the local store. He then rang me to say she left the house again and returned with two coffees which would indicate there may be two persons in the house.'

'I am not concerned. I know you will crack this case

and so does Lena,' she said, with a smile.

'Thank you.'

'My daughter is coming over for a break. She will be going to my parents first and then she wants to come and see me here. Would that be OK?'

'I think it will be OK as I do not think there is any danger anymore, but we had better clear it with Chief Constable Gregg. I will speak with him tomorrow morning.'

I rang the night crew, and they reported no sightings, and all was quiet, so tomorrow was another day.

TWENTY-SIX

I was awake very early; I did not sleep as well as I normally do. I rang the night crew; they reported it was a long night with no activity. Patience, I said to myself. Tuppence appeared early for a change.

'Can you not sleep?' I asked her.

'I'm excited to see my daughter and I can't wait. I need to book some time off – if that's OK?'

'That, I should think, will not be a problem.'

Soon we set off to the station and made our way to the incident room. I sat there contemplating where we were to date. I was concentrating when the name of Bryan Gates came to my mind. I had a brief interview with him at Helen Green's house when I first went there when he gave her an alibi. I need to speak with him again; I believe he is covering for her.

'Pop down and clear your holiday with Chief Constable Gregg. I am sure there will not be a problem,' I said, with a raised eyebrow.

'Sod off,' she mouthed to me and smiled.

I knew she would enjoy going to see him, I also knew Chief Constable Gregg would enjoy her visit.

I rang DC Taylor for an update, but there was nothing to report. I sat thinking of my plan as I was confident I would get the information I wanted.

- Helen Green was hiding Scott McKay in her house.

- Bryan Gates had supplied a false alibi for Helen Green. Why?

Patience, I said to myself. It will come together.

I got a call from DC Taylor to say Helen Green had gone to the local convenience store for some groceries. She had two full bags and made her way to the house; he had recorded the details in the log. I thanked him.

Two full bags of shopping were of no use as it proved nothing. I was not likely to go in the convenience shop and ask what she had bought; it was too risky as she may be a friend or known to the shop assistant. I could not take that risk.

I sat out the rest of the afternoon going over everything and then going over everything again, but I came back to the same starting point. I was convinced more than ever my line of thought was the right one; I just needed the evidence.

'Right, girls, it is time to go home.'

'Come on,' I said to Tuppence. 'We will go to The Scythe for some excellent food and alcohol for you, but none for me, at least until we get back to the apartment.'

'I am all for that.'

We headed for The Scythe. This was our first visit since the night I was pulled over, but I was looking forward to seeing Tom and Jenny and her fabulous food. After parking up we headed inside and as I got to the bar, I saw my brother with his wife, so we walked over to them.

'Tuppence, this is my brother Grant and his wife, Julie. Guys, this is Tuppence. She is working with me on the case.'

'It's great to meet you,' she replied with her usual smile.

'And it is good to meet you,' replied Grant. 'My mother has been telling Julie and me about you.'

Tuppence smiled. We joined them at their table and ordered our food.

'I decided we would eat out tonight and as you know The Scythe has always been a favourite place for our family,' I said, more for Tuppence than them. 'I am ready for this.'

The time went very fast and the conversation flowed. Tuppence and Julie got along very well; however, it was time to go. We bade our farewells and made our way back to the apartment.

'What a lovely family you have,' she said, smiling.

'My daughter will be in Cromley the day after tomorrow; she has decided to come to Cromley first. Chief Constable Gregg will run me to the station to pick her up so as not to interfere with the investigation. I have booked a few days off to be with her.'

'That is great news.'

It made sense for Chief Constable Gregg to pick her up as I feel things are now starting to move not just for me, but for her as well. I could see the relief on her face. We had just walked into the apartment when my mobile rang; it was from DC Kumar from the observation point.

'Sir, Helen Green left the apartment and walked round to the Indian for a takeaway, the Indian is about fifty yards from the house she is living in. The carrier bag was quite full and looked more than a meal for one. I walked to the Indian by the back route, and I said to the guy, "Can I have the same meal as the blonde woman had who has just been in?" He placed the order and we have it here in the apartment. It is a chicken tikka masala, a chicken korma, two rice and other minor items of food. I have recorded them in the log and verification from the Indian restaurant. Unfortunately, we have to eat the evidence as it is perishable,' he said, with a hint of humour.

I laughed. 'We are heading in the right direction. Enjoy the meal and charge it to expenses. Stick the till receipt in the logbook.'

'Good news?' enquired Tuppence.

'Yes, Helen Green has just bought two Indian meals from the Indian just up from her house. At the moment the only thing it proves is there may be two people in the house.'

'Patience is key,' she said.

She is such a positive woman. I wondered if her daughter was like her, although I got the impression she was.

TWENTY-SEVEN

The new day arrived. I rang DC Kumar but no further activities from the house were reported; they enjoyed the meal.

Tuppence made an appearance and our conversation centred on the arrival of her daughter; soon we were ready to go. We set off for the station, parked up and walked to the incident room.

I called Chief Constable Gregg and requested to see him. He agreed I could go to his office at nine thirty. In the meantime, I sat recording, as I usually do, the events of the previous day's events. These were my own personal notes and it is something I have always done. Tuppence and Lena are taking care of the case notes, so that the records are correct and above board.

The appointed time came, and I made my way to Chief Constable Gregg's office. I walked the corridors and stairs of this old building and knocked on the door. I was greeted with the now very familiar voice. I made my inside and sat on my now usual chair.

'Good morning, ADI Blackmore. I hope you have some news for me.'

'Good morning, sir. Yes, I have. I have set up an observation point close to Helen Green's house. It was reported she lives alone, but I do not believe that. The observation point is being used to monitor her activities and so far, she has bought coffees and sandwiches. Last night she went to the Indian restaurant just up the road from her house and she purchased Indian meals for two. I am now convinced Scott McKay is in that house.'

'What is your next step?'

'We continue the surveillance for now.'

I left his office feeling very good. He asked questions, but never questioned me. I felt I had his complete backing and confidence and that made me feel good.

I arrived back in the incident room and said to Lena, 'Are you OK here for a few hours on your own? I am available on my mobile and DC Taylor is also available.'

I noticed a puzzled look on Tuppence's face.

'Sure,' Lena said, with a smile.

'Grab your coat; we have a job to do,' I put to Tuppence.

We signed out and walked to the car and drove out of the car park.

'Where are we going?' Tuppence enquired.

'To Langton.'

'Where the hell is that?'

'It is about an hour and a half drive up the A1. I want to talk to Bryan Gates again; I do not believe his alibi.'

'Is he the guy you spoke to when you went to see Helen Green?'

'The very one. I thought a change of scenery would

be good for you.'

'I am all for that.'

The drive was uneventful, and Tuppence talked of her daughter's forthcoming visit. She was so excited about it all; so was I.

We approached Langton when Tuppence said, 'What is that large church over there?'

'That is Langton Cathedral.'

'It looks like an interesting building.'

'I have never paid a visit to it; I have not been in this area for many a year.'

We arrived at the building that employs Bryan Gates. I parked up and headed for the reception and I asked the receptionist for Bryan Gates. She made the call and shortly he joined us. He looked apprehensive as he approached us.

'Is there somewhere where we can talk?' I put to him.

'Sure, we can go to my office.'

He led the way. There was a meeting table in the far end of his office and by the look of his office he is a senior member of the company.

'How can I help you?'

'Quite simply by telling me the truth about your whereabouts on Saturday 6th June?'

'I told you; I stayed at the home of Helen Green,' he said without conviction.

'Bullshit. I do not believe you were anywhere near her house on that night, I believe you work away from home during the week and go home for weekends. It is, however, quite easy to check with your wife.'

He was now sitting very uncomfortably in his seat with a look of panic on his face; his hands were clasped very tight together. I leaned forward and said to him, 'I will be very direct with you, so we know where we stand. I am investigating the murders of Jake and Arthur Holmes carried out at Cromley Hall, along with some valuable heirlooms stolen on that Saturday night. It is my belief Helen Green may be involved in it. You have provided an alibi for her and if it proves it is incorrect, I will nail you to the fucking wall with a charge of conspiracy to murder and theft.'

I could see the look of panic coming over him and he did not know what to do. I had to get him to talk to me, so I adopted a softer approach.

'Look, I do not believe you were in her house that night. I think you unfortunately met her when you were in Cromley on business and an opportunity for sex presented itself. I believe she set a honey trap and you walked right into it. She has been blackmailing you ever since. Does that sound about right?'

He just looked at me, clearly panicking.

'I have no interest in placing charges on you, but that ball is entirely in your court, so tell me how you came to be in this mess.'

There was a silence for a few moments and then he started to slowly speak.

'I was in Cromley on my monthly visit to a factory

we supply; it is a big account, so I always make a personal visit. Helen Green was a new employee and over three months I got to know her, or should I say, she got to know me. She was quite flirty and attentive and, yes, I was flattered. I normally stay overnight at a hotel and on one night there was a knock on my hotel room door. I opened the door and it was Helen. She was dressed in a short skirt and a blouse opened down to her bust. She just walked in. One thing led to another and we had sex. The same thing happened on my next visit. She started asking for money and I refused, but she said she would inform my wife of our liaisons. She said if I gave her a hundred pounds a month, she would say nothing. I didn't know what to do and as it was only a hundred pounds a month, I agreed. I was at her house the day of your visit to pay her the money. I panicked when she said I was with her that night, so I just agreed with her. What happens now?'

'Do you have any contact with her at any time?'

'No, only on the day of my visit when I ring her. We arrange when I go and pay her the money.'

'I suggest you carry on with your arrangement until you hear from me. It is your decision whether you come clean with your wife about your liaison; I think it would be in your best interest to do so. I cannot guarantee Helen Green will not pursue her claim you were with her on that night, but that is something you have to deal with. For now, please keep me informed if anything changes.'

We said our goodbyes and left the building and

made our way back to the car.

When we got in the car Tuppence said, 'Bloody hell, I thought he was going to die with your questioning and then you become a humanitarian by giving him a way out.'

'I am not after him; he is just a very small pawn in this. He is a guy who was away from home receiving some flattery from a vivacious girl and he walked right into her honey trap. Yes, he obstructed the course of justice in a very small way, but to me it makes no difference to the outcome of the case. His biggest judge will be his wife.'

The journey back was uneventful. We arrived back in the incident room around four o'clock. I rang DC Taylor, but he had nothing to report; there were no sightings of her all day. The news did not dampen my spirits. I read a bit more about Burke and Hare, but it was soon time to call it a day, so we set off to the apartment.

Back at the apartment and over dinner, I asked Tuppence, 'With your daughter here, are you still going out with Chief Constable Gregg on Saturday night?'

'Yes, and Georgia knows I am.'

'What will she do on Saturday night?'

'You will look after her.'

'I would love to.'

'I know she will be in very good hands. Don't worry, she is more than capable of looking after herself and she is great company,' she said with a smile on her face.

'I look forward to it,' I replied.

TWENTY-EIGHT

Tuppence was already in the kitchen making breakfast when I got out of bed and made my way to the lounge.

'I couldn't sleep, as I am so excited to see Georgia,' she said.

I rang DC Kumar, and he had nothing to report; it had been a very quiet night.

'I am going for a shower. I will take some of my stuff out of the bathroom to make some room for your daughter.'

I looked at her and burst out laughing. She threw a towel at me, laughing at the same time.

I turned on the radio and the local news reported on a briefing this morning at nine o'clock.

'Better put on your best aftershave for Sue Bentley,' Tuppence said with a level of mischief.

'What time are you leaving for the railway station?'

'Chief Constable Gregg is picking me up at ten o'clock.'

I left for the police station and left Tuppence to her preparations for her daughter and, I dare also say, Chief Constable Gregg.

I was thinking about the radio bulletin and all they had to offer was a news briefing at nine o'clock that morning. I was really pleased that nothing had leaked to the media regarding our investigation and Sue Bentley was very quiet, just the way I wanted it.

I made my way to Chief Constable Gregg's office at eight forty-five and duly knocked on the door and was invited in.

'Good morning, sir.'

'Morning, ADI Blackmore. Are you ready for this?'

We left his office and made our way down the winding corridors and stairs to the briefing room. We walked in bang on nine o'clock to a packed room. We sat down and Chief Constable Gregg started.

'Good morning. The investigation into the crime at Cromley Hall is still progressing. However, at this time I can add no further information from the previous briefing,' he said firmly and directly.

'ADI Blackmore!' shouted Sue Bentley. 'Are you ready to make an arrest?' she asked, more I thought in a sense of desperation to get something.

'As Chief Gregg has already stated, there is nothing further to add from the previous briefing.'

'I can take from your answer the change in investigation teams has made no difference to the investigation into the murders of Jake and Arthur Holmes!' stated Sue Bentley.

'As I said, we have nothing to add from the previous briefing and I cannot go into the specifics of the investigation. When we have something concrete, we will report it. I do not get involved with speculation.'

'So, there is a line of enquiry?' asked the local

television reporter.

'There are always lines of enquiry and again I do not speculate,' I put to her.

'ADI Blackmore!' Sue Bentley directed. 'Due to your lack of progress, are you aware of the pressure you are putting on the police department and your inability to answer questions?'

'There is pressure on the Holmes family, as well as the police department. That does not excuse giving unfounded information for the sake of it. Information will be given once it has been proved to be correct,' I put directly but calmly to her.

'Thank you for your attendance, patience and questions. We will inform you soon on the next briefing,' said Chief Constable Gregg.

We got up and left the briefing room with a barrage of questions and we headed back to his office.

'How are you after that?' he asked.

'I am fine, sir; they are desperate for something to report. I believe Sue Bentley's report will again be negative and I believe that will play right into our hands. I believe it will give Scott McKay the impression we are no further forward so he will relax more.'

I left his office and when I returned to the incident room, I rang DC Taylor.

'Good morning,' he said brightly.

'Good morning. The news briefing this morning I believe will lead to negative reports on the local news and the Cromley Echo, so be more vigilant today and note it in the book and brief tonight's team.'

'Come on, Lena, let us take a walk to Queens Park and get a coffee.'

'I can make you one.'

'No, I want to stretch my legs. You can stay here, but I am going.'

'No, I'm coming.'

She grabbed her jacket and bag. The woman was clearly not used to my ways.

We left by the side door to avoid Sue Bentley's prying eyes, and walked leisurely to the park. We sat in the café and had our coffee. Lena was obviously not used to leaving the office except for normal break times. I on the other hand did it all the time.

Lena started to come out of her shell, relaxed and she had a great sense of humour; I could see why Tuppence likes her. We finished our coffees and made our way back to the station. We walked up the hill and made for the front doors. I could see Sue Bentley in the reflection of the big glass doors; I just smiled to myself and carried on.

Lunchtime soon came along, so I decided to visit my parents, who were at home, and my brother and sister were there. That was unusual, so I walked in expecting bad news. I should not have been so negative; all was fine.

'Where is Tuppence?' my sister asked.

'She has gone to the rail station to pick up her daughter, who has decided to come over from New

York to see her mother for a few days.'

'She is a wonderful woman,' said my mother. 'It's a shame she is not a little younger,' she said, with mischief in her voice.

'Do not go there,' I said to her. Secretly, I was really looking forward to seeing her daughter.

When I returned to the police station car park, I rang Tom Woods at The Scythe and booked a table for seven o'clock for three. I texted Tuppence to tell her about the booking and she messaged back she and her daughter were happy with the arrangement. I do not normally get nervous about meeting women these days, but my stomach was churning for a woman I had never met or seen, but felt something for.

I received a call from DC Taylor to say Helen Green had left the house and had been seen walking up and down the path in front of the shops and then returned to the house. I told DC Taylor to watch for Helen Green leaving the house to go and get a copy of the Cromley Echo.

The afternoon dragged on, so I decided to go to West Cromley Park and stretch my legs and reduce my stress levels. I normally deal with stress very well, but I guess it was the waiting around that was getting to me. I thought I would have to learn time management. I told Lena I was going out and I would return around four o'clock.

I drove casually to the park and parked up. I walked the path and through the trees, past the small lake and back to the visitor centre. I bought a coffee and made my way to the bench I had used many times over the years. I sat there deep in thought when I felt a tap on my shoulder. I turned round to see the smiling face of Amber.

'Hi, do you want a distraction? You seem miles away and, yes, I know you can't talk about it,' she said and sat down.

'I enjoyed our night together and I know deep down I have lost a lover. I could see it in your eyes, but I have gained a very good friend,' she said, with a smile.

'That sums it up perfectly. I will be delighted for us to be friends.'

We sat and talked for twenty minutes and then I had to take my leave and return to the station. I had just sat down at my desk when my phone rang. It was DC Taylor.

'Sir, Helen Green has left the house and she has bought a copy of the Cromley Echo and returned to the house.'

'Great, that is the reaction I was looking for, so stay vigilant.'

I walked to the car feeling very nervous and headed back to the apartment. I parked up and made my way up the stairs to the apartment door. I stopped at the door; I could hear laughter from inside. I put my key in the door and walked in. They were both in the lounge sitting and talking.

'Hi,' said Tuppence.

They both got up from the sofa and Tuppence said, 'Paul, this is my daughter, Georgia.'

I was stopped in my tracks as how beautiful she was. Sergeant Brown was right: she was definitely her mother's daughter. I got myself together and spoke.

'Hi, it is lovely to finally meet you.'

'How was your day?' Tuppence asked.

'Difficult, but I have to be patient.'

'Not your best attribute,' Tuppence replied with a laugh.

'Thank you for taking us out to dinner tonight. It was very thoughtful of you,' Georgia said.

'Beats your mother's cooking,' I replied with a raised eyebrow.

'Cheeky bastard,' replied Tuppence, and they both laughed.

We chatted for a few minutes and I left them to it. I grabbed my kit and headed to the bathroom and closed the door, something I do not normally do. I sat there soaking in the water when there was a knock on the door.

'Hello?' I called out. The door opened and Georgia walked in.

'Mum said you like a coffee when you are soaking and it helps you de-stress,' she laughed and placed the cup at the end of the bath.

De-stress? What, my hormones had gone through the roof. I lay there thinking about her: she was absolutely stunning. She had long, brown, wavy hair down to her shoulder blades. She was approximately five foot six inches tall with a figure to die for. She had a smile and demeanour like her mother, with the same sense of humour.

Soon we were all ready and we headed off. Tuppence took great joy in pointing out local sites and Cromley Hall as we drove past it.

'We will visit one day,' Tuppence said.

'I would like that,' replied Georgia.

'Perhaps Paul will be our guide as he is the local expert,' Tuppence said and laughed.

'That will be my pleasure,' I replied without hesitation.

We arrived at The Scythe and Tom showed us to our table. We ordered our food and Georgia commented on the character of the pub and how welcoming and friendly it was, a lot different from the bars of Manhattan.

'Have you been to New York?' Georgia asked.

'Alas, no,' I replied.

'Then you will have to come over as my guest and I will take you on the grand tour,' she said.

It was not what she said, but the way that she said it and the way she looked at me. My heart was pounding.

'I have told Georgia what happened at Cromley Hall without any details,' Tuppence said.

I nodded agreement to her.

The rest of the evening went well and eventually we made our way back to the apartment. I bade them goodnight and left them to spend time together and catch up. I went to my room. I rang DC Kumar and he had nothing to report. Tomorrow was another day.

TWENTY-NINE

I was awake early, so I sat on the sofa looking over the park with the usual morning activity. I was thinking deeply on the case; it is occupying my mind all the time now.

'Good morning,' Georgia said. 'Are you an early bird as well?'

'I have been rising early for my entire life and I enjoy this time of day. There is a serenity and purity about it,' I offered. 'Is New York your home now?'

'For now, but I miss my Englishness, my parents, my grandparents and the way of life here. Don't get me wrong, New York is great and it has been good to me, but it is not home,' she said with resignation.

'How do you spend your time in New York?'

'I love crafts and especially pottery. The apartment I share is too small to work in, so it will have to wait until I can do it,' she said with resignation.

Just then Tuppence made an appearance, looking bedraggled, and sat at the table. I went to make breakfast and left them to talk. We talked generally while we were eating.

'What are your plans for today?' I asked.

'Georgia came over lightweight so we have to go and buy some stuff for her, so a visit to the shops is what we will be doing. Will you drop us there?' she asked.

'Of course,' I replied.

I guessed Tuppence also wanted a number for her night out with Chief Constable Gregg. I dropped them at the shopping centre, and I decided to visit the guys at the observation point. I spent some time there, but it was very boring, but necessary. The guys were in good spirits despite the boredom. I left when Tuppence rang for me to pick them up. I took them to a hotel just outside Cromley.

'What are we doing here?' asked Tuppence.

'Coffee time,' I said, with a smile, and they both laughed. We headed back to the apartment so that Tuppence could get ready for her night out with Chief Constable Gregg. I knew she had been really looking forward to it. I dropped them off and left them to it and took a walk in the park.

I arrived back and Tuppence looked simply stunning. She was so excited about her night out and I was really happy for her. There was a knock on the door and Tuppence opened it.

'See you both later,' she said, with a smile and closed the door behind her. I was left with Georgia.

'I thought we could walk to The Lodge for something to eat and a drink,' I offered.

'That sounds good to me. I will go and get ready.'

My mobile rang and it was DC Kumar.

'Sir, Helen Green left the apartment and went to the local store for some groceries and, further, whilst she was out, there was movement at the small bedroom window, and we could see the outline of a person. I took some photographs. There is definitely a minimum of two people in the house,' he said, with confidence.

'That is good, so record it in the log and maintain surveillance.'

I imagine he is thinking, why we do not just go in there and arrest them? I feel the crunch time is coming.

I got myself ready and Georgia appeared.

'How far is the pub?' she asked.

'It is about half a mile. I thought it was nice to take a gentle walk to it. It has a nice garden, and we can sit outside in the evening sun.'

'That sounds really good and English to me,' she said and smiled.

We set off and gently walked the path and crossed the road of my recent incident to The Lodge. We arrived at the pub garden and selected a table.

'What a lovely setting,' Georgia said with a smile.

I went to the bar for some menus and drinks. I returned and sat down.

'I do not imagine they have pubs like this in New York.'

'They're mainly bars, but there are some Irish-themed pubs.'

'I guess it is a bit more vibrant than sleepy Cromley.'

'It is very busy and vibrant, but I am an English girl and I miss pubs like The Scythe and this one. I share an apartment and I miss a garden to potter about in and walks in the park. Central Park is not far from me, but it is not the same.'

We were generally talking when a familiar voice spoke.

'Paul! Why didn't you say you were out tonight?'

It was Richard (Yamma), with his partner Lucy, and beside him were John (Yak) and his wife Shirley.

'It was a late decision to come here,' I put to them.

I stood up and I introduced Georgia to them all and we all hooked up together. I looked at Georgia and shrugged my shoulders, but she just smiled. We all ordered food and drinks.

The evening went well with plenty of laughter and Georgia was chatting well with the girls. There was a definite connection between them. The time flew by and it was soon midnight. We said our farewells and we walked slowly back to the apartment.

'The lads are two of my best friends and we have been friends since we met at school. There is one other, George, who is away just now.'

'They are wonderful people, and you are blessed to have such good friends and I was really delighted to meet them. I have had two wonderful nights,' she said, with a smile.

'I have enjoyed tonight and it has been really good to meet you. Your mother always talks fondly of you I can see you both have a really good and close relationship.'

'She talks fondly of you. She was over the moon when you asked her to come with you to Cromley. She needed a change of scenery and it has done her the world of good.'

We reached the stairway to the apartment just as Tuppence and Chief Constable Gregg arrived back. We carried on up the stairs to leave Tuppence and Chief Constable Gregg some privacy. When we were inside, we were quiet, but not from nothing to say. I felt it was down to a definite connection between us, but I could not, at this time, allow anything to develop between us and, besides, she was only here for a few days.

Just then, Tuppence walked in, after leaving Chief Constable Gregg at the bottom of the stairway, with a lovely big smile on her face, and Georgia walked over to greet her. I went to the kitchen and made some coffees for us. I took them in to the room and they were chatting excitedly on the sofa. I sat down as Tuppence was telling us about her night out. Chief Constable Gregg had taken her to a cabaret night, including dinner, at a hotel, outside of Cromley and the music was a Tamla Motown night.

'How as your night?' Tuppence asked.

'We went to The Lodge for some food and drinks. It's a lovely place. We met two of Paul's friends and their partners joined us. They are all truly wonderful people. We had a great night,' she said, smiling.

I left them for a few minutes to call DC Kumar to see how things are and he reported all was quiet. I felt that tomorrow could not come quick enough for me.

I left them to talk. I went to bed with Georgia on my mind.

THIRTY

I was awake early as usual with an expectancy of the coming day. I rang DC Kumar and he reported all was quiet. I was standing at the window looking out over the park; I was miles away deep in thought about the case. A voice brought me back to my senses.

'A penny for them?' asked Georgia.

'I was thinking of the case and the coming days.'

'Sorry, I will leave you to them.'

'No, really it is fine, please stay!' I was almost pleading. We went to the kitchen to start breakfast, when I said, 'Are you like your mother where you will take over?' I said laughing.

'No, we will do it together.'

I put the radio on and we worked together with the breakfast, laughing at some of the songs played and changing the lyrics to others and generally messing about. I turned round to find Tuppence standing in the doorway with a lovely smile on her face.

'I think, unless you have something else on, we can go to Cromley Hall for a tour.'

I needed a distraction to occupy my mind.

'That will be fantastic,' said Tuppence.

Georgia approved.

I needed to take my mind off things, so I walked to

the local shops and I looked around. I bought a paper and headed back to the apartment; the girls were getting ready.

I sat and read the Cromley Echo, but the only thing interesting was the crossword, so I sat and filled it in.

The girls were ready and I remembered about the demand for tickets for Cromley Hall. I went online and I was lucky to get a slot for ten fifteen; we set off for Cromley Hall.

The main gate was open, but a barrier and cubicle were set up halfway down the drive. I stopped at the cubicle and showed our tickets, and we went on our way and parked up. We met up with the rest of the tour group and the tour started. The guide was very good and knowledgeable. I filled in my own bits that I knew and one or two I made up for a laugh. Soon the tour was over.

We left Cromley Hall, and I took them for a drive around the villages and historic sites around Cromley. I dropped them both at West Cromley Park to spend some time together. I returned to the apartment and put on the Test Match and sat going over the case and where I was to date.

- I had the entry point to the hall.

- I had DNA results off the phlegm, confirming Scott McKay was at the hall.

- Helen Green lied about her alibi with Bryan Gates.

- Bryan Gates lied about his alibi with Helen

Green.

- Screwed up autopsy.

I had to admit to myself I had come to a halt. I needed some hard evidence to tie Scott McKay to the murders of Jake and Arthur Holmes; so where was it? I needed to find Scott McKay; if I found him, I was certain I would find the evidence.

I believed it was time to force the issue and raid the house of Helen Green. I would speak with Chief Constable Gregg tomorrow morning.

THIRTY-ONE

The new day brought a new but nervous optimism. I felt it was now time to force the issue. I believe Scott McKay is holed up with Helen Green and the evidence I am looking for is with him. If it does not come to me, I will have to go and get it.

I was ready and just on the point of going to the station earlier than usual and giving Tuppence and her daughter time together. They both appeared just as I was leaving, so we said our goodbyes and I headed for the station.

I know Chief Constable Gregg is at his desk early every morning, so I rang him. I made my way to his office and knocked on the door and was invited in.

'You are early this morning, which means there is something on your mind.'

'Sir, I have reached a stalemate in the case where I have to force the issue. I have DNA evidence to put Scott McKay at Cromley Hall, but not the murders of the Holmes brothers. I believe Scott McKay is holed up in Helen Green's house and I believe he has the evidence with him in terms of his clothing, shoes, etc. The surveillance team have confirmed there are two people in Helen Green's house and I believe Scott McKay is that second person.'

'So, tell me the next step.'

'I need to carry out a forced entry to the house and a forensic search. He is showing no signs of coming out, so I will have to go and get him.'

'What makes you think it is Scott McKay who is in the house?'

'I know Helen Green has lied to me when she told me Bryan Gates was with her on the night of the murders; Bryan Gates has confirmed she lied. Helen Green was at Cromley Hall the other morning. I saw her acting suspiciously and she panicked when she saw me.'

'Very well. When do you plan to carry this out?'

'I want to do a plan today and carry it out early tomorrow morning. I believe they think they are safe, so there is no urgent rush. I have the house under surveillance. The element of surprise will be with us.'

I left his office in a buoyant mood and returned to the incident room to put my plan in place.

- I would need a team of police officers to break down the door to gain access and secure the premises.

- My guys and myself would make the arrests.

- I would need Graham Coleman and his crime scene team for forensics.

- A specialist crime team would go in and search the premises.

I set up a meeting for eleven o'clock that morning with Chief Constable Gregg, Graham Coleman and myself.

Eleven o'clock soon came around and I headed for

Chief Constable Gregg's office. I met Graham Coleman along the corridor. He was curious to what was going on, but I made him wait. I knocked on the door, then we were invited in, and we duly sat down, Chief Constable Gregg spoke.

'ADI Blackmore, will you, for Graham Coleman's benefit, put your plans for tomorrow?

'To date, we have DNA evidence that belongs to Scott McKay, but this only places him at Cromley Hall. We have found the secret entry point to Cromley Hall and by the DNA evidence we can place Scott McKay there as well. The trail to Scott McKay is cold and I believe this is due to him being off the radar.

'We have set up an observation point close to the home of Helen Green; we have evidence and a partial sighting of a second person in the house. I firmly believe Scott McKay is holed up in the home of Helen Green. As the evidence is not coming to us, I believe we will have to go and get it. I intend to raid the house of Helen Green early tomorrow morning.

'I suggest we go in at six o'clock tomorrow morning to make the arrests and recover the evidence we require: clothing as they may have blood on them, shoes to match the cast prints we have so far.'

'Where will we meet tomorrow morning?' asked Graham Coleman.

'I suggest we meet in the car park of The Larches shopping centre, just inside on the left of the entry point to the car park. It is about half a mile from Helen

Green's house. We will carry out the following: we will force entry to the house tomorrow morning at six o'clock and make the arrests; Graham and his Scene of Crime team will enter the building and carry out a forensic examination; then a specialist search team will carry out a detailed search of the house. They will be particularly looking for a holdall, a bag, shoes, etc.'

I requested extra police officers to assist and my request was granted; we were now set for tomorrow morning.

I met with extra police officers assigned for tomorrow. I showed them a photograph of the area and a plan of attack. I wanted an officer at the side of the building and two in the rear garden in case he legs it out of the window. After further discussions, we were set.

I set off to the observation point to see the guys and brief them on tomorrow's events. They were both fired up and ready for it. They would join us at five thirty am in The Larches car park. They would brief the night crew and I would ring them later. Everything was now fully set for tomorrow.

I called it a day and set off back to the apartment. In reality, I was looking forward to seeing Georgia. I opened the door to find Tuppence sitting alone.

'Georgia has left to visit her grandparents. She did not want to tell you as you are fully focused on the case,' she stated.

To say I was disappointed was an understatement, but I know she was right. I had to fully focus on the case.

'How did your day go?' Tuppence asked.

'We are set to force entry into Helen Green's house early tomorrow morning. I have to move the case forward as we have stagnated; I have to go and get the killer and the evidence. I fully believe both are in that house.'

I rang the night crew; they were as positive in their outlook. They would meet us as we parked up outside the shops just up the road from Helen Green's house. I suggested they took it in turns to get some sleep as tomorrow could be a long day.

Myself and Tuppence went for a walk in the park mainly to walk off some of the adrenalin flowing through me. I had never felt that level of discomfort in my own body; my heart rate had increased, my breathing was deeper than normal, and I could feel the blood pumping through my veins. I knew, without a doubt, this was the highest profile case I had ever worked on. I also knew that Scott McKay was holed up in Helen Green's house. I remained calm and focused; I knew I would get the bastard.

THIRTY-TWO

I awoke alert, fresh and pumped up for the new day. This was my day of destiny, so bring it on.

I rang the night crew and they reported all was quiet; they were ready for the day ahead.

I dressed and made my way from my room, and I found Tuppence in the kitchen. She had made me a bacon sandwich.

'I can't have you going into battle on an empty stomach,' she said with a smile.

I bade her farewell and made my way to The Larches car park. I was first to arrive. Within five minutes everyone had arrived. I briefed the teams on the order of events, then we set off.

I drove the half mile and parked up outside a row of shops. The teams parked up behind me, then we all gathered outside the shops. The morning was very still as we walked slowly and quietly towards Helen Green's house. We stopped outside; we were set.

I gave the order. The door was smashed in with shouts of 'Police!' with a lot of noise to create a level of confusion and disorientation. The guys charged up the stairs, batons in hand and ready for anything.

'Sir, someone has run up a ladder into the loft.'

'You two go after him,' I shouted.

I ran into the bedroom and found Helen Green sitting up in bed with a sheet pulled up to her neck. She looked scared.

'Taylor, Kumar, cuff her and take her and put her in the back of your car for now,' I ordered. 'The rest of you, outside with me.'

We made our way down the stairs to the front of the house.

'I ain't done anything!' she screamed.

She continued to scream and plead her innocence as she was taken to the car.

'You three go around to the left of the houses to the other side, but remain quiet. Graham, when Helen Green is removed from the house, take your team and carry out your forensics. The rest of you, come with me and, again, quietly.'

We made our way around the right-hand side of the houses. I stopped them at a point and motioned for them to remain quiet and we waited. By now the whole area was awake, with people hanging out of windows and phones videoing the events. A man was pointing down to one of the gardens, Scott McKay was heading my way. The man in the window was laughing and continued to point. I did not need him; I knew the route Scott McKay would take.

I could hear noises from a fence, so we were ready as Scott McKay jumped over and landed between us.

'Hi, nice of you to drop in,' I put to him.

He motioned to make a run for it, but DC Kelly

rugby tackled him. He was cuffed and under control in moments. I then spoke to him.

'Scott McKay, I am arresting you as you have been identified as a suspect of the murders of Jake and Arthur Holmes on Saturday 6th June at Cromley Hall. You do not have to say anything, but it may harm your defence if you do not mention when questioned, something that you later rely on in Court. Anything you do say may be given in evidence.'

He offered no comment.

'Take him to the car and to the station; the custody sergeant will be waiting for him.'

We walked back to the front of the house to Helen Green. She was sitting in the back of the car protesting her innocence. Due to the now very public interest I decided to charge her in the car.

'Helen Green, I am arresting you as you have been identified as a suspect of the murders of Jake and Arthur Holmes on Saturday 6th June at Cromley Hall. You do not have to say anything, but it may harm your defence if you do not mention when questioned, something that you later rely on in Court. Anything you do say may be given in evidence.'

'What the fuck, I ain't done anything?!' she screamed, tears running down her face.

'Take her to the station; the custody sergeant will be waiting for her.'

The Scene of Crime team were still in the house carrying forensic checks, so I needed patience for now. I decided to ring Chief Constable Gregg.

'Good morning, ADI Blackmore. You have news for me?'

'Good morning, sir. Yes, we have gained entry to the house and arrested Scott McKay and Helen Green. They are both en route to the station in separate cars. Graham Coleman's team are carrying out forensic checks and when they have finished the specialist team will go in. I will leave DC Kelly in charge at the scene, and I will head back to the station.'

'Very well, we will speak later.'

I spoke with DC Kelly and left two further officers with him, as a crowd was gathering. It was time to go to the station.

I reached the entrance to the station and noticed Sue Bentley frantically waving her arms at me. I ignored her and drove to the barrier. The barrier raised and I saw her running towards me, but I drove on and parked up. She reached the car.

'ADI Blackmore, what was going on this morning?' she said breathlessly.

'You are on police property, so I suggest you leave,' I said to her whilst walking to the entrance.

She eventually realised her attempts for information were fruitless and started walking to the barrier. She did not have a code to get out, but that was her problem.

I went to the custody room and found DC Taylor and DC Kumar in there. I walked over to them, smiling, and they were all smiling.

'Have they been booked in?' I asked.

'Yes,' said the custody sergeant. 'All items have been removed from them and their shoelaces, as well. They have been put in separate cells at opposite ends of the cell block. Helen Green is still screaming her innocence, so I have put an officer stationed there to keep an eye on her.'

'Thank you,' I replied.

'What next?' asked DC Kumar.

'Breakfast,' I said with a smile.

'What about the prisoners?' DC Kumar asked.

'I am not buying their breakfast.'

There was a pause and we all laughed.

'We will go to the café down in Queens Park; they do a great bacon sandwich and coffee.'

I rounded up the team, except DC Kelly who was back at Helen Green's house. He would not miss out. We headed to the park. We reached the door of the café when I noticed Sue Bentley heading our way. She clearly was able to escape the confines of the police station car park. We went inside and ordered our food and coffees and sat in the corner. I deliberately sat with my back to the door when she entered and headed towards us.

'ADI Blackmore, what was going on this morning? Is it related to your investigation? Don't deny it, as you are all over social media.' She was demanding, in a high level of agitation.

'I have nothing to say to you unless it is in an official capacity and this is not one of them, so I advise you go away before you get yourself in trouble,' I put to her firmly, but not lifting my head to look at her.

She turned round and stormed out of the café slamming the door hard, which brought out the owner.

'If the door is damaged, charge it to the Cromley Echo,' I said to the owner. 'You have four reliable witnesses here.'

We all laughed together. I turned to the team.

'Well done for the observations on the house and the arrests this morning and all the work you have all done. It has been a great team effort,' I said, with all sincerity, 'but we still have some work to do to put our case together to allow us to close the case and seal a conviction.'

'One thing: how did you know where Scott McKay would appear after he tried to escape?' asked DC Taylor.

'A friend of mine lived a couple of doors down from Helen Green's house. The planned layout of the houses is a square block, so the way the gardens are laid out there is a natural route to the point where he emerged. He entered the loft and made his way along and went through a hole he had knocked through to the neighbouring house and out through the back garden. I just figured that is where he would show himself.'

'I can say on behalf of all of us, it has been a pleasure working on the case and feeling involved,' DC Kumar put to me, with nodding heads all round.

We finished our breakfast and headed back to the station.

'Are you going to interview them now?' DC Taylor enquired as we walked up the hill.

'No, I want them to stew for a while. We will go back to the incident room.'

I looked and there was no sign of Sue Bentley. I guess she got the message.

We arrived back at the station and the atmosphere was really good. Lena was wondering what was going on, so we enlightened her. My mobile phone rang, it was Chief Constable Gregg.

'Yes, sir?'

'Will you come to my office?'

'I am on my way.'

'I am going to Chief Constable Gregg's office, so start formally putting the case together. We will fill in the missing bits as they arise.'

I left them to it and made my way to Chief Constable Gregg's office. I knocked on the door and the usual booming voice called out.

'Come in, ADI Blackmore. We have been inundated with phone calls as word has spread around on social media, so as I said to you earlier, there will be a briefing at two o'clock and I believe it will be lively.'

'I will be ready, sir.'

I left the office and headed back to the incident room, where I found them all working quietly and with determination. I sent a text to Tuppence telling her all went well, and she replied with a smiley face.

Graham Coleman rang me to say his team had

completed his forensic checks and left the building and DC Kelly had sent in the specialist search team. This was a phase in the investigation that was over, so we had to crack on.

'DC Sharp, will you set up an interview for me and include DC Taylor? Then go to the hotel where Bryan Gates was staying and look at video footage off the security cameras when Bryan Gates was staying there. We will be interested in Helen Green's visits.'

'Right, we will start the interviews. I will take you in turns to do them, so, DC Taylor, you are first.'

Just then I received a call from DC Kelly.

'Sir, the specialist team have recovered a holdall, male trainers and clothing. They have been handed over to the forensics team, bagged and are on their way to the lab.'

'That is great news. Seal the house and make your way back to the station.'

I rang Graham Coleman to notify me the second he finds anything and have DNA analysis carried out straight away.

The interview was set up, so DC Sharp and DC Taylor and I made our way down to Interview Room One. We entered the room and Scott McKay was sitting facing us. He appeared arrogant, as if we had nothing on him. We sat down and DC Taylor turned on the tape to record the interview. He identified us all to the waiting recording machine.

I sat for a few seconds looking directly at Scott

McKay and then I leaned forward and looked directly at him and asked, 'Why did you murder Jake and Arthur Holmes at Cromley Hall on Saturday 6th June?'

'I didn't kill anyone. I was nowhere near Cromley Hall on the night you said,' he replied sneeringly.

'Is there anyone who can substantiate that?' I asked.

'Yes, I was with Helen Green on that night. She will tell you that.'

'That is interesting. Helen Green has given a statement that she was with someone else on that night,' I put to him.

I sat back in my chair and watched the panic wash over him.

'She is lying; she was with me!' he yelled in a mixture of panic and great agitation. 'I want a solicitor; I'm entitled to one,' he demanded.

I suspended the meeting for the duty solicitor to be summoned and he shortly arrived. His name was Rhodan Mackerel. He was tall, very thin, gaunt and would not have looked out of place in an Alfred Hitchcock movie. Scott McKay spent time with his solicitor and then we cracked on.

'As I put to you earlier, Helen Green has given a statement that she was with someone else on that night.'

'No comment,' was his response.

'You went to Cromley Hall on Saturday 6th June. You entered the old servants' quarters, searched and found an exit point at the back in the corner behind an old wardrobe. You walked along the top of the wall around to the back of the kitchen. You walked down to the ground level and found an entry point at the point between the kitchen and scullery. You made your way down the passageway, pushed a panel and gained entry to the passageway between the kitchen and the scullery. You made your way to where the heirlooms were on display and stole them. Sometime between these points you came across Jake and Arthur Holmes and deliberately murdered them. On leaving the hall you found an alcove in the passageway where you stored the heirlooms, which we now have in our possession. You had planned to return for the heirlooms once things had quietened down.'

'No comment,' he answered.

'I have your footprints in the earth, from the top of the wall, and your trainers that made them. I have your DNA from the passageway alcove where you placed the heirlooms. You were not too clever about where you sneezed. Perhaps you thought with confidence you would never be caught.'

'No comment,' he replied.

DC Taylor stopped the tape and left it to the custody sergeant to do the legalities. I and DC Taylor left the interview room and headed back to the incident room.

We all sat at the table and DC Kelly asked, 'How did it go?'

'He denied everything at first and then presented with the evidence he retreated to a no comment mode.

He has requested a solicitor and that was arranged. We have evidence to tie him to Cromley Hall and I am very confident there will be evidence of DNA from the findings at Helen Green's house to tie him to the murders.'

I received a call from Graham Coleman to say they had found a T-shirt with blood splatters, trainers with a bit missing that matched the casts from Cromley Hall and the DNA, and it was great news.

'DC Sharp, will you apply to hold Scott McKay and Helen Green for a further forty-eight hours? The DNA results should be in by then.

'I want you, DC Kelly, and Sharp to set up an interview with Helen Green. I want you to ask her about her alibi with Bryan Gates. Just record her answers and we will meet later to discuss. I have a meeting with Chief Constable Gregg before we meet the media scrum, so I will catch up with you later.'

I walked to Chief Constable Gregg's office at one forty-five pm and knocked on the door and I was invited in.

'Are you ready for this? It will be mayhem in there.'

'Bring it on,' I replied.

We made our way along the winding corridors and stairway. We were both walking with confidence. We entered the room and the volume level rose sharply, with random shouting of questions raining at us.

Chief Constable Gregg raised his hand and asked for silence and then said, with authority, 'I will make a statement and answer some questions afterwards. This morning an operation was carried out in the early hours where persons of interest were arrested on suspicion of the murders of Jake and Arthur Holmes and the theft of valuable heirlooms from Cromley Hall.'

'How many people were involved?' asked a voice or face I did not recognise.

'I can't reveal this information just now, but it will be revealed when the time is right,' replied Chief Constable Gregg.

'ADI Blackmore, how do you feel after solving this case and bringing arrests so quickly?' asked Sue Bentley.

'First of all, it is never down to one individual. It has been a great all-round team effort, which I am proud to be a part of.'

'But you must take credit for this?' She shouted.

'As I have said, it has been a great team effort,' I repeated.

'ADI Blackmore, where does this leave Roderick Holmes?' the television reporter asked.

'That can't be answered just now,' answered Chief Constable Gregg.

'Chief Constable Gregg, are you confident of getting a conviction?' Sue Bentley asked.

'Yes, I am very confident we will secure a conviction,' he answered.

'Where does that leave SIO DI Grainger?' another face I am not familiar with asked.

'As I have reported recently, he is investigating

other cases,' Chief Constable Gregg replied. 'Thank you for your time and there will be another briefing when all the interviews have been concluded.'

We stood up and left the room with a barrage of questions following us. We made our way to his office. We discussed the briefing and we agreed we will never make all of them happy, but we also cannot stay there all day.

I left his office and made my way back to the incident room where all the guys were together chatting away.

'We have just been watching the news briefing and you and Chief Constable Gregg handled it well,' said DC Sharp.

The others nodded agreement.

'Cheers, guys,' I answered with sincerity.

'How did you get on with Helen Green?' I put to DC Kelly and DC Sharp.

'She was very emotive and constantly sobbing, saying she did not kill anyone. She said she was with Bryan Gates over and over,' reported DC Kelly.

'Scott McKay has said she was with him,' I said, 'so we will interview her again at five o'clock, so if you can set it up.' I looked at DC Sharp. 'Then you can join us at the café in the park for a coffee.'

We all laughed and made our way. I beckoned to Lena to join us.

DC Sharp caught up with us at the entrance to the café in Queens Park. I bought the coffees and we sat outside in the afternoon sun. We talked about general things, but not the case; we needed to have a break from that. The lads were curious about Mortley, so I enlightened them on its finer points and not so finer points. The general opinion was Cromley was a better place to be. We wandered back to the station and prepared for Helen Green. I would be taking DC Kelly with me this time.

The appointed time came and we made our way down to the interview room we used earlier. We walked in and Helen Green was sitting facing us. We sat down and DC Kelly started the tape and identified everyone to the tape. I made sure there was a female officer in the room, just in case there was a problem. Like Scott McKay, I sat for a few seconds looking at her; I wanted her to feel uncomfortable.

'I didn't kill anyone. You know where I was on that night. I told you that when you came to my house and Bryan Gates proved it,' she said, crying in desperation.

'That is not correct, and you know it,' I said, provoking her.

'It's true and you know it is,' she screamed and got to her feet.

'I suggest you sit and calm down,' I said to her. She was panicking. 'Bryan Gates was at home with his wife that night. He comes to Cromley once a month to see his client and it is always during the week. He has never been to Cromley at the weekend. You befriended him and turned up at his hotel one night with the sole intention of blackmailing him by seducing him; he paid you one hundred pounds a month. He was at your house that day to pay you the money,' I put directly to her.

'He's lying,' she said, sobbing. 'I want a solicitor,' she demanded.

We suspended the interview and returned to the incident room. I wanted to stick with her, as she would crack. I did not think she could take the pressure.

A solicitor was sourced by the name of James Brown. He was a dapper dresser with a neat-cut suit, he was well groomed and assured. He spent time with his client and then we cracked on.

'On the night of 6th June, Bryan Gates was at his caravan on the east coast. This has been verified by witnesses and the site manager; he and his family were in the site club sitting with another couple. We have video footage from the hotel of you visiting Bryan Gates at the hotel on two occasions. The video shows you walking to Bryan Gates' room, knocking on the door and being allowed to enter the room. The video shows you leaving the room one and a half hours later.'

I waited for her comment but none came.

'I suggest you stop this charade and tell the truth.'

She looked at me with defiance and spoke. 'Scott McKay turned up the night before you smashed my door down!' she yelled.

'Alas, that is not true. We have been monitoring your house and we have videos of you going out for takeaways for two people from the Indian restaurant. No one except you has entered or left your house,' I directed at her.

'I didn't kill them men!' she screamed in panic.

'I am closing this interview for you to think things over. I suggest you talk to your solicitor and start telling the truth. That is the only way you will protect yourself, because right now you are digging a hole for yourself that is getting deeper.'

DC Kelly and I got up to leave the interview. When I got to the door I stopped for a moment and looked at James Brown and then left the room. We went back to the incident room and the lads were still there.

'Do you think she is involved in the murders?' DC Sharp asked.

'No, I do not believe she was involved directly with the murders and quite honestly I do not believe she was aware of Scott McKay's involvement. She is scared stiff and panicking. I believe if she just sat back and thought about everything, life would be easier for her. I hope her solicitor will see that,' I put to them.

'You opened the door for her,' offered DC Kelly.

'I had to, I needed her to calm down and start thinking. I am not after her, she is just a silly girl, I want Scott McKay,' I said, with venom.

'Right, lads, it is time we called it a night. It has been a long and satisfying day and it has been a great team effort and we can do no more now.

The lads set off home and I went down to see the custody sergeant and said to him, 'Keep a close eye on

Helen Green overnight; she is unstable right now.'

He said he would arrange it.

I got in my car and sent a text to Tuppence to say I was on my way and would see her in fifteen minutes. I set off for the apartment.

'How was your day?' Tuppence asked.

I told her all the day's events, the briefing and interviews. She sat with her mouth open taking it all in. I grabbed a beer from the fridge and sat looking out of the window over the park. I was thinking of Georgia. Tuppence came and sat beside me.

'Georgia said if you want to call her, she would love to talk to you,' she said with a smile.

'Thank you, I would really like that.'

I put my arm around her and gave her a big hug. A nice end to the day.

THIRTY-THREE

I slept better than I have over the last few days. The new day brought an enforced confidence. I believe we are getting closer to the conclusion, but not quite there; we still had work to do.

Tuppence was up early, but of late she has not been so grouchy. I think Chief Constable Gregg is a lot to do with the change in her. I really hope the relationship develops to a permanent conclusion.

I turned on the television and put on the local news, we had breakfast as we watched the bulletin. The room was packed, and Chief Constable Gregg was in full control over the proceedings and my part as I answered the questions.

'Sue Bentley of the Cromley Echo looks a bit subdued; don't you think?' Tuppence commented.

'Her line of communication has been cut, for now, to the station. She is like a raft drifting on the ocean, looking for a sail to bring her ashore,' I offered.

Domestics done, we headed for the station and found the team already there. We all exchanged the usual morning greetings. I called them all together for a group discussion, so I started.

'We have evidence tying Scott McKay to Cromley Hall by way of footprints and DNA, but not yet to the murders. The forensics team have found a T-shirt with blood splatters, in the bottom of a bag. They are processing DNA analysis; we should have the results hopefully soon. We know he hit them over the head, but that did not kill them. Following a comment from DC Taylor, regarding Burke and Hare, I went to Bradford prison, where I found out Scott McKay had read a book on Burke and Hare from the library whilst he was in prison. There are bruises around the noses of the two Holmes brothers, but nothing else.'

'Perhaps they were suffocated at his point,' said DC Sharp.

'In what way?' asked DC Kelly.

'I will demonstrate,' offered DC Sharp.

He stood up and walked around to the back of DC Kelly. He put his hand around his head in front of his face just in front of his nose.

'What if he pinched their noses with his thumb and index finger and had a cloth or something in his hand and suffocated them?'

'I do not think the murders were premeditated, so knowing Cromley Hall, a cloth or rag would be very unlikely to be lying around,' I offered.

'What about a handkerchief?' asked DC Kumar.

'Interesting theory,' I said. 'I will ring Graham Coleman now and discuss it with him.'

I rang his number.

'ADI Blackmore, I do not have the DNA results yet.'

'That is not why I am ringing. Will you check Scott McKay's clothing and see if there is a handkerchief or some type of cloth in any of his pockets and if so, will you do a DNA analysis? It is possible the Holmes brothers were suffocated with either of them.'

Graham Coleman agreed to my request, so I returned to the team discussion.

Next for discussion was Helen Green.

'Helen Green is a very scared young woman who is prone to emotion and not thinking straight. We have blown her alibi out of the water; she does not have a clue what to do,' I put to them.

'Perhaps a little more pressure would break her?' said DC Sharp.

'I think we should use a softer approach,' offered DC Taylor.

'I agree,' I said. 'She is scared, so a softer approach would I feel be the best option. We need to get her on our side. We need to lead her to the answers we want by gaining her confidence. She is a misguided, silly woman and I believe that is all to her; we will find out when we talk to her. DC Kumar, you will be with me this time, so will you set up the interview for eleven o'clock?'

Just then Tuppence informed me Chief Constable Gregg wanted to see me. I set off to his office. I knocked on the door and was called in and I sat in my usual spot.

'How are the interviews going?'

'We are making progress, sir. Scott McKay is now "no commenting". Helen Green is scared stiff so we will be adopting a softer approach to get her on our side, I will be talking to her at eleven o'clock this morning. Graham Coleman is carrying out DNA analysis, so we are awaiting results. I have applied, due to the seriousness of the charges, to hold Scott McKay and Helen Green for a longer period and it has been granted. I am confident we will have the DNA results and interviews completed by then.'

'Good. The CPS want to talk to discuss the charges.'

'If we could make it this afternoon, sir, at three o'clock, I would be grateful.'

'I will make it so.'

I left his office and headed back to the incident room. DC Kumar gave me the thumbs up for the interview room at eleven o'clock.

The appointed hour arrived so DC Kumar and I headed to the interview room. We walked into the same seating arrangement as yesterday and she looked as scared as the last time I saw her. The custody sergeant informed me she has not eaten anything since she was brought in. DC Kumar and I sat down, and DC Kumar set up the formalities. I sat looking at Helen Green; my thought process was broken when Helen Green spoke.

'Do you really think I was involved in the killing of those two old men? I don't want to go to prison.'

She spoke in a softer tone than yesterday. Gone was the angry, emotive voice. She obviously has been thinking hard overnight. She must have picked up on our vibes to take a softer approach with her.

'That is down to you. So far you have been evasive and uncooperative and quite frankly it could very much go against you.' I leaned forward looking directly at her. 'I suggest we forget everything you have said before, as I can prove it is nonsense. I do not think Scott McKay will protect you, so a fresh start will be in your best interests. I want to know how you got involved with him and why you are shielding Scott McKay.'

She looked at her brief and he nodded to her; she paused for a few seconds to get herself together.

'I met him in a pub. I was with some friends; he was on his own. I got talking to him and he seemed nice. We talked for a time, so I decided to stay with him when my friends moved on. He walked me home and left me at the door. I gave him my phone number and we agreed to meet the next night in the pub.'

'Did he turn up?'

'Yes, but he was late and out of breath when he arrived. He said was sorry he was late, but he just carried on talking and it was soon forgotten. Later he walked me home and I invited him in; we had some coffee and he went home.'

'Did you start seeing more of him?'

'Yes, as each day passed, and we eventually saw each other every day, and thinking about it, I didn't see him all day on Saturday 6th. He said he was going to see his mum.'

'When did you see him again?'

'Late Sunday afternoon. He had a bag and he looked

327

anxious. I asked him what was wrong, and he said he'd had a row with his mum and she had kicked him out.'

'What happened next?'

'He asked if he could stay with me for a few days until he got a place of his own. He looked so lost with his bag in his hand, so I agreed.'

'How was he during his stay with you?'

'He was agitated, but I put that down to the row he'd had with his mother.'

'How was he towards you?'

'He was all right at the start, but he became more agitated as time went on.'

'Did you think it was still to do with the row he had with his mother?'

'He went out one day and came back very late and very flustered. He said he was being chased. I asked him why and he said he was going to come into a lot of money and others wanted to get their hands on it. He said when he got the money we would go away somewhere and live together.'

'Did you believe him?'

'Yes, as he always seemed genuine to me,' she said, with her head lowered, and her words tailed off.

'When did he start to become a recluse in your house?'

'From that day onwards. I asked him why he was so scared of these people. He said he had been in prison for something stupid, but it was behind him now. He said he had met some nasty people and bumped into two of them that day, but he wanted nothing to do with them. He didn't want them to take his inheritance, so he would lie low for a while.'

'What happened when I came to see you?'

'I panicked when I saw you. Bryan was there and, yes, I was blackmailing him and…'

James Brown interrupted. 'I want to speak with my client before we go any further,' he requested.

'It's all right. I want to be fully open and not have this on my mind for the rest of my life. Bryan Gates was there that day to give me the money. I just said I was with Bryan on that night on the spur of the moment. Bryan agreed because he did not know what to do. When you left, he said, "What the hell are you doing to me? I'm out of here." I have not seen or heard of him since,' she admitted with a level of embarrassment.

'I think it is time for a break so we will stop. We will continue at five o'clock this afternoon,' I put to them.

All parties agreed.

DC Kumar did the formalities and we headed back to the incident room. The team were there, so we had a discussion.

'She is hanging herself,' stated DC Kumar.

'I do not agree. She is just being honest and getting it off her chest. She just wants it over with and to get on with her life and take her punishment, if any, that comes her way,' I stated.

'Surely she will be charged with blackmail and obstructing the course of justice,' DC Kelly replied, with concern.

'I will not be looking for it. She is just a silly girl and things just got out of control. She wants it over with and to get out of here. Bryan Gates just wants to forget about it and is not looking for any charges. His greater higher authority is his wife and that is one sentence he will have for life. They are very small bit-part players in this crime. Scott McKay is the one we want, so we must fully focus on him.

'The final decision will not be down to us. I am meeting the Crown Prosecution Service this afternoon, so I may have a better idea then. Right guys, it is time for lunch.'

We used the station canteen for the first time and headed back to the incident room. The team were there bringing their notes up to date. I am a stickler for correct paperwork; I want nothing to come back to us. Three o'clock soon came around, so I headed for Chief Constable Gregg's office. I knocked on the door and was summoned in. He was sitting at his desk and another guy was sitting next to my normal seat.

'ADI Blackmore, can I introduce you to Rupert Squires of the CPS,' Chief Constable Gregg indicated to him to continue.

'ADI Blackmore, I felt it was time to have a talk to see where you are with your investigation.'

Just then my phone rang; it was Graham Coleman.

'Please, I have to take this call,' I requested and was granted. I returned to the desk after my call. I started the briefing to Rupert Squires.

'There are three individuals in this case, two minor individuals, Brian Gates and Helen Green. One major individual, Scott McKay. They are as follows.

'Bryan Gates, a salesman who visits Cromley once a month, got involved with an employee of the company he was visiting, a Helen Green. She set a sexual honey trap at his hotel and he walked right into it. She blackmailed him to the tune of a hundred pounds a month. He was at Helen Green's house when I interviewed her. He provided an alibi for her. He is not involved in the crime at Cromley Hall.

Helen Green met Scott McKay in a pub and got involved with him. Scott McKay moved into her house and became a recluse to hideaway. She did not know he was involved in the murders at Cromley Hall.

Scott McKay found a secret access to Cromley Hall. He made his way in, where he murdered both Jake and Arthur Holmes and some stole valuable heirlooms.'

'Can we now talk in more detail regarding each individual?' asked Rupert Squires.

'Bryan Gates was drawn into a sexual relationship with Helen Green when she got to know him. She turned up at his hotel room one night with the intention of seducing him; we have video footage of her at his hotel room door. She succeeded and then blackmailed him. He is not involved with the Cromley Hall murders. He was a silly man, and his judge will be his wife and he is on a life sentence with that. He does not want any criminal charges made against Helen Green. I do not believe applying charges would not be in the public interest and would destroy lives with no benefits.

Helen Green is in custody with ongoing interviews. At first she was frightened, and now she is being incredibly open and cooperative. She was not involved in the murders. Scott McKay told her he had an argument with his mother, and she threw him out. He went to Helen Green's house, where she took him in. She said she panicked when I turned up to interview her and Bryan Gates was there at the same time to pay her some money. She said, out of panic, she was there with Bryan Gates on that night and he confirmed it, but had also panicked. Scott McKay had told her he was waiting for a very large inheritance, which I believe to be the heirlooms, and take her away for a better life. She did not know he murdered the two Holmes brothers. She is a silly girl who naively got involved with Scott McKay. Like Bryan Gates, I do not think there would be any benefit in bringing charges against her; she is being very cooperative.

Scott McKay was thrown out of Cromley Hall on occasions due to snooping around and he was eventually banned from Cromley Hall. He was in prison and upon release he planned entry to Cromley Hall, where he found the secret access point on a previous visit. He entered the hall by the old servants' quarters and he made his way across the top of the wall. We have his footprints that he left embedded in the earth, and we also have the trainers he was wearing. He gained access via the secret entry point where we recovered the heirlooms. The forensics team recovered phlegm off the wall where they obtained DNA that was confirmed to belong to Scott McKay. When we raided the house, a T-shirt was recovered with spatters of blood, and the phone call I just received was to tell me the DNA results proved to be of Jake and Arthur Holmes and Scott McKay. The blows to the head did not kill Jake and Arthur Holmes, they were suffocated first. There is bruising around the nose and face of the brothers, and I believe this is how they were suffocated. I believe they were killed separately. I believe he attacked them from behind by putting his thumb and index finger clamped to their noses and with a cloth, possibly a hankie, put it over their mouths. The forensics team have located a hankie in Scott McKay's jacket and a DNA test is ongoing; we should have the results tomorrow afternoon. We have enough to charge him with the murders of Jake and Arthur Holmes.'

'There is a lot of good work there, ADI Blackmore, but do you consider yourself to be judge and jury?' Rupert Squires asked.

'Not at all. You asked me where I was with my investigation and that was my answer. I will complete my investigation and hand over the reports; it is your department's decision whether they should all face the courts. If I were called, I would be sympathetic to them. Bryan Gates and Helen Green have both been very open and cooperative during the interviews. Scott McKay is where the real focus will be,' I said directly to him.

'It is my belief we have enough to formally charge Scott McKay and release Roderick Holmes, so I will set this in motion,' Rupert Squires said directly.

'I would be grateful if we could formally charge Scott McKay tomorrow after I receive the DNA results from the forensics team. Perhaps Roderick Holmes could be released to clear the way,' I suggested.

We discussed other things, but we had an agreement all round. I left Chief Constable Gregg's office and headed back to the incident room. I also knew the final decision would not be mine.

I found DC Kumar waiting for me for our five o'clock interview with Helen Green. I said to Tuppence I could possibly be late; she could get a taxi back to the apartment. She said she anticipated that; Chief Constable Gregg would drive her back to the apartment.

DC Kumar and I made our way down to the interview room bang on five o'clock. We walked into the room and found her appearance as she was earlier, relaxed and relieved to get this whole episode off her mind. We sat down and I took a few seconds to just look at her. I wanted her to think I was looking directly into her mind to ensure she was not lying to me.

'Did you ever do any washing for him,' I asked her.

'No,' she replied.

'Did he do any of his own washing?'

'Yes, just the clothes he was wearing. He washed

them at least twice.'

'Did that not strike you as being a bit odd? He moved in with you with a bag that one would assume had his clothes in.'

'Yes, I did think it was strange, but he kept the bag by his side all the time and never opened it. He would not let me near it.'

'And that did not appear odd to you?'

'No,' she said with tears in her eyes.

'I saw you at Cromley Hall and when you saw me you panicked and left very quickly. Why were you there?'

'I wanted to get out of the house for a while, so I walked to Cromley Hall to stretch my legs, no other reason.'

'You were keen to buy a copy of the Cromley Echo. Why was that?'

'I was interested in what was going on and I spoke to Scott about it, but he was not interested. I now know why,' she said, crying.

'What did Scott McKay do whilst he was in your house?'

'He was in the loft. He said he could hear something moving about. He thought it was rats.'

'He was preparing an escape route,' I put to her.

'I know that now,' she said as her voice tailed off.

'This will be a good time to finish for today.'

All parties agreed, so DC Kumar did the formalities and we went back to the incident room.

We sat and chatted, and DC Kumar agreed that she

has been a naive, silly woman who was scared stiff. We called it a day and headed off home.

I headed to the car, and I sent Tuppence a text to let her know I was on my way, mainly to give Chief Constable Gregg time to leave the apartment.

I arrived and Tuppence was talking to Georgia. I joined in the conversation. It was good to see and talk to her.

THIRTY-FOUR

I was awake early as usual. There was no sound from Tuppence's bedroom, so I sat by the window and looked out over the park. It was a quiet, serene morning to prepare me for what I knew would be another busy day. I could feel the sun rising in my heart from all angles in my life.

Tuppence appeared and headed to the bathroom with a smile. She is in a particularly good place in her life right now.

We got ourselves ready and headed to the station and to the incident room where the team were all there and in good humour.

'I want to talk to Scott McKay this afternoon at four o'clock, so DC Taylor, will you set it up and join me?' I requested. 'The reason it will be late is I am waiting for DNA from Graham Coleman.'

Lena shouted to Chief Constable Gregg wanted to see me, so I made my way to his office and duly knocked on the door in an enlightened mood. The call to enter came. I entered to find Chief Constable Gregg with the company of Rupert Squires of the CPS. I made my way in and sat at the desk.

'Good morning, ADI Blackmore. Things are moving along very quickly to the point where decisions have to be made. Would you agree we have enough to charge Scott McKay?' asked Chief Constable Gregg.

'Yes, sir. We have the evidence to charge him. The DNA result I am waiting for is to prove he killed them by suffocation. I am very confident the result will be positive,' I responded.

'Good,' he replied. 'I will let Rupert Squires explain.'

'We can't delay the charge. You have enough to charge him, so this can't be delayed. Roderick Holmes will be brought in and all the charges against him will be dropped, and he will be free to go. The media are demanding information and we must give it to them. A briefing has been set up for two o'clock this afternoon, where it will be revealed that Scott McKay will be formally charged with the murders of Jake and Arthur Holmes. I appreciate you are waiting for one more DNA result, so we do not have to reveal the charges at this point,' he put to me.

'I do not have a problem with that, as I will be formally charging Scott McKay this afternoon at four o'clock.'

'Then we are all agreed?' said Chief Constable Gregg with a sense of relief. 'Be here at one forty-five for a chat before we face the masses.'

I left Chief Constable Gregg's office with my sense of wellbeing from this morning still intact and headed to the incident room, where I called the team together.

'I have had a meeting with Chief Constable Gregg and Rupert Squires from the CPS. The charges against

Roderick Holmes will be dropped and he will be free to go. No doubt he will return to Cromley Hall.

'A media briefing will be held at two o'clock this afternoon to announce to the waiting world Scott McKay will be formally charged with the crimes. We will have to bring forward the interview with Scott McKay where we will formally charge him, so DC Taylor, will you arrange this for eleven o'clock?

'We need to finalise our reports for the CPS and it must be a priority, so let us focus. Write your reports, then Tuppence and Lena will formalise them in a format for the CPS.'

The room was a hive of activity. When the time came to charge Scott McKay, we were just about to set off when Tuppence shouted loudly, 'Scott McKay is trying to escape!'

We all ran down to the cell block where Scott McKay was being held. He was swearing and kicking whilst being restrained by two officers and my guys jumped in to help. He was brought under control and cuffed. He was in a very agitated state; it was my guess he knew what was coming. I had him taken back to his cell to calm down.

I walked in and said directly to him, with a smile, looking directly into his eyes and with a bit of venom, 'Get used to it. You are going away for a very long time.'

He got up to make a lunge at me, but DC Taylor and DC Kelly grabbed him and soon put him back on his bed very quickly and stood menacingly over him.

'Come on, we will return to the incident room.'

We walked the short walk along the corridor and stairs, when DC Sharp asked, 'How long are you going to leave him?'

'As long as it takes for us to have a coffee.'

We all laughed.

During our unexpected coffee break, Graham Coleman rang me and I answered with expectancy.

'ADI Blackmore, I have some positive news for you. Your hunch was right; we have recovered DNA from Jake and Arthur Holmes, along with the DNA of Scott McKay on the handkerchief.'

'Thank you,' I replied.

Then, 'Yes!' I cried out. 'We have Scott McKay and the Holmes brothers' DNA on a handkerchief, so we can say with confidence that is how he killed them, by using his thumb and index finger to pinch their noses to stop them breathing through them, and then, with his handkerchief in the palm of his hand, he put it over their mouths and suffocated them. That will explain the bruising on their noses and faces. The murderous bastard then clubbed both over the back of their heads and just walked away. Come on guys, I want you all there while we nail the murderous bastard,' I said, with as much venom as I could muster.

We walked down to the custody sergeant, who looked shocked to see us.

'I want Scott McKay brought to the custody sergeant's desk right now,' I ordered. 'We will assist if required.'

The sergeant grabbed the cell keys and we all walked to his cell; I wanted him to feel very intimidated. The cell door was opened. He was sitting on his bed.

'We are all going for a little walk. I suggest you cooperate and come quietly. Your choice,' I put directly to him.

He rose slowly and paused for a moment looking at eight police officers looking menacingly at him. I think he decided the game was up. His body language changed as his shoulders drooped and he walked slowly surrounded by the officers. We arrived at the custody sergeant's desk. His brief was already there.

'Scott McKay, you are being charged with murder. On Saturday 6th June 2020 at Cromley Hall, you unlawfully killed Jake Holmes, being under the Queen's peace, with malice aforethought. You do not have to say anything, but it may harm your defence if you do not mention now something you later rely on in court. Anything you do say may be given in court.'

'No comment,' he replied.

'Scott McKay, you are being charged with murder. On Saturday 6th June 2020 at Cromley Hall, you unlawfully killed Arthur Holmes, being under the Queen's peace, with malice aforethought. You do not have to say anything, but it may harm your defence if you do not mention now something you later rely on in court. Anything you do say may be given in court.'

'No comment,' he replied.

'Scott McKay, you are being charged with stealing valuable family heirlooms on Saturday June 6th at Cromley Hall. You do not have to say anything, but it may harm your defence if you do not mention now something you later rely on in court. Anything you do say may be given in court.'

'No comment,' he replied.

I looked at the custody sergeant and motioned towards his cell. The sergeant and his two officers went to him, so the team and I left the room and blocked off the external exit. He walked slowly to his cell and entered it without argument and the cell door was locked.

'Well done, lads. Time for lunch.'

We returned to the incident room and the mood was buoyant, so I said, 'Who is for the café in the park?'

They all were so off we went. We ordered our food and drinks and sat outside at one of the benches. I could see Sue Bentley across the park, but she made no move towards us. Tuppence took the opportunity to tell us some good news.

'The charges against Roderick Holmes have been dropped and he has been released a free man.'

'Well, the day just gets better and better, so enjoy your lunch,' I put to them.

Soon it was time for me to return to the station as the news briefing was looming. I told the team and Lena to have an extended break; they had earned it. I also told them if they wanted to attend the news briefing, they could and to stand at the back of the room. I left them to it, but Tuppence walked back with me and spoke.

'I started this with you, and I want to finish it with you together.' She was looking straight into my eyes.

'I would not want it any other way,' I said, with an enormous smile.

I left Tuppence in the incident room and made my way to Chief Constable Gregg's office. I knocked on the door and was invited in with a softer tone from him this time. He was in good humour and spoke.

'Are you ready for this?'

'Absolutely!' was my positive reply.

'Good.'

The room was packed and fell silent as we entered the arena. All eyes were upon us, the questions rained down on us as we were sitting down. I noticed Tuppence, Lena and the guys at the back of the room. Tuppence smiled at me, and I relaxed.

Chief Constable Gregg put his hand up and requested a level of order until finally the first question arrived from Sue Bentley of the Cromley Echo.

'Roderick Holmes has been released. Does that mean you have, as you say, another person of interest?'

'In answer to the first part of your question,' answered Chief Constable Gregg, 'I can confirm Roderick Holmes has been released and is no longer a person of interest in this enquiry. I will leave ADI Blackmore to answer the second part of your question.'

'A man, one Scott McKay, has been arrested, interviewed and subsequently charged with the murders of Jake and Arthur Holmes on Saturday June 6th at Cromley Hall. A further charge of stealing valuable family heirlooms will also apply,' I put directly.

'Is he a local man?' asked the television reporter.

'Yes, he is,' I answered, directly.

'You must feel delighted to have solved the case, ADI Blackmore,' said Sue Bentley.

'I did not personally solve the case; it has been a great team effort all round, with a lot of work and commitment put into it by a very dedicated and talented team that I am very proud to be a part of,' I said directly.

'ADI Blackmore, will Roderick Holmes sue the Cromley police force for wrongful arrest and imprisonment?' asked the local television reporter.

'My concern relates to this case and nothing else,' I replied directly.

'When will Scott McKay appear in court?' asked Sue Bentley.

'That will be down to the Crown Prosecution Service. Thank you all for your time and we will inform you if anything changes,' Chief Constable Gregg replied.

We stood up and made our way out of the room and back to Chief Constable Gregg's office. We entered to find Rupert Squires waiting for us. He was in a more relaxed mood; he was the first to speak.

'The news brief was very impressive and to the point,' he said, with a smile. 'Scott McKay will appear in court to face the charges put to him. I would appreciate all the paperwork is completed for us by close of play tomorrow,' he requested.

'It will be done,' I answered directly. 'What about Bryan Gates and Helen Green?'

'We all agree there would be little public interest in charging them and the damage it would cause would be far greater than a slap on the wrist from the courts. I have spoken with the relevant parties and as far as we are concerned you can release Helen Green,' he said, with finality. No charges will be brought against Bryan Gates.'

'Thank you,' I said with relief. 'I will read the riot act to her before she goes.'

'Now,' said Rupert Squires, 'we need to discuss your investigation and all the details. I know you have provided some already and you are awaiting results from one more.'

'I would like the team involved in it, so can I suggest we meet in the incident room at ten o'clock tomorrow morning? And, sir, it would be good for you to be there as well. It would be good for them also,' I said directly.

They looked at each other and they both agreed.

I left for the incident room in a buoyant mood and found the team in the same frame of mind, I was proud of every one of them and walked in with a smile. They turned to look at me and they were smiling as well. I finally spoke.

'Tomorrow morning at ten o'clock, the Chief and Rupert Squires of the CPS will be here to discuss the case against Scott McKay. I wanted you all to be involved in this process, so ensure you all shave and smell nice for them.'

We all started laughing.

'I have not told them about the final piece in the jigsaw with the DNA result on the handkerchief; we can drop that on them tomorrow. Scott McKay will appear in court the day after tomorrow, so we need to have all the reports completed by the end of play tomorrow. I know a lot of it is done, so go over them to ensure they are correct and factual,' I said, looking at all of them.

'What about Helen Green?' asked DC Kelly.

'She has been a silly, naive woman, but no charges will be brought against her, so shortly we will go down and tell her, but not without reading the riot act to her before we let her go. Will you have her brought to the interview room and ensure her brief is there,' I put to DC Kumar.

The interview with Helen Green had been arranged for four o'clock and it soon came round, so we made our way down. She was sitting with her brief, James Brown, and I hoped after we had spoken with her, he would feel good. I sat as usual and looked at her for a few seconds. I could see her shuffling extremely uncomfortable in her seat. I leaned forward and spoke.

'After a lot of investigation and discussion, it has been decided not to press charges against you and, quite frankly, you are an incredibly lucky woman. You got yourself involved with someone without engaging your brain. I suggest when you leave here, you think back over the last few weeks and how you have lived your life and the people you meet with and change it. I also suggest you stay away from Bryan Gates and if you do not, I will be knocking, extremely hard, on your door. DC Kelly will escort you to the custody sergeant where your personal belongings will be returned to you. If there is someone you want to call, DC Kelly will take care of that.'

I looked at James Brown and said to him, 'I suggest she leaves by the side door as there are likely to be members of the press hanging around. DC Kelly will show her the way.'

I got up to leave when Helen Green spoke.

'ADI Blackmore, thank you and I will heed your words. There will be no more trouble from me.'

I looked at her and nodded.

I made my way back to the incident room and DC Kelly arrived back forty-five minutes later.

I rang Bryan Gates; I had a similar conversation with him as to the one I had with Helen Green.

There was a sense of relief from him, and he felt he could move forward with his life. He told his wife of the events in Cromley and there has been a lot of arguments and tears, but they are making a go of it. He has learned a valuable lesson and greatly regrets what happened. I told him of Helen Green. I felt assured he would never hear from her again, but if he did to let me know straight away.

The day was coming to an end and the team were heading home, so I suggested to Tuppence we go to The

Scythe for dinner. A big smile came across her face, so I knew her answer.

We had half an hour until the pub opened, so I took a longer drive through the villages as we headed off to The Scythe. Tuppence loves these detours looking at the houses and scenery. We drove through the village of Harpingworth and under a long railway viaduct. Tuppence was excited, so we stopped and parked up for a while. I felt the most relaxed I have been for a long time; it felt good.

The viaduct is 1,275 yards long. It stands sixty feet high with eighty-two arches. It is built entirely of brick and in my opinion is a great feat of engineering. It was built in the latter part of the nineteenth century, so very labour intensive. Sadly, lives were lost, and many injuries and severe injuries were sustained in the building of the viaduct. I have been here many a time over the years with my dad and my brother. Tuppence was enthralled by the viaduct and loves the history of this type of structure, so I thought she would return to it.

We reached The Scythe, and we were welcomed by Tom Woods, and his wife Jenny came out from the kitchen to see us. We chatted for a few minutes before Jenny had to return to the kitchen. We sat down and ordered our food and chatted about the last few days. Generally, it is not something I do, but I have not seen very much of her.

A thought occurred to me to book a table for Saturday night and, if Tuppence was agreeable, to invite my parents, my brother and sister and their partners. Tuppence was delighted with my suggestion and said she would look forward to it. I spoke with Tom and provisionally booked a table for eight to be confirmed tomorrow.

We had our food and headed back to the apartment, where Tuppence spoke with Georgia and I said hello. I just wanted to see her. I made my phone calls to the family and everyone agreed, so Saturday night was set.

THIRTY-FIVE

Tuppence was already up and sitting on the sofa looking out over the park when I made an appearance. She was sitting very quietly and deep in thought.

'What is on your mind?' I asked.

'I'm sad because we are coming to the end of the investigation and my return to Mortley will be soon. I really like Cromley. It is so much more interesting than Mortley.'

'I do not know what the future holds right now, so we will cross that bridge when we come to it, so come on, keep your chins up,' I said, laughing.

'Sod off,' she said, as she threw a cushion at me.

Tuppence went for a shower, so I quietly snuck into the bathroom and threw a cup of cold water over the top of the shower curtain and legged it.

'You bastard!' she yelled. 'I'll get you for that.'

I laughed my head off.

Somehow, I think Tuppence's life will change, as she is so taken with Chief Constable Gregg. Perhaps her wish to stay in Cromley will become a reality.

After the domestics, we headed for Cromley station and to the incident room. The team were all present, so I had them all lined up for light-hearted inspection, including the girls. It was good to see Lena coming out of her shell and joining in the banter, I think, however, Tuppence is behind the change in her.

We spoke about the part each one of us would play and ten o'clock soon came round. We were all assembled waiting for Chief Constable Gregg and Rupert Squires, and presently we heard them coming down the corridor and they both entered the room.

'ADI Blackmore, will you do the introductions and then start us off?' requested Chief Constable Gregg.

I stood and walked over to the information board.

'Ladies and gentlemen, may I introduce Rupert Squires, representing the Crown Prosecution Service. Chief Constable Gregg you already know – and if you do not, you will be in serious trouble.'

A lot of laughter ensued and that broke the ice.

'The purpose of this investigation was to investigate the murders of Jake and Arthur Holmes and the theft of valuable family heirlooms carried out on Saturday June 6th at Cromley Hall. The case was puzzling due to a lack of an entry or exit point at the hall. The assumption was it was an inside job, but that did not stack up. There is no need to go into the details, as it is of no value just now. We carried out a detailed examination of the externals of the hall and a secret entry point was found. DC Sharp, will you start the route into the hall?'

'Scott McKay gained entry by first accessing through Blaggards' Door and then he walked along to the far end of the Peasants' Walk. He climbed a stairway and walked into the old servants' quarters to the far corner of the building and moved an old wardrobe. Behind the wardrobe he found an opening in the outer wall of the building and made his way through to the top of the wall. He walked along the top of the wall, where he left footprints in the soft earth. A mould was taken of the footprints and forensics matched to one of the trainer shoes he was wearing. He walked around the top of the wall and made his way down to the rear of the kitchen scullery.'

'Thank you. DC Kelly, will you take us through the next part of the route?'

'There was evidence of Scott McKay's footprints walking back and forth behind the building; we have further forensic casts of them. He found a cleverly concealed access point cut into the wall that took him down a passageway to a wooden panel. When pushed, the panel opened and he gained access to the corridor between the kitchen and scullery. In the passageway there is an alcove and that is where the heirlooms were recovered. They were wiped clean and no fingerprints or DNA were recovered. He was, however, careless; some phlegm was recovered off the wall adjacent to where the heirlooms were found. In the phlegm there were some hair particles, and the DNA of Scott McKay was recovered.'

'Thank you. DC Taylor, will you take us through the next part of the route?'

'Scott McKay made his way along the corridor of the hall to the long room where he encountered first Jake

Holmes and then Arthur Holmes. It was thought at first a blow to their heads was the initial cause of death. A lack of blood around their heads indicated they were possibly dead already. The second autopsy report reported the cause of death was by suffocation. Bruising on their noses and around their mouths was investigated, but nothing at the scene was found that would have suffocated them. The forensics team during their detailed search found a handkerchief in the pocket of the jacket Scott McKay was wearing. DNA analysis was carried out and the DNA of Jake and Arthur Holmes was recovered, along with that of Scott McKay. This evidence arrived this morning.

'It is clear he approached them from behind and covered their mouths with his hand that held the handkerchief, and he then pinched their noses. He applied pressure to suffocate them, and it was after this he hit them over the head with a blunt instrument. A T-shirt recovered from a bag belonging to Scott McKay had tiny blood splatters and the DNA analysis confirms the DNA belongs to Jake and Arthur Holmes.'

'Thank you, DC Taylor.'

'So how did we connect Scott McKay with the crime? I believe, like me, he was convinced there was a secret access to the hall. He has been caught a few times snooping around the hall until he was eventually banned. I myself was caught in the church in the hall grounds looking for a tunnel to the hall. I was sent packing with a clip round the ear from the verger Mr Holloway; I was twelve at the time.'

The laughter released a bit of the tension.

'The Cromley Hall security system has been replaced and updated, so it was obviously no good to us. Fortunately, they had still the old video system and the old videotapes. The Cromley Hall security manager went through the videos and managed to find a twenty-second clip of Scott McKay, which confirmed to me he was the person of interest I was looking for.

'He seemed to disappear, so I thought he may have served a jail sentence. We trawled through court records from three years ago and finally came across an individual sentenced around that time and released recently and there was one, a Scott McKay.

'There was a likeness between the photo on the court file and the video. I believe he was the person of interest I was looking for. I had no address for him; all avenues were met with a dead end.

'I was at Cromley Hall talking to John Holmes when I noticed a former employee, Helen Green, walking around the grounds. What struck me was she was in an agitated and anguished state and that made me suspicious. I had interviewed her, but she had an alibi with a Bryan Gates. I decided to go and talk with Bryan Gates and after questioning he admitted he had panicked and supported Helen Green. I felt then there was a connection between Scott McKay and Helen Green.

'My gut feeling told me Scott McKay was holding up in Helen Green's house. However, I had at that time no evidence to go charging in there and scare him off. We set up an observation point close to the residence where Helen Green was staying. Our observations clearly showed there were two people in the house, but only Helen Green would leave the house and that was to purchase goods, coffees and cakes for two and takeaway food for two. Graham Coleman provided DNA evidence from the phlegm sample he found in the passageway to be that of Scott McKay. It was at this point we had enough to tie him to Cromley Hall, but not the murders.

'It got to the point where we stagnated. Scott McKay was not coming to me, so I had to go and get him. I spoke with Chief Constable Gregg, he agreed to my forced entry to the house. When access was gained, Helen Green was found sitting up in bed. Scott McKay was seen running up a ladder to the loft area. I figured he had set an escape route. I arrested them on suspicion of the murders of Jake and Arthur Holmes and the theft of the valuable heirlooms.

'Scott McKay actions were aggressive and once challenged with the DNA analysis that placed him at the crime scene, he went to a "no comment" situation. As we went down to formally charge him, he had tried to make a break for it, but he was restrained.

'Scott McKay has been formally charged with the murders of Jake and Arthur Holmes and the theft of the valuable heirlooms, which I hasten to add, we have in safekeeping,' I finalised.

There was silence for a few seconds and then Chief

Constable Gregg stood up to speak.

'Thank you all for your presentations. Rupert, is there anything you want to say?' he directed.

'Thank you for all your detailed work and conclusive evidence. Your investigation has been thorough and a credit to you all,' Rupert Squires concluded.

The meeting was concluded, Rupert Squires returned to his office. I was invited to Chief Constable Gregg's office. We entered the office and closed the door. Chief Constable Gregg turned to me and spoke.

'Well done, Paul, a great result.'

He shook my hand.

'Thank you for your support all the way through this investigation, sir. It was the bedrock to it all. It was an all-round team effort; I am proud of every one of them for the work and dedication they all put into it. We must finalise the finer details for reference and filing and wrap it up.'

We talked a little more, then I left and made my way back to the incident room. The atmosphere in the room when I entered was electric with high fives all round and the biggest smiles I have ever seen. They had a right to be so satisfied. I told them to take an extra hour for lunch and then we would finalise the details.

I rang John Holmes at Cromley Hall to request to see him and he said he would be delighted to see me. I went over to Tuppence and spoke.

'Come on, we are going to Cromley Hall to see John Holmes. We will grab some lunch whilst we are there.'

'Yeah, I'm up for that.'

We headed for the car, and as we were driving out past the barrier I noticed Sue Bentley leaning against the window frame of her office. I looked up at her and thought to myself, I was not bad for a novice.

As we made our way Tuppence said to me, 'I thought you might have asked me to tell them about my surveillance on Helen Green at the hall.'

'You are a civilian. If Chief Constable Gregg found out you were doing surveillance work, my balls would be slowly growing back now.'

'Oh yes, I forgot about that.'

We both laughed our heads off. We arrived at Cromley Hall and stopped at the barrier and I pressed the intercom.

'Can I help you?' enquired the gorgeous Irish voice.

'DI Blackmore to see John Holmes.'

'Yes, he is expecting you.'

I drove to my normal spot. We walked over to the door and rang the bell that has been rung for hundreds of years. Today it sounds great to the ear. John Holmes opened the door and spoke.

'Welcome, DI Blackmore and Tuppence, welcome indeed,' he said with a smile as he invited us in.

We walked into the hallway and Cynthia Holmes appeared and ran to us with arms outstretched to give us both a great hug.

'Thank you on behalf of the family for everything you have done for us. We will be eternally grateful,' she

357

said with a warm smile. 'I have made some lunch, so please join us.'

'It would be rude not to,' I returned with a smile.

Cynthia Holmes led us along the corridors to the large dining room with a high ceiling. The walls were decorated with dark brown pictures. How I enjoyed the Pre-Raphaelite Movement and the vibrant colours they used. To me, they brought British art out of the dark ages. There are a lot of antiquities, accumulated over the years, around the room and together they all add to a great atmosphere. We sat at the grand table and the lunch was brought out to us. The lunch was good and went down very well. The conversation turned to the case.

'Is the case against Scott McKay solid?' asked John Holmes. I knew the sentiment of the question was relating to his nephew.

'You can appreciate I cannot discuss the case. However, with the evidence we have, I would say the answer to your question is yes,' I said with sincerity.

'Thank you for your honesty and believing in my nephew and us all.'

I nodded in agreement.

'The main reason I am here is to discuss two things with you.'

John and Cynthia Holmes looked at me intently; so did Tuppence.

'First, I know you and Chief Constable Gregg are members of the same golf club and have played golf together on numerous occasions, but during this case, because of your connection, he has had to keep a distance. I sincerely hope this does not affect your friendship with him and life will move on.

Second, I want to bring the investigating team to the hall to show them around the hall. We have discussed it and I want them to see the reality,' he concluded.

'The answer to your first question is simple. I have a very high regard for Chief Constable Gregg. I look forward to taking money off him once again on the golf course and return it over the bar afterwards,' he said, with a smile. 'The answer to your second question is, yes, of course. It is the least we can do.'

'Arrange it for a late morning and we will arrange lunch for them,' Cynthia Holmes said, excitedly.

There was agreement all round.

'I will arrange it with Tuppence,' she said smiling and looking at Tuppence.

It was time to return to the station. We said our farewells and made our way to the car and set off. We arrived at the station to find them all at work finalising the evidence and reports for Rupert Squires. We were on target to complete by close of play today. I told them of the visit to Cromley Hall and lunch put on by Cynthia Holmes. There was a lot of banter and general looking forward to it. By the end of the day, we had completed our task.

Tuppence and Lena emailed them to Rupert Squires; our work was done. I found out Scott McKay would be appearing in court tomorrow morning at ten o'clock. I said the team would all be there. We called it a day and we all went our separate ways.

Tuppence and I walked to the car and Sue Bentley was looking out of her office window.

I said to Tuppence, 'She must spend a large proportion of her day looking out of her office window. Perhaps we should speak with Chief Constable Gregg to have a neon sign put up for her to keep her up to date with events.'

We both laughed as we set off. We reached the apartment and parked up.

We were walking towards the stairway when I said to Tuppence, 'Are you fit for a drink at The Lodge?'

A silly question to ask I know, as the answer was yes. As we had a large lunch, we had a light snack at The Lodge and the couple of drinks went down well. We made our way back to the apartment and relaxed. There was one thing playing on my mind and I thought now would be a good time to talk to Tuppence.

'Tuppence!' I called to her. 'Come and sit down for a minute. There is something I want to talk to you about.'

She made her way over and sat on the sofa.

'I want to talk to you about Georgia, and quite frankly I cannot get her out of my mind, and I really do not want to. She is a fantastic woman and I want to see more of her,' I said, looking directly at her.

She moved closer to me and took my hand and

answered, 'Paul, Georgia feels the same way about you. I have never known her to feel that way about a guy before. I don't believe she could find a better guy to be with, so I am happy for the pair of you.'

'I am the luckiest guy in the world and looking forward to seeing her.'

I gave Tuppence a big hug and felt incredibly happy.

I made my way to the bathroom, stopped, turned round and shouted to her, 'I have just realised you could be my mother-in-law.'

I carried on walking and laughing.

'Sod off, asshole!' she shouted.

I was soaking happily in the bathwater when Tuppence quietly entered the bathroom and tipped a saucepan of cold water over me.

'Revenge is sweet,' she said as she left the bathroom.

THIRTY-SIX

I was up early as normal and sat on the sofa at the window. It was a sunny morning; it reflected my mood. I was glad I had a chat with Tuppence last night and it was good to know Georgia felt the same way about me. I saw Amber running around the park and all the feelings and questions I had for her had left me; I now see her as a friend.

My mind turned to the forthcoming court case. I was certain Scott McKay would plead guilty and, if so, the case would be wrapped up very quickly. That would be good for all concerned.

Tuppence made an appearance and made herself some tea and sat beside me. We sat overlooking the park taking in the early morning serenity and runners gracing the park. It was time to get ourselves ready for the day ahead and we did so with good humour and enthusiasm. We turned on the TV for the local news and a reference was made to Scott McKay's appearance in court later this morning. I turned off the TV and turned on the radio to the sounds of Bill Withers singing 'Lovely Day'.

I turned to Tuppence. 'I hope that is a good omen for the day.'

We made our way to the station, parked up and

walked to the incident room. The team were all there and looking forward to the court appearance of Scott McKay.

The time came for us to make our way to the court. We sat in the seats reserved for us. I could see Sue Bentley in the press section and she glanced up at us. I saw John and Cynthia Holmes sitting quietly in the public gallery and he nodded acknowledgement to me.

The court was brought to order and Scott McKay was brought in from his cell. He walked with his head bowed and walking slowly; he looked a broken man. He would have a lot of time to reflect on what he had done. He did not look at anyone.

The session began and he was asked to confirm his name and address, which he duly answered. He was going to be asked the key question, as far as the team and I were concerned. The charges were read out to him, and he was asked if he pleaded guilty or not guilty.

'Guilty,' he said, without looking at anyone.

He was remanded in custody to appear in court at a date to be set for his sentence; there was no request for bail. He was taken back to his cell.

I turned and shook the hand of each member of the team, and we made our way outside. John and Cynthia Holmes were waiting for us. He shook the hand of us all and thanked us all for the conclusion of the case. After a few more words, they made their way back to Cromley Hall to convey the good news. We were making our way back to the station when Sue Bentley called out to me. I stopped and told the guys I would join them shortly.

'Congratulations on the conviction of Scott McKay. You must be delighted.'

'He has not been sentenced yet, so you are being a little premature.'

'Yes, but that is just a formality,' she said, exasperated.

'When he appears back in court and is sentenced, I will answer any questions you ask,' I put to her. What I did not tell her was I would probably be back in Mortley.

I joined the guys in the incident room. Chief Constable Gregg joined us and made a small speech thanking the team for all their efforts, hours put in and most of all their desire to seek justice. This case would be with them for the rest of their lives. I knew he was right. He left us to it, but said to me to pop in and see him. I said to the guys and Lena to take the rest of the day off as they had all earned it. It just left Tuppence and me in the room.

'Come on, we will go and see Chief Constable Gregg.'

'No! It's you he wants to see,' she said, in an alarmed state.

'We started this together and I promised you we would finish it,' I said, with a smile.

We walked down the corridor and knocked on the door, we waited a few seconds and the call came. I walked in first, closely followed by Tuppence. Chief Constable Gregg looked up and looked surprised. I thought I had better explain.

'Sir, I started this investigation with Tuppence and now that we have come to the end, I would like her to be here for the end.'

Chief Constable Gregg thought for a moment or two and then spoke.

'Very well, please sit down,' he said, with a smile.

Tuppence was looking softly at him. I could feel the chemistry between them and it was good. He then spoke.

'You are quite right by saying we are at the end of the investigation. I wanted to personally thank you for agreeing to return to Cromley and the calm and detailed way you have dealt with the investigation and the people concerned.

'I take it, sir, I will be returning to Mortley the week after next,' I put to him.

'Yes, that's the plan. But you will return when Scott McKay appears in court for sentencing when it arises. Finally, I would like to thank you, Tuppence, for your support to ADI Blackmore. Chief Constable Mondell and I had reservations regarding the arrangement, but it turned out to be the right one in the end and your assistance has been invaluable,' he said, directly looking at her with a smile.

'Thank you, sir. I have enjoyed my time here. Will I be returning to Mortley on Monday?' she said, with almost a tear in her eye.

'Yes, as the case is now closed, I can't keep you here,' he replied.

We left his office a bit deflated at the thought of

returning to Mortley. We returned to the incident room. The place was eerily quiet without the team.

'Come on. I promised you a tour of the area, so are you up for it?'

'Of course. I'm surprised you need to ask.'

We made our way to the car and headed off to the old town of Stalford, with its cobbled streets and protected buildings. We had lunch in a quaint old pub and did a little shopping. Tuppence liked the character of the town and said she could live there.

We left Stalford and drove across the country and around the reservoir and back towards Cromley Hall. Tuppence started to get her bearings as to where we were. We continued, so I decided we would call in and see my parents, Tuppence was delighted with that.

My parents were at home. I could hear the lathe running in my dad's workshop as we walked down the path to the house. We went into the house and my mother was delighted to see us. We spoke for a few minutes and I decided to let them chat together, while I went to see my dad.

I walked down the path and as I got closer, I could hear the familiar music I had heard many a time over the years. I opened the door and walked in. He stopped working when he saw me and came over and shook my hand. We exchanged the normal dad-to-son questions, and then he said to me, 'After all these years, do you still like this tune?'

'Dad, you can be assured. I will never tire of hearing

'Tubular Bells'!

We sadly returned to Mortley the next morning.

THIRTY-SEVEN

The time to return to Cromley soon came round and Tuppence and I met with the team in the incident room. It was good to see them all and we were on a high. I went to see Chief Constable Gregg and he was in a buoyant mood. We all headed to the Crown court and sat together.

The court was brought to session and Scott McKay was brought in. He had lost weight and was a broken man. As I said to him previously, he would have a lot of time to think about what he had done.

The court was brought to session and the judge entered and took his seat. He spoke of the evilness of the crimes that Scott McKay had committed on Jake and Arthur Holmes, and further added.

'You suffocated Jake and Arthur Holmes and then callously clubbed them over the head; you then just left them lying there on the floor. You thought by finding a secret passageway you would get away with it and return at a later date to collect the heirlooms you had stolen and concealed in the hidden passageway.

'What you did not take into consideration was the superb and dedicated police work carried out to solve this crime. The police worked very meticulously and logically to solve the case and it is a great credit to them.

Taking everything into consideration and that you have shown no remorse, I consider you to be a dangerous and evil individual. The sentence I bestow on you will reflect the seriousness of your evil crime. I sentence you to two life sentences where they will run concurrently for twenty-five years with no parole.'

The judge ended the session. The case was over.

We made our way back to the station in a buoyant mood with a lot of handshaking, hugs and back-slapping. Chief Constable Gregg came in and thanked us all and he told me there would be a briefing at two o'clock and to meet him at one fifty in his office.

The time came round I made my way to his office and then to the briefing room to the masses.

We entered, but the atmosphere was a bit more serene and even Sue Bentley was smiling. Chief Constable Gregg opened the meeting.

'As you will be aware, Scott McKay was sentenced this morning to two twenty-five-year sentences to run concurrently with no parole. This concludes a difficult case solved by a dedicated and motivated police team, so we will take some questions.'

'ADI Blackmore, I apologise for calling you a novice. I was wrong. How are you feeling with the result?' Sue Bentley put, directly but softly.

'It has been a great team effort throughout and there have been contributions and discussions, and the dedication shown by the team and the other teams involved along the way to achieving this result and we are happy with it,' I put to her.

'Do you ever take credit yourself?' she asked.

'It was a great team effort, and we are immensely happy with the result.'

'What happens to you now, ADI Blackmore?' asked the television reporter.

'I will return to Mortley.'

'How do you feel about that?' asked Sue Bentley.

'I do not have a problem with that.'

Chief Constable Gregg put up his hand and spoke.

'Thank you, ladies and gentlemen, and we will close at that. It has been a complicated case with the right result. Thank you for your patience throughout.'

We got up to leave and headed to his office, we entered and he shut the door. He shook my hand and told me how much the result had lifted everyone and also that a review of the department was in progress. I had no doubt he would complete his task.

I went back to the incident room to the team and the atmosphere was electric. I told the guys when I was back in Mortley I had arranged to have a couple of weeks off as I badly needed a break.

I had arranged a tour and lunch at Cromley Hall. We set off and this time Chief Constable Gregg joined us. Tuppence was in a very good frame of mind, so I asked her why.

'I have resigned. I will be moving permanently to Cromley to start a new life with Robert Gregg. He has proposed to me and I have said yes. I never thought I could be this happy and content. I will be staying in Cromley for a while, so I will not return with you to Mortley.'

'That is fantastic news. I am very happy for the both of you.'

We arrived at Cromley Hall to be greeted by the lovely, gorgeous Irish voice. She opened the gate and I parked in my now usual spot. We made our way to the door, where we were met by a fully dressed butler; in fact, all the staff were dressed in period costume and a lavish banquet was laid before us. They had made sure we had a great time. I met Roderick Holmes in a private room, where he thanked me for believing in him and the family.

When the meal was over, I told them all I had a surprise for them. I asked Tuppence to take Cynthia Holmes and Lena to the corridor between the kitchen and the scullery. I summoned the team, Chief Constable Gregg, John and Roderick Holmes. I asked John Holmes if he would get the key to Blaggards' Door.

I opened the door and made my way down the Peasants' Walk up the stairway to the old female servants' quarters. We entered the building and made our way to the far corner. I looked at them and then I moved the wooden cupboard, and then removed the bit of wood covering the opening to the outside. I looked at the look of puzzlement on their faces.

'Gentlemen, we will be going through this opening and make our way along the top of the wall around to the other side. Please walk in single file and take your time. I will lead the way.'

We left the building and made our way around the wall and down through the vegetation to the rear of the kitchen area and I stopped at the access hatch to the hall.

'Gentlemen, I have left the best until last.'

I put my hand on the access door and I gently pulled it open. There was a gasp from the team; John Holmes was standing opened-mouthed with his hands on his head. The internal passageway was now accessible, so we made our way down to the wooden panel at the other end. I removed the securing peg and opened the door and stepped into the passageway. We met Tuppence, Lena and an astonished Cynthia Holmes. John and Roderick Holmes were astounded and could not believe the journey they had just taken.

I said to them all, 'This is how Scott McKay entered and exited the hall and as you can see, it is years old.'

John and Roderick Holmes were speechless. Finally, John Holmes spoke.

'There have been rumours of a secret tunnel or passage for many years and I confess in my younger days I did look for one, but I was always unsuccessful. I am truly astounded by this revelation.'

'Now that you are aware of it, I suggest the access door is securely locked from the inside and the hole in the wall in the old female servants' quarters is filled in.'

'You can be assured I will the work started straight away,' he pledged.

We all made our way back to the great hall and I

slipped away and left them to it for a few minutes. I had promised Mr Holloway I would go back and see him once the case was over. I made my way down to the church and I found him in the church preparing for the next service. He was delighted to see me, so we sat down and talked. I filled him in on all the events of the case and then told him about the secret passageway. He was delighted and astonished it actually existed, so he would speak with John Holmes to see for himself. I re-joined the group in the great hall where Tuppence said to me, 'Where did you go to?'

'I had promised Mr Holloway I would see him once the case was over, so I found him in the church and told him the events of the case and, of course, the secret passageway.'

Finally, the day was over, so we made our way back to the police station and to the incident room. We had a couple of hours to kill before my train back to Mortley; Chief Constable Gregg was dropping me at the railway station. My flight to New York was booked for six o'clock the next morning and I was looking forward to seeing Georgia. We were talking about New York when my mobile phone rang. It was Bryan Gates.

'Sorry to bother you, ADI Blackmore. I received a package today with five hundred pounds in it with a note that said "Sorry, H". I think it's from Helen Green.'

'Leave it with me and I will get back to you,' I promised.

'I have to pop out,' I said to Tuppence. 'I am going

to call on Helen Green.'

I arrived at Helen Green's house as she was loading a car with bags. I walked up to her and she smiled. She was a lot more relaxed than the last time I saw her.

'I guess I know why you are here.'

'Then tell me.'

'It has been on my conscience, taking the money off Bryan Gates. I wanted to return the money to him to free my mind. I am moving to Cornwall to my aunt's. She has a small business down there and I will be working for her. I want to put all this behind me and make a fresh start,' she said openly with total honesty.

'OK, I will let him know.'

'Inspector Blackmore,' she called out. 'Thank you for making this fresh start possible for me and I will not let you down,' she smiled.

I waved to her as I walked off, so I rang Bryan Gates.

'Mr Gates, Helen Green is freeing her mind of her past and she is moving to pastures new. She has returned your money to free her conscience to enable her to move on. It is nothing more than that, so I suggest you take it and treat your family.'

'Thank you,' he replied.

I made my way back to the police station; my work in Cromley is now finally finished. I was met in the incident room by Tuppence, so I explained to her my visit to Helen Green and the positive outcome.

Soon it was time for me to leave. Chief Constable

Gregg and Tuppence dropped me at the railway station. I looked at them both and I thought how well they were suited to each other. I was just about to board the train when I asked Tuppence, 'What time is my train to Heathrow?'

'Midnight!' she answered.

I looked at her and we both burst out laughing, with Chief Constable Gregg looking on a bit bemused.

EPILOGUE

My flight to New York went smoothly and I was met by Georgia at the arrivals gate at JFK airport. She had the biggest smile on her pretty face and gave me a massive hug when she greeted me. We made our way to her apartment in Manhattan and there was just the two of us. The girl Georgia shared the apartment with had moved out whilst I was there to allow us to spend time together. We had a great time touring New York and became very close to the point where I want to spend the rest of my life with her.

Georgia moved back to England to reclaim, as she said, her Englishness and for us to be together. Georgia got a job with one of the big London tabloids, it was a temporary situation. We bought a house with large outbuildings where Georgia could do her art, especially her distinctive pottery. She has become very successful and in demand to the point where she packed in her job to work full-time on her art. Tuppence now works for Georgia with marketing, sales, etc. She is very good at it, they are a good team.

I am now a Detective Inspector in a new district and the area is where we work and have our house. I still have contact with the Cromley Hall police team and advise them when they request my help.

Tuppence and Chief Constable Gregg married at Cromley Hall and also had their reception there. Tuppence got her wish and now lives just outside of Cromley. She has a continuous smile on her face and Chief Constable Gregg knows he is a lucky man.

The team and I had a great night out along with everyone else involved with the case. SIO DI Grainger took early retirement and left the area. He has not been seen or heard of since. Chief Constable Gregg has completely overhauled the department and made it more flexible. Overall, it is in a damn better shape.

I could not imagine how life would turn out when I returned to Cromley to investigate the murders at Cromley Hall. The impact on my life has been awesome and I feel truly blessed.

ACKNOWLEDGEMENTS

To Gill for your wonderful support, good advice and fun nights at the quiz.

To Mary for your honesty. Soft options are always the easy way out but thankfully you did not take it and that, I greatly appreciate.

To Angela for your support and understanding of my 'word blindness.' This is a secret I have kept to myself over the years and as a teacher your help has been invaluable. I no longer see it as a flaw in my intelligence and character.

To the special person to whom I owe so much, thank you for your guidance and support.

ABOUT THE AUTHOR

Reef was born and raised in Northamptonshire and still has a property in the county to this day.

Reef was never motivated by the school system he attended but was educated to an adequate level and left school without any qualifications. Reef suffered from what he called 'word blindness.' He kept it hidden from the world when one of the teachers called him a 'stupid boy'. Reef would read but struggled to store the information in his grey matter; he learned to deal with it in his own way. After recently discussing the problem with his sister, he decided not to hide it anymore.

The subject Reef enjoyed the most was English; in later years he attended night school to study English Language and Literature. He achieved O & A levels in each subject and proved to himself a personal achievement. Reef also went on to study History and Art History. He was a member of a study group, and this helped him enormously.

Reef always enjoyed reading but it was his Aunt Violet who installed the love of books to him at an early age. That love of books has remained with him to this day.

Over the years the desire to write was growing within him until it could not be held back anymore. The result is the release of his first novel, 'Two Heads Are Better Than One.'